THE OLD MEN IN BLUE

KEN MOORE

THE OLD MEN IN BLUE

By Ken Moore

Transcendent Publishing
PO Box 66202
St. Pete Beach, FL 33736
www.transcendentpublishing.com

Transcendent
Publishing

ISBN: 9781090928351

Printed in the United States of America.

DEDICATION

This book is dedicated to all who have served their community wearing a blue or any other color of a police uniform. Past, present and future who conduct their job faithfully and with honor.

CONTENTS

INTRODUCTION

It was about 10 o'clock Friday night the week after Memorial holiday weekend at the Bradford Ranch. The ranch belongs to the Bradford family and has been in the family for the last four generations of Bradford's. The ranch is nearly one hundred thousand acres. It's located on a mountaintop and is surrounded by valleys. The ranch has about two hundred acres of wheat fields, ten thousand acres of timber, but mainly large grassland areas for grazing herds of cattle. Although many ranches have fancy names, by using their cattle brand or a nearby landmark, this ranch is just known as the Bradford Ranch.

The ranch is in the northern end of Wallowa County in eastern Oregon. It is only a few miles from Washington and Idaho. The county is known for the natural beauty of the big mountains, several rivers and Wallowa Lake. It is also known for fantastic mule deer, whitetail deer and rocky mountain elk hunting. Because of the large numbers of big game, there are also many black bears, cougars and some wolves that roam the mountains. The county covers an area of three thousand fifty-three square miles with only a resident population of around seven thousand people.

The county encompasses the rugged Wallowa Whitman National Forest. The only paths of motor vehicle travel into the county are roads from Washington on Highway 3 or from Union County on Highway 82. Both highways end at the county seat, the city of Enterprise. There is a remote paved county road named the Imnada Road that will take travelers in or out of the county only 9 months of the year due to being closed from the deep annual snowfall.

Because of the limited roadways, big mountains and just being remote, the county is somewhat isolated from most of Oregon. It is the destination for a tightknit group of well-seasoned retired cops.

At the ranch, Kyle Morris sat relaxing in deep thought near their campfire. He was thinking about his life; he was now fifty-two and he'd had a long police career. Kyle was born and raised in SE Portland, his father an Oregon National Guard fighter jet crew chief for years based at Portland. All he wanted to do was become a fighter pilot as his Dad had encouraged. While in high school his rifle team coach was a Portland Police Officer. Kyle learned a lot about shooting and police work from the coach. The coach's stories and information about police work steered Kyle away from jets. During that time, he started seeing the darker side of humanity in SE Portland and on the local news.

Some guys he knew where dropping out of school and starting into drugs, and some bragged about breaking into homes and stealing to get money to buy them with. The nightly news ran stories about victims of all types of evil crimes. He went to a junior college majoring in Law Enforcement. Kyle's instructors were all local police officers and deputy district attorneys. Most had talked on and on about the "Thin Blue Line": The few who protect society from the bad and evil people. Police work was the career that Kyle had been destined to follow. He knew in his heart he could stop bad guys and evil and would do what he could to get criminals off the streets to make his community as safe as he could.

He met his future wife, Claudia, after being a police officer only a few years. They had two sons who were now in their twenties. They had a good marriage of just over thirty years. Claudia was kind enough to understand her husband needed to work all the long and odd hours to do his job. Many marriages cannot get through that.

Kyle had been shooting rifles since around the age of 10 and hunting big game at age 12. The high school Kyle attended had a .22LR rifle team and was in a shooting league of several hundred high school marksman, both male and female. As a freshman, Kyle tried out for the team. After a few months of training, he was good enough to be a dependable performer at competitive matches. The rifles they used were highly specialized of the type of rifles used in the summer Olympic games. Normally only junior and senior students shot on the team. He was already shooting as good as or better than the older team members, and they needed him. By his junior year, few shooters could shoot better than Kyle in the whole state of Oregon. In his senior year, Kyle was in the master class level, the highest level of match shooting. He also won the state championship the same year. Shortly after high school a local rifle club asked Kyle to join their club and shoot on both the smallbore .22LR caliber rifle and highpower .308 caliber rifles. While on the team, they went to the National Championships. At his best, Kyle placed seventh of all US smallbore shooters and fifth place in the US in all highpower shooters during the next three years.

This team used the national match M-14 rifle for the highpower matches. Those M-14s were shot at ranges from 200 to 600 yards. In all these types of competition, the shooter must rely on the standard sighting devices. The rifles cannot have a scope and are fired while only supported by the shooter. No supports such as bipods or sandbags are allowed.

Kyle had been winning the local, state, national and international matches. He had been in the top ten of all shooters in the United States in those rifle events for several years. At home, he had a wall of medals and trophies from just a few years of shooting competition. He was on the road to be on the next US Olympic rifle team.

But there is no money in amateur competition, so he joined the Clackamas County Sheriff's Department. After two years with the county, Kyle was accepted by the Oregon State Police (OSP) and assigned to the Patrol Division.

His shooting hobby was put on hold because of the time taken up working many long hours, weekends and nights in the Patrol Division. But, there was no one in the police community that had fired half as many rounds, knew how to understand the wind's effect on bullets, knew ballistics or how to hold a rifle to shoot it accurately shot after shot as Kyle did. Kyle was put on the special weapons and tactics (SWAT) team as a sniper. At the end of that first year, he became the team lead sniper, also training the other team members in rifle marksmanship and many other police department snipers.

In the patrol division, Kyle found the police work was not as rewarding for him. Although investigating traffic crashes is important, it took time away from tracking down wanted criminals and in the metro area there were many. He had met many good people who had become victims of various types of crimes, and would use his skills to investigate and arrest the ones who had committed those crimes.

After a few years he was reassigned to the Detective Division to a newly formed street crimes unit, tracking down and arresting only wanted hardcore felons. A felon who has been arrested over and over again for burglary, sex crimes, drug crimes etc. This was what Kyle found best to his liking. His job was locating and taking the criminals who only knew violence and evil against society off the streets. He used informants and good old police work to get them. They all had their chance to change, but wouldn't. He even arrested several he knew from his high school years that had become drug dealers, car thieves, burglars and even one who had become an outlaw biker gang member. He worked in that unit until retiring five months ago.

At OSP all SWAT team members work in normal police assignments, and after stressful training can become a SWAT member, ready to respond to a call for their specialized help at a moment's notice, traveling anywhere in the state. Some think the SWAT team is deployed to kill a bad guy. That is simply not true at all. Their job is to contain the criminal from harming others and get him or her to surrender without firing a shot. Only when that cannot happen, then deadly force may be used. The team had received many awards for a SWAT callout/mission ending with the criminal walking out and surrendering. For a number of reasons, the last few years had more callouts ending up with unstable people wanting or forcing the police to shoot them. It is called suicide by cop.

Kyle was really looking forward to a long and happy life without any more of that stuff or even the need to get up and go to work in the morning, or having his cell phone ring during a family member's birthday party, a holiday, or a sporting event of one of his sons. Or, cancelled vacations.

This camping place has been the site of many yearly vacations and group gatherings. The group had been coming here for years to work on their former boss and close friend's ranch. Kyle's group includes some of his former coworkers and their wives. The men had all worked together during part or all of their careers at the Portland Office of the Oregon State Police. They are now all retired.

All of the men have worked hard maintaining their physical strength and endurance during their careers. They had to remain in better shape than those they arrested. They always had to win every fight, because losing meant they might also lose their lives. Even in retirement, they still workout at a gym every week. Now, because they are not on differing shifts, they can work out together.

Retired Lieutenant Bill Bradford had been their station commander. It was Bill's ranch where the men were gathering. They all looked up to Bill for two reasons: he was taller than any of them, and he had been their boss. He seemed to always have the right advice or right answer to any question. Bill is the only member of this group who was not on the SWAT team. He was too busy managing the office of about sixty state troopers and five Sergeants. Bill is the oldest of the group and was the first to retire eight years ago. He returned to the family ranch as the only living child of his parents.

When he did, Bill and his wife built a new log home from their own timber about ¼ mile from the home site of his folks. The members of the group still address Bill as "LT" out of their respect toward him.

Lonnie Hall was the next to retire six years earlier. During Lonnie's career, he became the Sergeant in charge of all department training. He really brought the department up to and beyond most other police departments in Oregon by getting the troops better equipment and training. Under his leadership, Lonnie updated the troopers' service revolver to a semi-automatic pistol, the Glock 9mm model 17. He was key in organizing the first SWAT team for OSP. He even helped with the monthly training for the members of the SWAT team until he retired. He was also instrumental in the training and arming of all patrol troopers with AR-15 rifles, another first for OSP.

Mac Randall was next to retire and left right away to work overseas as a private security operator for two years at an unnamed company. At OSP, Mac was a member of that first SWAT team and remained on it until retirement. It was Mac who encouraged Kyle to leave the Sheriff's Department and apply for the State Police. Because of Kyle's background in marksmanship, Mac wanted him on the SWAT team. Mac and Kyle had become lifelong friends. At Mac's regular assignment, he was assigned to the gang unit for many of his years at OSP. In that unit, he mostly went from one gang shooting to another or conducted high-risk search warrants arresting the gangsters. Mac's favorite SWAT team position was on the entry team. Even after years of being on the team, he still wanted to be the first to enter any home or building.

Rick Barnes retired almost two years ago. Rick was the nicest guy of the group. He worked his whole career and never had anyone file a complaint against him. No one else in the group could say that. Rick's normal assignment was in the Patrol Division at Portland. Rick became the SWAT team hostage negotiator and armored vehicle driver. That meant he did all maintenance and upgrades to the vehicles. Those vehicles were two 1965 V-150s from military surplus. Rick added a tractor blade and 8-foot ram to the front of the vehicles so he could breech walls or any building when needed. The ram was put on or off the blade as needed and was always carried by the vehicle mounted along its side. It was years later before any other local police departments had a vehicle with that much power and armor. Because of that, Rick and the V-150s were loaned out to assist other police department SWAT teams th-roughout Oregon.

Mac and Kyle had taken down plenty of bad guys and had to shoot some of them during their careers, and all in this group had to protect and save each other a time or two.

Now, that life was behind them... freedom from being ready at a moment's notice... freedom from calls because someone needed help... no more bad guys to arrest. Others were now doing what they had done for years. Kyle was happy it was over and knew it was time to move on. He was happy that he was with his loving wife and friends at a place they called a second home. Kyle and his pals went to sleep that night not knowing of the giant shitstorm that was going to hit Oregon and Washington that would be waiting for them in the morning.

CHAPTER 1

It was just after 7:30am, Kyle sat in the front passenger seat of an armored Humvee, one of three armored vehicles the guys had been assigned since the war had started. All three were traveling as fast as possible with police lights and sirens on to a call for help about 80 miles away from the ranch; a deputy sheriff had been shot while on routine patrol.

Kyle thought back. It only seemed like a few days ago they were only thinking about working at the ranch, not fighting a war against an invading army and bad people entering the county to take what they wanted. Now they were a SWAT team again, this time "The Ghost Team."

This morning their breakfast was cut short from a radio call from dispatch.

The dispatcher said, "All Ghost Team members activate. Ghost commander, phone the dispatch center. All off duty Sheriff's Deputies, report to the office."

The Lt phoned into dispatch right away and listened as the dispatcher explained the situation.

She said, "A deputy had been shot and is being taken to the hospital in Enterprise. The two-man patrol was in the Wallowa Lake vacation homes area. They had radioed in seeing a male body. The passenger deputy had gotten out to check the body and was shot above his bulletproof vest, and he might not live. The uninjured deputy sped away with the wounded deputy and took more gun fire as they left.

"The Sheriff is enroute to the hospital along with all other on duty deputies."

Lt told dispatch, "All Ghost team members are enroute to the city of Joseph to plan an assault. Have a city fire truck and ambulance met us there. We will have our plane in the area after we arrive."

Sheriff McCabe phoned the Lt, "The injured deputy has died. He did not have a chance. He was shot by a high-power hunting rifle.

"The deputies left a fully loaded M-16 in the street when the wounded deputy dropped it outside the patrol vehicle. I have the address of where the gunfire came from, and a person phoned dispatch to give us more information about the target house. We believe they have a woman hostage in the house and the dead man seen earlier was her husband."

"Give me the phone number of the informant," said the Lt. "I will have Rick talk to that person. Sheriff, this may not help, but if those in the house do not surrender right away, they all die!"

When the Ghost Team vehicles arrived in Joseph, the EMS and fire truck were standing by along with six deputies and the three local state troopers. Rick had just finished talking to the informant.

The Lt. yelled out, "Everyone here, circle up around me. Rick has intel about the target after just talking to a person who knows the guys in the house."

Rick explained to the group, "The unnamed person I spoke with is basically a local bar fly.

She will not tell me her name. She said she has been in the house with these guys during the past week over two nights. The house is about 6 miles from here. They act like bullies and talk about taking over the city of Joseph. She went home with them to make some extra money having sex with them. There are four guys in the house. They bragged to her about killing and stealing on their way here from Portland in the old classic car they stole. "She further said they have two AR-15 style rifles and several more hunting rifles with scopes. One of the guys told her he was going to kidnap and rape a woman that lives nearby because she is pretty and is too stuck up to talk to him."

Rick then explained the house layout to the group.

LT told the team, "Kyle, get your sniper rifle and find a position on a roof top about two blocks in front of the target. Jim, get into a sniper position with your sniper rifle that faces the main level, left side of the house. You guys give us intel about what you see. We will have three men behind the house behind hard cover. Another near the front area also behind hard cover. Remember, bullets may be coming your way. We will have a four-man assault team in the rear of the V-150. Everyone else stay back with the EMS vehicles unless called into action."

Rick told the group, "I will mount the ram to the front blade on the V-150, and if they do not surrender, instead of dropping tear gas, we drop a frag grenade inside the house."

Jim found a position and placed his .308 bolt action sniper rifle pointing at a main level bedroom.

He radioed, "I am in position, I can see into a bedroom window. There is a naked woman tied to the bed. I can see her breathing, but she is passed out or asleep."

Kyle radioed, "I am on a roof top straight out from the front of the target. All windows on both levels have the blinds closed. I see the dead man and there is no rifle near him, assume the bad guys have the M-16."

Kyle had his R-25 .308 semi-auto sniper rifle ready with a ten-round magazine in it and two spare twenty round mags placed on his shooting mat nearby.

The Lt radioed to everyone, "The air unit will be overhead in fifteen minutes. At that time, the V-150 will move into position."

At the sight of the plane overhead, Rick drove the V-150 to the house. He stopped in front of it and turned the massive vehicle facing the house while in the street. Rick used the PA system and said, "This is the police, you in the house come out now! You are surrounded! Come out with your hands up!

Jim radioed, "The woman is now awake and looking around."

Kyle said, "I see the blinds moving in the upper left window."

At that moment a burst of automatic gunfire was shot through the window at the V-150. Kyle could not see the shooter, but took a shot. He then aimed the scope to the wall and placed the crosshairs about where a person might be standing and fired several more rounds. He knew the heavy high-speed bullets would easily travel through the wall and still be able to kill a man.

Then suddenly four rifles were being fired from the windows at the front of the house. All the gunfire was directed at the thick armor of the V-150. The bullets just bounced off, causing simple scrapes in the black paint. The sound of the gunfire was deafening, and many bullets could be heard ricocheting after hitting the armor.

After the start of the gunfire, Jim saw a guy enter the room of the hostage. The guy was holding a scoped hunting type rifle. He took a step toward the hostage and started to raise the rifle, pointing it at the woman.

Jim did not pause, he reacted and fired his .308, and the bullet hit the bad guy center of his chest. The bullet knocked the bad guy back into the wall behind him. Jim quickly cycled the rifle's action and fired again. This time he aimed for and hit the bad guy right between his eyes. A sure and instant kill. Jim watched through his scope as the bad guy's lifeless body slid down the wall. There was a mess of brains, skull and blood trailing the body to the floor. Jim cycled the bolt, ready to shoot again if needed.

Jim then took a deep breath and calmly radioed, "One armed enemy killed, bedroom."

Rick yelled over the hail of bullets striking the vehicle, "Lt, time to ram through the front door and drop the frag." Rick shifted the vehicle into gear and floored the throttle. The V-150 sped across the yard as bullets still bounced off the armor. As the ram went crashing through the front door, Rick stood on the brake pedal.

The Lt pulled the cord that released the grenade from the steel box into the living room. As the grenade was released it automatically released the firing spoon. Rick was already backing away as the grenade went off. A large dust cloud and debris went up into the air above the house after the grenade was fired. All around the front of the house it became hard to see through the dust and smoke. Everyone within a mile or more could hear the gun battle. Some said it sounded like a war zone in their community.

When the grenade went off, the ground shook, and everyone engaged in the fight felt it and heard it. Jim's ears starting ringing. Although Kyle could not see anyone, he fired into each front window and around them into the walls.

The Lt yelled to the gunner to fire the 240B machine gun into the upper level. "Just short bursts, traverse the gun across the upper level!"

The dust was still in the air and the 240B rounds were still hitting the house when all gunfire from the house stopped. Everyone around the house could smell the burnt gun powder drifting in the air.

The Lt radioed, "Cease fire, cease fire, all Ghost Team units cease fire."

Everyone waited in case more gunfire came from the house. After several minutes passed, the assault team entered the house through what was left of the doorway. They spotted a body; it was missing a leg and most of his chest, clearly dead. The room appeared to have been splashed with red paint, blood from the now deceased bad guy. They entered the bedroom and found the woman hostage still tied to the bed. She was dirty and beaten up, just staring at the officers with guns aiming around the room. They saw another body with a rifle still it its hands lying on the floor from Jim's shots.

Two deputies with the Ghost Team quickly cut the woman loose and covered her in a blanket as the two Ghost Team members pointed their M-4s up toward the upper level. The deputies rushed the woman out the front doorway and ran her to the waiting EMS unit. She was in a state of shock and never said a word.

The two Ghost Team members slowly walked up into the upper level. Dust was still floating around, and the smell of blood was strong in the air. They both saw two bodies lying near the front windows. Both have multiple bullet wounds. One was missing most of his head. Blood and flesh were all over the area on the walls and floor. The Ghost Team guys left the house and told the Lt that all four are dead; the house was cleared and now safe.

At that point the Lt radioed dispatch, "Hostage recovered safe, all hostiles killed, all officers are uninjured."

Kyle got his gear and climbed off the roof to meet up with Mac and Jim. They looked at one another, then hugged. Kyle said, "How did this place we think is like heaven turn to hell in just a few days. What will happen next?"

CHAPTER 2

The story started a few years before when the relationship between the United States, The People's Republic of China, and the Democratic People's Republic of Korea became more complex and unstable. The United States, through the United Nations (UN) attempted to put an end to the buildup of arms in North Korea, mainly their missile and nuclear programs. All attempts, ranging from giving North Korea money and oil to sanctions on imports, have failed. North Korea now has more military weapons, developed short and long-range missiles, and is making nuclear weapons. In recent years North Korea has made over 85 missile test launches. They are outright telling the world the weapons are to be used against the United States.

China has said publicly that they are also trying to stop the North Korean military buildup. But, China still sells North Korea nearly all of the goods that it imports. Including large amounts of coal and food grains. Recently a cargo ship carrying American grown wheat was seen by United States spy satellites unloading at a North Korean dock, clearly in violation of current UN sanctions.

The President of the United States made a speech on national television saying,

"After years of United Nations sanctions, North Korea continues to develop missiles and nuclear weapons in defiance. China supplies North Korea with most of its needed fuel and food. If China will not stop the North Korean missile and nuclear programs, the United States will consider sanctions on imports to China."

After that speech, the Chinese president told the world, "China will stop all exports into North Korea until the missile and nuclear programs stop."

The Chinese have claimed this in the past, but the past shows they know what to say to the world to deflect criticism.

In an attempt to verify China's promise, hidden tracking devices were placed into coal and wheat shipments that China shipped from the states of Oregon and Washington to be used only by the Chinese. After several weeks, some of those devices were detected in North Korea.

Armed with that evidence, the US President met with his cabinet. During the meeting he told the cabinet, "I want to keep putting hidden tracking devices in coal, wheat and timber that we sell to China. No one outside of some special government agents know of the trackers."

He further said, "I want a UN sanction of a 100% embargo against North Korea until they stop the illegal weapons programs. "We will give that a few weeks. If we have more proof that China is still exporting aid to North Korea, I will close all trade with China, and all North Korean banking accounts and other funds in the United States will be frozen."

All cabinet members around the table responded affirmatively and energetically proceeded to accomplish the President's plan.

That same week the United States ambassador to the UN made a speech saying, "Because the United States is aware of the continued violations of the UN sanctions against North Korea regarding their missile and nuclear programs, I ask that the UN take a vote to stop 100% of all aid to the North Koreans by all countries until they stop violating the sanctions. Currently, North Korea is a clear danger to international peace and security. If North Korea fails to stop their missile and nuclear weapons programs, the next step will be military action. I now ask for a vote."

Eight of the UN Security Council members voted in the affirmative. The Chinese ambassador then said, "Under article 27, China is vetoing the ruling."

With that done, it was the end of any help from the United Nations regarding North Korea.

For decades the Chinese government has sent personnel to visit American companies and government installations like the power grid, dams, freeways, railroads, bridges, schools, nearly all of the United States infrastructure. Many times, it was an honest attempt to bring their country into the modern world. Sometimes it was to get information helpful in case of a future war.

Among the "visitors" were members of an espionage unit run by a general known as Yang. Yang was in charge of interviewing the returning spies. Not long ago, a returning spy met with General Yang.

The General asked the spy, "What did you develop from your visit to Bonneville Dam on the Columbia River?"

The spy said, "General, I got many good photos of the whole site, including the electrical generating turbines. Those American fools even taught me how to run the dam from the control panel. It can be completely operated from one desk."

"Very good, now go and write a complete report. You are dismissed," growled Yang.

China has always been able to keep many military upgrades in weapons secret from the outside world. They have made new weapons far more advanced than anyone would believe. Some weapons only few in China even knew about.

During a recent trip, General Yang went to a secret weapon testing area. There he had a meeting with the top scientist.

"Welcome General, I have good news for you," said the scientist. "We have finally finished the new Electro Magnetic Pulse (EMP) missiles. They do not produce any radioactive fallout. Our army can occupy the area right after the blast. And they are able to fool radar."

"What is the blast range?"

"General, it is a 70-kilometer circle. Within that circle most electronics and anything with a computer will never work again unless it is protected in a Faraday Cage. No other country has any weapons like these. General, our tests prove the Faraday Cages we made work."

"You must never mention this work to anyone outside of this area." With that said, the General turned and left.

Just a few weeks later, the US President had an emergency meeting with his cabinet. The President asked the Department of Defense Secretary, "Ed, report on the tracking devices in the exports to China."

"Mr. President, roughly a quarter of the wheat, timber and coal shipped by Chinese ships was off-loaded in China and moved into North Korea."

"Any other news to report, Ed?" asked the President.

"Yes, Sir. Mr. President, North Korea is about to launch two more test missiles this week." The President stood and pounded his fist on the table. He looked around the table then said, "That's it! I am through playing games with China over the little fat bastard in North Korea. If they launch any more missiles, we'll place an embargo on China. No more United States imports, exports, and all Chinese money in any United States banks gets frozen. Maybe that will stop China from helping North Korea."

The Department of Agriculture Secretary stood and said, "Mr. President, China has agreed to buy nearly 70 million worth of wheat, corn, soybean and timber from Washington and Oregon this year. They are buying millions of dollars of coal shipped through those same states. The United States has sold over one trillion dollars' worth of stock and bonds to China. Many are government bonds."

"So, they will not get the wheat or timber. We will sell those to another country."

"Mr. President, China pays 18 months ahead of what they plan on buying during the following year. This year's shipments have mostly already been paid for last year. They will not be happy, they will lose about 60 million dollars."

The President said, "If North Korea launches any more missiles, I will inform the United States citizens as to the embargo against China."

The week after the two North Korean missile test launches, the embargo was announced on national television. The President told the world of the proof that China is still giving aid to North Korea.

The president of China followed by saying publicly, "China has done nothing wrong and hopes that the United States and China can come to an agreement soon."

He phoned General Yang and told him, "Proceed with military plans to get our grains, coal and timber before the people of North Korea and China starve and are without building supplies."

Several months ago, General Yang, acting as a president of a mock Chinese company, arrived with the Ground Force soldiers and the Strategic Support Force soldiers to lease out two abandoned ship docks: one in Portland, Oregon and the other in Seattle, Washington. The General opened up an office at the Portland site. There they unloaded container cargo ships onto the acres of the secure dock and surrounding land. United States Customs agents inspected the containers of trade goods as they left the docks, but many containers remained and escaped inspection.

General Yang called his subordinate, Colonel Li, into his office for an update. The General asked Colonel Li, "How is our plan working out?"

Li said, "We have been getting all of the secret containers moved off the dock unseen by United States Customs at night. More of our ships are being brought into the Columbia River and into the Sea Tac area on schedule and are anchored near those cities."

"How is it possible the ships are not being inspected?" Yang asked.

"Anchoring ships in the rivers before they get off-loaded is a completely normal everyday sight in the international shipping world. The United States Coast Guard knows the ships' names and locations at all times while the ships are in the United States waters because of a transponder that all commercial ships carry. The Coast Guard knows the cargo and crew through the shipping documents that they get faxed to them from each ship. The Coast Guard does not know if the ships are providing the correct information. And, none will be inspected to know what and who they really carry. They quit doing ship inspections shortly after President Bush left office as a way to save costs."

So far, the Chinese plan was coming along perfectly.

At 3:00am Saturday morning, the Chinese invasion started to go operational.

At the United States Coast Guard Portland Station, there were two young officers working the night shift in the tracking and intelligence office. The office has a giant wall of video monitors.

On these monitors the Coast Guard can see the names, and locations, to track all of the cargo ships. Suddenly, the video monitors go blank.

"What the hell just happened?" asked the senior officer.

"I don't know, I had nothing to do with it, I was almost asleep," was the reply.

"We just lost all the tracking and locations of all commercial cargo ships between Coos Bay, Oregon and the Canadian border," said the senior officer.

The senior officer, clearly upset, shouts at his co-worker, "Hey, shithead, get the monitors back online. Now!"

"Boss, I am trying. I am going through the checklist. It says it will take up to thirty minutes to do all the tests."

"Okay, keep on it. It's really no hurry since no ships travel into the Columbia River or Sea Tac at night. Those in the river at anchor stay at anchor. So, I will not wake up the Captain. I am not going to sound an alarm. I will go and make a fresh pot of coffee. In case you need help, I will be back in a couple minutes."

At the same time, two men wearing all black bicycled onto the I-5 freeway bridge across the Columbia River. They are Chinese Special Forces soldiers. The two leave the bicycles on the sidewalk. They remained silent as they then climbed up to the control office and looked inside through a glass window.

They find the bridge operator sitting reading a newspaper while facing away from them. They then climb back down several feet.

One of the soldiers speaks up and says, "I will take the shot."

The other shook his head. "Affirmative."

They both return to the window. The soldier drew his semi-auto pistol, a Chinese QSW-06 with a suppresser attached to the muzzle. He took aim at the back of the bridge operator's head and pulled the trigger the moment a truck traveling on the bridge passed below them, making a loud rumbling noise on the steel roadway decking. The soldier thought to himself, *what prefect timing*. The bullet traveled about eight feet after passing through the glass window. The bullet from the 5.8x21mm cartridge entered the back of the bridge operator's head. The operator died before his head hit the desk. His brains and skull splattered all over the newspaper.

The soldiers entered the room and activated the lift span of the bridge. The crossing arms go down across the traffic lanes and sidewalks, blocking anyone from crossing the span. There is only light traffic on the freeway at that hour. Those drivers that cross on the bridge regularly understand the bridge will be closed to crossing vehicles for as long as twenty minutes to allow ships to pass under. After the bridge was fully opened, the two men smashed instruments and cut wires controlling the span controls. It was now locked in the up position. The two men leave the control room and bicycle to the railroad bridge.

That bridge is a mile away further west on the Columbia River. The railroad bridge is not manned at night. They simply break into the office and raise the span, and then destroy the controls again to prevent it from lowering.

"Our work here is done, let's get back to the dock," said one of the soldiers as they begin the thirty-five-minute ride.

The other man answered back, "I'm glad to be involved in such an important mission. These dumb Yankee's will get just what they deserve. I wonder how many will be dead by this time tomorrow."

"Many thousands my friend, many thousands throughout this area."

Not far from the bridge mission, several black vans were traveling around the Portland area with a team of Chinese and North Korean soldiers in each vehicle. The first van parked at one of the Portland International Airport public parking lots. There the team has full view of the Oregon Air National Guard base flight line. They had four surface to air handheld missiles stored in EMP-proof boxes. They could see the two F-15 fighter jets that are armed, standing by on alert.

The other van has arrived at Bonneville Dam, which supplies electricity to most of the Portland and Seattle areas and also provides flood control. This team approached on foot in a darkened area.

The team stopped at the unlocked eight-foot-tall chain-link gate and fence at the entrance. They find the lone armed security guard in the security booth. The inside of the booth was lit up, allowing anyone nearby to see into it and the guard unable to see outside of it. The security guard was sitting with his head tilted down reading a gun magazine. The Chinese soldier was twenty feet away. That soldier sticks the barrel of a type 64 suppressed submachine gun through the fencing, aims and fires one bullet. The bullet entered the guard's chest and went through his heart. His body was driven backwards off of the stool he was sitting on and onto the floor. His bulletproof vest was unfortunately left hanging on the coat rack at the door of the booth. He is dead seconds later. His life's blood was now mostly drained from his body and pooling on the floor.

The shooter waved at the rest of his team. He then signaled for them to drive the van through the gate. He said to the last team member, "Lock the gate. We all go on foot from here to locate the other guard."

They soon found the other guard asleep in his security vehicle with the driver's door window fully open. His head was tilted back, snoring loudly. Another member of the team signaled the others that he would shoot this guard. He drew his pistol with attached suppressor. Because this guard was wearing a bulletproof vest, he aimed at the left temple, pulling the trigger twice. The guard never felt anything after the first shot.

The team leader said, "Now that the security has been taken out, go and get the van. We will travel in the van to the dam operator's center. It is almost one mile from here."

The on-duty dam operator was deep inside the dam monitoring the water flows and electricity output. The team did not need the operator alive. All team members have been taught how to monitor and operate the controls. They know what every switch does and when to turn each one on or off. They parked outside the doorway of the generator control room. The team must walk down into the dam through three stories of stairs attached to thick concrete walls. At this point, they were far below the river level. The team quietly approached the dam operator's desk area. They found him fully asleep with his head down on his desk.

Team leader signaled the others that he will take the shot. The operator gets one bullet to the back of his head at close range from another 5.8x21mm pistol cartridge. Now, they had full control of Bonneville Dam.

The team leader said to the others, "Toss the three bodies into the river. After that is done, we split into the two teams. Team #1 go to the North end of the dam. Team #2 go to the South end.

If anyone else arrives at the dam before our other teams get here, just shoot them. Looks like the other teams will be here in three to four hours. Expect to be shooting Americans before our brothers arrive!"

CHAPTER 3

For some hours, multiple two-man teams of Chinese and North Korean Special Forces soldiers on motorcycles traveled south from the Portland area and north from Seattle. Most used the I-5 freeway, but some veered east to use smaller parallel highways and county roads. They carried explosives and had been at their assigned places now working hard. Their job was to place explosives to blow up bridges on highways near the southern border of Oregon and northern border of Washington. There was no need to take down the whole bridge because taking out only a section of each bridge would stop all traffic. Where there are no bridges, the teams would place explosives near the highways to block them from the blast debris.

The bridge on highway 101 near Gold Beach over the Rogue River was blown. Also, the I-5 freeway at Medford, again over the Rogue River, was blown. The seven other highways on the southern border would have landslides blocking them only for a short time until more damage could be done.

In Washington, the bridge near Bellingham on I-5 would be destroyed. The other five highways crossing into the United States from Canada would be blocked by road damage or hillside debris. None of the highways bordering Idaho were targeted. All explosives were timed to go off at

4:05am. Another team was at Kinsley Field. It is the Air National Guard air base in Klamath Falls, Oregon. There they have two F-15s parked on alert outside of the hanger. The Chinese team was in position nearby to launch SAMS if they started the jets. In Portland the other team was watching the Air National Guard air base. Several other large teams had been traveling to remote areas of Oregon and Washington.

In Oregon, the team leaders' radio General Yang. They only say, "Oregon team 1 and 2 are in position and ready."

The Generals radio operator said, "Copy, over."

The Washington teams radio the General and repeat the same message.

In each state were two other Chinese teams with three semi-trucks and trailers and two small 4x4 old style jeeps. In Oregon, they were parked on remote county roads in the south central and eastern regions of the state. One was near Fort Rock and the other near the Burns Junction. In Washington, the same types of two teams were set up in remote areas of the Colville Indian Reservation in north-east Washington in very remote areas and unseen by anyone.

Captain Lee and his men were at the Fort Rock site. He got his men together for a pep talk. "Men, soon we will be launching missiles to remote Oregon highways and will destroy the roadways so that no person or vehicle can travel on them. We must be ready in case of an air attack, the surface to air missiles will be manned at all times. Any known military aircraft flying in the area will be shot down. Private aircraft fleeing Oregon will be allowed to leave. By afternoon, we will be resupplied with food, water, more personnel and weapons."

Cargo Ships that were at anchor in the Columbia River near Portland started moving at 3:05am. The Lead ship radioed to the General, "Ships one, two and three moving to position."

Each ship that was out at sea, unseen by the Coast Guard since the monitoring system went down, moved close to the shores of the two states. Each ship radioed, "Moving into position."

Motor vehicle traffic was stopped on the I-5 Bridge. The drivers stood outside of their stopped vehicles. All people on the bridge could see three large ships traveling upriver towards Troutdale, Oregon. One driver shouted over to the driver in the other lane, "No wonder the bridge is up for so long, there are three ships coming through."

Another stopped driver said, "Yeah I see that, but what's weird is none have any lights on and there are no docks upriver for any ships that big to tie up at."

The team leader at Bonneville Dam said, "Now kill the power, turn off all the electrical power being generated at the dam."

One of the team members said, "Finally, I got to help destroy the west coast," as he flipped every switch to off.

This act put the whole west coast power grid into trouble. A chain reaction would happen. Switches will flip to off to save themselves from overloading, and some would have transformers blow at nearly all western state power stations. While many of those stations can go back online, it could take days to have the correct safe routing of electricity bypassing this dam.

Ten minutes later, each Chinese ship sailing in the ocean off of the coasts of Oregon and Washington launched their newest weapon. The midrange missiles loaded with a small EMP warhead.

One of the ship's Captains said to his ship's pilot, "Now that we launched missiles, I can tell you what we are doing. When each warhead detonates, all modern motor vehicles, aircraft, ships, train engines and anything with a computer in it within a 70-kilometer radius of each missile blast will shut down. The targets of the missiles are all the cities along the I-5 corridor and coastal areas. We have put all the major cities into a long-term electrical blackout."

The pilot replied, "I guess we are at war with the United States."

The Captain confirmed, "Yes, we are. If the Americans are smart, they will meet our demands very soon and we will get the food and timber our people need and have already paid for."

The remote semi-truck teams were outside of any of those blast effects. They launched their missiles armed with conventional warheads to the highways blocked by the earlier motorcycle teams. The railroads near the state lines were also targeted. Minutes later, the truck teams launched missiles loaded with anti-personnel mines. Those mines were dropped as the missile traveled over the target area and spreads hundreds of mines. The motorcycle teams then traveled to meet the truck teams. They have been given the "Okay" to kill anyone they saw on the way.

CHAPTER 4

Some citizens realize the power has gone out but, do not know why. All those driving gradually coast to a stop with a dead engine. Police on duty are without working vehicles or police radios. Most walk back to their offices or homes.

Officer Viles in Portland was walking back to his office when he saw a man sitting in a yard chair. The man yelled to Officer Viles, “Do you know what happened? It seems that all electrical power is out in the city.”

Officer Viles walked up to the man and said, “I’m not sure, the patrol car and police radio just quit. The few others I met just had their cars quit like mine. Some are waiting by their cars so when their cell phones work again they can call a tow truck.”

The seated man said, “I think it was an EMP. I heard a loud explosion and some others a long distance away.” He pointed at the West Hills of Portland and continued, “At that moment, all power went out. We may be in a radioactive fallout area.”

“Who would do that to United States?” asked Viles.

The man replied, “I don’t know for sure. If we are still alive in a week or so, maybe we will find out. If I was to guess, I think North Korea or the Chinese did it.”

"Wow, I was going back to the office. But, I have a family and live about 2 miles away. I am going home, not back to the office," Viles exclaimed.

"Good luck officer," said the man. "I hope I am wrong about the EMPs, but I doubt it."

"I hope you're wrong, too," said Viles.

The Oregon State Emergency Management center in Salem also went completely offline. It was supposed to provide all police, fire and medical responders in Oregon, including the National Guard communications and organization during any emergency. Moments later, while on-duty personnel were switching over to generator power, the building was destroyed, killing all inside by a direct missile strike from a conventional warhead.

The two teams watching the F-15s saw the power go out. They put on night vision goggles and watched for any activity at the alert planes.

The team leader at PDX says, "Men, get the missiles out, then spread out around the parking lot. We will wait to see if the planes start. If they don't, I will give the order to fire anyway."

The men moved to positions for a clear shot at the planes.

All they saw were some airmen walking around with flashlights. After several minutes go by, the team leader said to the first two men, "Fire your missiles into the alert planes on my order. You other two fire into the Air Guard plane hangar. After that, walk back to our base at the dock. If anyone tries to stop us, shoot them and keep going. Ready, one and two... fire… three and four… fire."

The two F-15s suddenly exploded, sending large fire balls of jet fuel up over one hundred feet into the sky. The ordinance on the wings exploded from the heat of the fire. The fifteen men and women on the flight line were all killed instantly. Before anyone at the base knew what happened, the hangar exploded, destroying six more F-15s and killing more airmen. The team at Kingsley Field enjoyed similar success. The Oregon Air Guard, the country's only combat air assets in the Pacific Northwest, is no longer a fighting force.

The three ships proceeding east from Portland in the Columbia River have stopped near the city of Troutdale at the site of an eighty-acre aluminum plant. It had been closed and not operating for decades. From the ship, portable ramps extended. They start unloading troops, shipping containers and vehicles. The troops were from both the Chinese People's Liberation Army and the Korean People's Army. The containers all had EMP shielding. Inside the containers were military weapons and supplies. Armored personnel carriers (APCs), type 89 tracked vehicles and the type 92 wheeled vehicles were being unloaded. They also unload four Z-10 attack helicopters and 8 M-171 transport helicopters.

Colonel Li radios General Yang and said, "General, we have secured the Troutdale outpost area.

By the end of the day, it will be a military fortress surrounded by a wall of shipping containers with armed men and SAM sites set up. The helicopters are being made ready for flight. We will also secure the thousands of gallons of aviation fuel at the Troutdale airport. That runway will then be destroyed so no planes can take off or land."

General Yang said, "Remember to take trucks over to the nearby truck stop on the I-84 freeway and take all fuel truck trailers back to the outpost. If you don't, the fuel we need may get stolen by others. Do not let anyone stop you in your duties."

"Yes sir, it will be done as soon as I have the trucks ready," Li replied.

The docks in Portland and Seattle operated by Chinese companies have been busy. They were now unloading the hundreds of containers of military supplies. Then the steel containers were stacked around the dock boundary, forming another fortress wall.

Soon a vehicle transport cargo ship arrived at each dock. From these, many armored personnel carriers, SAMS and more attack and transport helicopters along with several thousands of soldiers were unloaded.

Teams of Chinese and North Korean troops were forming up in the APCs getting ready to drive out onto the city streets in Portland and Seattle.

General Yang walked over to the vehicles. Upon finding Captain Sima, he said, "Our intel shows the streets are easy to travel on since there was only light traffic when the EMPs struck."

Sima replied, "Yes, General. I thought travel would be easy. Do we know yet if the Oregon governor is at the Salem mansion or his Portland home?"

Yang said, "Captain, our spies say he is with his family and one state trooper bodyguard at his Portland home. Bring back the governor and his family, no one else. Also, we confirmed the mayor of Portland is with his wife in their Portland home. Your work today will be easy."

"Good news General!" exclaims Sima. "My two teams will take them to the assigned high school and hold them there as prisoners. Is the school secured and ready for them?"

"Yes, get going as soon as you're ready," the general said as he walked back to his office.

A short time later, Captain Sima and his troops in APCs arrive one block away from the Governor's home.

Sima told his troops, "We go to the front door and kick it open. The spies say the governor and body guard are sitting in the kitchen. His wife and two boys are upstairs still asleep.... Let's go!"

Six soldiers went to the front door and opened it with one hard kick. Several seconds later, Captain Sima was standing in the governor's kitchen. As the bodyguard stood up and drew his Glock pistol, the Captain fired his suppressed submachine gun into the trooper. The trooper was hit eight times in his chest and dropped to the floor dead.

Captain Sima in nearly perfect English said, "You are under arrest, you and your family will not be harmed if you do as I say. Otherwise ONLY YOU will leave here alive."

The Governor was clearly upset and shaking. He looked down toward the dead trooper and cried out, "Please don't hurt my family, I will do whatever you ask."

"Good," said Sima. He explained, "We will all go upstairs to your family. Each person will pack one bag of clothing. We must leave here soon."

The Governor asked, "Why are you doing this, who are you...?"

Sima was silent. He motioned to the governor and the group hurried upstairs. They woke the rest of the governor's shocked family. With a packed bag of clothing, they left while being covered by the soldiers' submachine guns. They were all placed inside an APC and driven away to the school, or what is now named Prison #1, Portland. As the family was unloaded from the APC, another APC arrives with the mayor of Portland and his wife.

Captain Sima tells the group, "We now hold and control all of Oregon and Washington states. You will be held here until we decide when to release you. While here you will have food, water and sleeping areas. You must follow all orders given by me or my men. No questions at this time. I will talk with you later today."

The governor and mayor started to ask questions. "Why are you doing this to us? What do you want? Why did the power go out? Did you cause the power to go out? Finally, the governor said "The US government will not stand for this! You will never get away with any of this!"

"Shut up, no questions at this time! Follow my men NOW," shouted Sima.

The two families were taken into the school gym where beds are set up for them. They noticed armed guards standing in every corner.

It was now 6:00am in Oregon and Washington, but 9:00 am in Washington DC. The belief was that there was a massive power grid failure on the west coast. They had received some satellite phone calls from California saying the power was out, but everything else was working. No news from the western parts of Oregon and Washington. The White House receives a fax from the Chinese government. It was a demand letter addressed to the President of the United States:

Since the United States of America is not willing to allow the People's Republic of China to have what we already paid for, the People's Liberation Army with assistance from the Korean People's Army has landed fifty thousand soldiers in the states of Oregon and Washington. Our armies are there to take what we are rightfully owed.

The armies have successfully taken control of all areas west of the Cascade Mountain range. We have destroyed all electrical power and communications to the lands west of this. Anyone entering those lands will be destroyed. All United States military in those lands must leave. Any United States military intervention against China or North Korea will result in North Korea destroying South Korea. We hold hostage hundreds of United States citizens, including both states' governors and major city leaders. They will not be harmed unless you attack. We have ships approaching that have equipment to restore electrical power, food and water for your citizens. Our ships arriving and leaving must not be harmed.

The People's Republic of China demands:

1. All United States military and all NATO troops in South Korea must leave and not return.

2. Since we have paid for grains and timber in Oregon and Washington, all harvested wheat, corn, soybeans, timber and coal in Oregon and Washington now belong to the People's Republic of China.

3. The citizens in Oregon and Washington must give up all firearms.

The People's Republic of China will be available to discuss our demands.

The White House aide that removed and read the fax yelled, "HOLY SHIT! Wake the President now. We have been invaded by the Chinese!"

The President had run his election on downsizing the military and military spending to save tax payer money so that he would be able to provide free health care to everyone except the rich and help all who do not have a job by giving them free housing and free college. Since in office, he already closed down Joint Base Ft. Lewis-McCord in Washington State.

The President is awakened and handed the fax from the Chinese. After reading the document, he became worried about the lives of the Americans in the control of the Chinese. He told his aide, "There will be no United States military intervention. All ships from China must have free transit to and from Oregon and Washington. Arrange a meeting to be held on Wednesday to speak with the Chinese. Now, go get the cabinet together so we can have a meeting on this matter ASAP!"

CHAPTER 5

The morning of the invasion, just after daylight at the Bradford ranch, a Golden Eagle takes flight from its roost high in the rim rock. The eagle stretched out its wings. From wing tip to wing tip, the eagle measures eighty-five inches. The powerful wings allow the eagle to climb quickly into great heights above the ranch. From that high altitude, the eagle looks at the ground for breakfast. No man-made sounds can be heard; no horns honking, no engines running, no people talking, no city sounds… just a few young deer calling for their mothers.

The eagle flew over the site of the old ranch homestead. It could see four RVs parked alongside of each other with some large pickups, an SUV and a boat near a newly constructed building. The building is the meeting hall for ranch visitors and workers.

The eagle continued soaring on the morning updrafts over large grassy fields and scattered ponderosa pine trees. It flew over the new ranch house, a big beautiful log house about a quarter of a mile from the meeting hall.

The eagle looked down at the woodshed where cords of firewood were stacked. At this time, it is only half full. The eagle sees a mouse sitting on some of the wood. It passes up on that meal and continues looking down near the field edges for prey. It sees something larger! A rabbit is sitting eating grain, unaware of the eagle above. The eagle makes one circle and silently dives at the rabbit. Moments later, the eagle has the rabbit in its talons and is flying back to its roost for breakfast.

Mac was the first to awake and went into the meeting hall to get things ready for the group's breakfast. He then realized the power was out. He went back out and checked the power to his RV. There was no electricity at that connection, either. He went to Kyle's RV to get some help.

While knocking on Kyle's RV door, Mac yelled, "Get up! Are you going to sleep all day? I need your help. The power is out again."

"Hey, I'm up. Be out in a minute," replied Kyle.

A few minutes pass and Kyle stepped outside. Meeting Mac, he said, "You know it's nice to be sixty plus miles from Enterprise, but mountain weather sure causes enough power outages."

"Yeah, but the cell phone service is out this time along with the electricity. That's a little more than normal," replied Mac.

"Well old buddy, let's get the meeting hall generator running along with the propane furnace and cooking stove. At least the RV's have switched themselves over to the on-board battery power."

Just before 9:00am, the group was finishing up their breakfast. Most were having their second or third cup of coffee and talked about the work that needed done at the ranch that day.

Suddenly, an alarm sounded from the fire lookout loud speakers. All the men know that sound; they have heard it many times over the police radio. For ten seconds, high and low alarm tones are heard. It means to all police EMERGENCY, standby for details.

"What the heck… do they have tests on that system?" asked Rick.

Mac replied, "They're never supposed to test it, only use it for real emergencies."

Kyle's wife Claudia asked, "Could it mean there is a forest fire?"

Mac said, "Could be, but whatever the problem is, we need to get to the lookout and find out."

Rick said to the men, "I will get my truck started. We'll all fit into it."

"Before we go to the lookout, everyone needs to go outside and look around all directions for smoke. We may need to bug out if a forest fire is close. Remember the last big fire. It was within several miles of the ranch. We only got lucky it was stopped at the river," Kyle said to everyone.

The group, minus Rick, looked around and sniffed for smoke. No smoke was seen or smelled. Rick drove over to the men standing outside the meeting hall and yelled out, "Let's go guys!"

As they approach the ranch home they saw the Lt's wife, Mary, standing on the porch. She waved to them and yelled out, "Bill is in the lookout talking on the radio. We don't know what's happening. The power is out along with the home phone and our cell phone service. We are running off the generator again."

Rick waved back at Mary and drove to the lookout. As they walked into the radio room, Lt was talking on the radio. They heard him say, "Okay, we will be there soon."

He put the microphone down on the table and turned to face the group standing in the doorway. His hands were shaking and his voice trembled as he spoke. "Men, that was Sheriff McCabe. He just said that the state has been invaded by a foreign army, ahhh, the Willamette Valley already appears to be controlled by them. All electrical power is out along with landline phones and cell phone service. It appears nothing with a computer chip is working in the valley. Satellite phones, at least around here, are working. The Sheriff's Office is operating on a standby generator as is the rest of Enterprise. All motor vehicles in this area are working, so it appears the grid is down."

The four guys just stood there not saying a word.

The Lt continued, "Men, the Sheriff got the information from an Oregon National Guard Captain in La Grande through the county emergency satellite phone. The Captain explained a lot about the event to the Sheriff."

Lt then looked into the faces of each man and said, "Men, the Sheriff needs our help. We need to get to Enterprise ASAP. Anyone not wanting to go just say so, I will understand."

All the men turned and looked at each other.

Mac said, "We are all going, that's what we do. We help when others can't or won't. We are a team."

The other guys nodded with their heads.

"Okay," said the Lt. "Get geared up, bring rifles, handguns lots of ammo and all your tactical stuff. No telling when we will get back home. Tell your wives what we know, sorry it ain't much at this time."

Lonnie turned to the group and said, "Lt, we will be back in a short time. Sounds like we were just damn lucky to be here and not home in the valley. We will need to put some hurt into some unknown army bastards soon."

The group decided years earlier to become a kind of "prepper" group and the ranch would be their bug out place. Because of that, they had a shipping container half buried near the meeting hall loaded with ammunition and ammunition reloading supplies along with other emergency equipment. In the meeting hall basement, among other items, each guy had a safe containing their weapons. They had been given most of their OSP tactical gear at retirement since they were now OSP reserves. Just in case of a state-wide emergency, they could be called back into service. All that gear was kept at the ranch.

Each man in the group told his wife everything he knew, which was not much at that point.

Kyle told Claudia, "All you gals need to go meet with Mary. Set up a rotation so someone is always in the radio room. It may be the only way to get information as to what is happening throughout the county and in Oregon. We should be able to radio back here when we might be able to return."

Claudia said, "But, you guys are all retired old men. What can you do now?"

"Yes honey, we are old, but the SO only has about five road deputies and there are only three local state troopers to cover the whole county. They have never done any police work like we have. If nothing else, we can train them. Honey, sorry but I need to go." Kyle kissed Claudia and left the RV.

The group hurried to the meeting hall basement and put on their old blue police utility uniforms, old Danner leather boots, duty belts, drop down leg holsters, tactical vests and grabbed their helmets. They got their Glock 17s along with grabbing their AR-15s. They put extra magazines into their bulletproof tactical vests.

Kyle looked at the others and said, “Maybe I should also grab one of my sniper rifles.”

They all agreed. Mac jokingly said, “Which one, Kyle?”

After a minute of thinking, Kyle said, “The R-25, the semi-automatic .308 caliber rifle. This rifle-scope combo is accurate to six hundred yards with the 168 grain match bullets that I load.”

He packed the rifle into a hard-plastic case along with five loaded 20 round magazines. Lastly, each man had an old sweat stained blue baseball cap. Across the front in white letters it read, “Oregon State Trooper.” They put their caps on and headed out of the basement.

Rick looked around at the others and said, “Wow, we still fit into the old clothes and gear. Let’s get the Lt and head for town.” A short time later, all of them were racing into town in Rick’s big Chevy crew cab pickup to meet with Sheriff McCabe. Sheriff McCabe is the typical small county Sheriff. He grew up in Wallowa County. He was the star high school football player, who received a football scholarship. He came back home after collage and started working as a deputy sheriff. A few years later, he ran for Sheriff and easily won the election. He was now in his third four-year term as Sheriff. He was always seen wearing a clean white cowboy hat, cowboy boots and jeans. Unlike many Sheriffs, if he was working he wore the department uniform shirt, not a suit and tie.

Instead of the standard police duty gun and belt, this Sheriff proudly wears a western style gun belt with a real

Colt .45 single action peacemaker in the holster. He stood in front of a mirror at his home and said to himself, *Am I up to the job the county needs me to do? Can I protect the citizens who elected me to do just that?*

CHAPTER 6

Earlier that same morning in Troutdale Oregon, Lenny, the unmarried younger brother of Lonnie Hall, had gotten up early to go to the small plane airport in Troutdale. Lenny had been in the Marines and seen combat, and after that he worked at OSP as a patrol trooper for several years. He left OSP to become a pilot flying cargo planes for a living. He thought today he would fly his personal plane before the afternoon winds picked up, which would make flying his little plane no fun at all. One of his toys was a 1961 Cessna 172 airplane. It is a high-wing, four-seat single engine light aircraft. The only modern things it has in the cockpit are a GPS and the radio.

Lenny got up around 7:00 am. He was not sure of the time since the apartment had lost electricity during the night. He looked outside and noticed no vehicles were moving. He saw one vehicle abandoned in the street. He also noted that his cell phone had no service. He got dressed, packed his backpack with a lunch and some bottles of water. He put on a shoulder holster with his Glock 9mm handgun. He donned a jacket to cover the gun. He went to his car and discovered it would not start. He then walked to the airport. He didn't see any other people during his walk.

Lenny thought about the possibility of an EMP when he saw more abandoned vehicles on the city streets. There was no freeway traffic or aircraft flying.

Both are a normal sight even this early. Even a train was stopped across a street, completely blocking it. No one was around, not even police or fire crews anywhere. He was convincing himself that maybe an EMP really had been detonated in the area.

At the airport, a fellow plane owner was near his hanger.

The guy asked, “What do you think is happening around here?”

Lenny told him, “Maybe an EMP struck and knocked out all electrical devices.”

“No way, maybe a truck hit a power pole,” replied the man.

“Could be, but why is the cell service out along with the electrical power?”

“How would I know? I am a doctor, not an electrical repairman. But, it is strange. I had to walk to get here, my BMW would not start. I cannot get my Cessna Sky Catcher to start. Nothing works, and I paid 150,000 bucks for it last year.”

Lenny then said, “If my plane runs, I will fly around the area and see if I can learn more and then come back. The flight should be fifteen minutes or so.”

“Okay great, maybe by then I can get a maintenance person on the phone to help me.”

“Good luck with that, see you in a little while.” Lenny walked off to his plane.

Lenny tossed the backpack into the plane and did the preflight checks. The fuel tank was full. The engine started right up and ran great, although, the radio and GPS did not work. Lenny took off and circled around Troutdale. He saw the same everywhere: no vehicles moving and few people walking around. He banked over toward the Columbia River.

Lenny was shocked. Could he really be seeing what was down below? He looked at the old aluminum plant. It was now bustling with activity. Ships in the river nearby were moving vehicles off and onto the shore. It all looked like military equipment and men in uniforms. A gun atop a cargo container started tracking him.

Lenny yelled out, "OH SHIT!" He pointed the plane into a steep dive, pulling up just above the water surface of the river. He saw the bright streaks of tracers passing above and in front of him.

"What the fuck is happening around here and whose army was shooting at me?" *The helicopters did not look to be US military. Maybe the helicopters will take off and shoot me down.* "Shit, I need to get out of here, NOW!"

Lenny pushed on full power and continued flying low over the river for several minutes, trying to decide what to do. He wondered where to go. Then he thought about his brother and sister in-law at the ranch in eastern Oregon.

Lenny yelled out, "Hey big brother. I will be seeing you in a couple of hours. God, I hope you guys are okay." A six-hour car trip to Enterprise is less than three hours in the Cessna, and he had plenty of fuel to make it. So, Lenny flew eastward, mainly staying in view of I-84 and the Columbia River so as to not get lost.

A few minutes later he passed the Bonneville Dam and saw men in black uniforms. One man pointed up at him and another nearby fired a long burst from a machine gun at him. He jammed the throttle to the firewall and climbed over some nearby cliffs out of the range of the gun fire.

He yelled out, "Why me, what the fuck is going on around here? Is everyone going to try to kill me today?"

All along the freeway he saw stopped semi-trucks and a few cars. He passed the city of Cascade Locks. Some people were walking around, but no vehicles were moving. Later, as he passed over Hood River, the city seemed a repeat of Troutdale and Cascade Locks. Only a few people moving around, walking or bicycling. Around 90 miles east of Portland near the city of The Dalles, he saw a massive vehicle crash involving trucks and cars, several of them burning. The whole freeway was blocked in both directions. There was a long traffic back up behind the crash in the west bound lanes.

In The Dalles, cars were backed up at gas stations and people were standing around. He noticed a few vehicles actually moving, only headed east on the freeway. As he continued east, he noticed more normal traffic movement.

Lenny finally neared the city of Enterprise and circled the airport. Not seeing any planes in the pattern or on the runway, he landed.

Lenny saw a guy working on a nearby plane. He walked over to the guy and excitedly said, "I came from the Portland area and until I got to The Dalles I did not see any vehicles moving. Is all the power out here? Are the cars working? Do you know what happened? My plane's radio does not work."

The guy said, "I really don't know what's going on, but all electricity is out around here including cell service and land line phones. The vehicles run just fine. Some people think maybe it is a big power grid problem. The Sheriff is having a meeting now with county managers and other police at the high school gym to talk about it."

Lenny asked the guy, "Do you know what time it is."

"Yeah, it's 10:15," he replied.

CHAPTER 7

The school was about five blocks from the airport and Lenny walked into the gym. Soon, he spotted his brother Lonnie and some other OSP guys he knew. They were retired, but they were all now wearing OSP SWAT type gear. It made no sense. Lenny thought about today, nothing today made any sense. He yelled, "Hey Lonnie!" and waved at his older brother.

Lonnie waved for him to come up front where the OSP guys and Sheriff were all standing.

The Lt's group had arrived at the gym just minutes earlier and noticed that the county emergency mangers, county department supervisors, the three local state troopers and the whole Sheriff's department was arriving. The group walked in and saw Sheriff McCabe. The Sheriff waved to them to come over. Together they walked away from all the others.

The Sheriff said, "I have a lot to say and will make a speech to everyone attending. But first, the State of Oregon is without any top leadership. We are on our own here. After the meeting, I want to deputize you guys to help me and this county. At this time, the job is without pay. If you take me up on the offer, then you need to drive to La Grande and meet with the National Guard company commander Captain Westbrook and bring back some military equipment."

The Lt, "Bill," spoke up saying, "We already decided we're going to help you. But, these men," pointing to the group, "are my close friends. We are an established team. I want to continue leading them as a team. Would that be okay?"

The Sheriff said, "Yes. Bill, I want you to be my second in command for all law enforcement in this county and we will work together. You know your men, you know exactly what they can do and how they get it done. They will be under your direct supervision. They have much more experience than any of my guys. I think the county will need them working as a team."

Lonnie introduced Lenny to the Sheriff. "This is Lenny, my younger brother. He is a retired Marine with plenty of experience in combat and was an OSP Trooper. He is now a pilot and should also be deputized. His plane is parked at the airport. Sounds like he will also be needed."

The Sheriff replied, "Of course," and thanked all of the group for volunteering to help.

The Sheriff then asked everyone attending to be seated. He began speaking to the crowd.

"Thanks everyone for coming on such a short notice. I have a lot to say, please hold all questions until I am done with my speech. First off, we all know each other except these men in the front row. Men please stand and face the crowd."

The Lt's group stood as they turned toward the crowd.

The Sheriff continued, "These men are all friends of mine and are retired from the Oregon State Police. They were members of the State Police SWAT team in Portland for many years. I trust them as any other men in my department. They will be deputized and will work for me. They will be wearing blue uniforms instead of our normal brown uniforms, but carry the Wallowa County Sheriff's office badge."

Each one starting with Bill Bradford waved and said his name. All of the people present knew him. Most county employees at the meeting had heard stories about the others but had never met them.

The Sheriff continued, "As everyone present knows, we are off of the grid. This morning I received a phone call through the county emergency satellite phone from the Oregon National Guard in La Grande. The Captain there informed me that as of this morning Chinese and North Korean troops and equipment have landed in western Oregon and Washington. They fired weapons that took the electrical grid offline and disabled anything that has a computer chip running it.

"The Chinese told Washington DC that they now consider the two states to be under their law. They want all the timber harvested and grains here to be shipped to China now and in the future. They said they have the means to destroy any military that attempts to stop them. They have taken US citizens hostage including our governor. The state-wide emergency management center in Salem is offline. My belief is it was destroyed.

"The Guard Captain said state police, city police, some central Oregon Sheriffs along with the National Guard leadership are meeting today in the city of Bend. Bend is outside of the Chinese control at this time. Our President said he will not approve any US military intervention and is attempting to hold talks with China later this week. We are on our own. We must do everything we can to make Wallowa County as safe as possible for its citizens. We may have American citizens enter our county to loot or kill us. We may need to decide to fight the Chinese or surrender to them.

"The Guard Captain is loaning us equipment and troops as soon as he can. The Idaho National Guard is going to help Oregon. No regular Federal military is allowed to help us in any way. We expect thousands of people to be fleeing from the Willamette Valley to eastern Oregon. For now, the Guard is going to help those fleeing as much as possible. The Captain expects the National Guard to prepare to fight the Chinese in Oregon."

Everyone listening just sat with their mouths open, many shaking their heads. Several started crying.

"I realize most people in this county carry firearms and they know how to use them. I expect all citizens allowed to have firearms to be armed at all times. To help keep citizens of the county safe, we will be manning roadblocks on the highways into the county. You may be asked to show your ID to police or National Guard soldiers at roadblocks. Please do it. It is for your safety. Each vehicle coming into the county, unless it is military or police, will be searched. Delivery trucks will be allowed to bring goods into the county. But, mostly no outside citizens will be allowed to enter the county unless they own vacation homes, property, or have relatives in the county. We will keep records who the new residents are and where they will be living. As of now, the I-84 freeway is still open from around The Dalles to Idaho. We have been told food and aid will be coming from Idaho. I will be working on getting together as many able-bodied men as possible to form a county-wide militia. Please call 911 if you suspect or know about anyone who might be connected to the invasion of our state."

The Sheriff paused for a moment, then started speaking again.

"Please hold all questions for several more minutes. I need all county Search and Rescue personnel and the OSP guys up here."

At that time, the Sheriff deputized Bill's group and the 20 Search and Rescue personal, bestowing them with full enforcement authority.

The Sheriff asked the Lt and the 20 new deputies to stay and sent the others from the ranch to La Grande. The Sheriff tried to answer questions from others attending the meeting. He just did not have any answers yet. After the meeting ended, the Sheriff and the Lt got busy making plans for the highway roadblocks.

CHAPTER 8

That same morning, Kyle's two sons Justin and Eddy were at their apartment in Milwaukie, Oregon. Eddy was first up needing to go to work that morning. He found out his cell phone was without service and there was no electrical power in the apartment.

Eddy woke up his older brother Justin and said, "Hey the power is out, could you give me a ride to work? We could stop and get breakfast together, I'm buying."

Justin rolled over in bed and said, "Yeah, I need a shower, then let's get going."

"Me too, fifteen minutes and I will be ready."

After getting ready, the two of them walked out into the parking lot to Justin's SUV. Justin pushed the door unlock on the key fob and said, "Hey, my door won't unlock."

"Just use the key in the door like in the old cars," said Eddy.

"Yeah, smart ass, what do you think I was going to do?"

As they got into the SUV, Justin tried the key in the ignition. He said to Eddy, "Well smart ass, nothing in this car is working. Now what?"

They looked around and noticed that no vehicles were traveling on the nearby highway. So, they walked over to the sidewalk and saw vehicles stopped in the roadway and a few people walking or bicycling. Justin said, "Remember dad talked about natural disasters and even mentioned an EMP? There is something strange going on."

"Yeah, the plan is everyone in the family would grab a bug-out bag, some weapons and head to the ranch near Enterprise. But, without a vehicle it would take days to get there," replied Eddy.

Justin told Eddy, "This may not be an EMP, but let's bicycle to Mom and Dad's home to see if this blackout is the same there. We should pack backpacks with water bottles, a few clothes and our Glock 17s with holsters and two spare magazines. The ride is only eight miles."

"Okay, I guess I'm not going to work today. Whatever happened, I think we need to stick together."

"Yeah little brother, I will protect you."

They packed up and rode to their parents' house. On the way, they noticed no one had power and all vehicles were parked or stopped. The exception was a 1950s-Ford truck with an old guy driving it past them. As the vehicle passed, the driver honked and waved.

At their parents' home, it was the same: no power and no working phone. Both began to worry about what to do and how could they get to the ranch.

Justin said, "Man, it's about three hundred fifty miles to the ranch. We need to get stuff together to take on the bicycles."

Eddy went to his dad's gun safe and opened it. Inside the safe he found a Bushmaster AR-15 carbine and a Remington 870 12-gauge shotgun with an 18-inch barrel. In another safe, he found more ammunition than most small stores stock.

Justin sat thinking for a few minutes about the bicycle ride to the ranch. It was too far for a bicycle trip. Chances were they would never make it. He spoke up, "Remember one of Dad's close friends, Jim Hellman? He retired from the Clackamas County Sheriff's Office several years ago. He was on their SWAT team and was also a firearms instructor."

"Yeah, so? Most of Dad's friends were SWAT team guys, what about him?"

"Well, Jim has a restored 1957 Chevy Carryall 4x4. He lives just about five more miles away. Maybe his truck is running like the old Ford we saw. Let's ride our bicycles over to see Jim."

"Okay big brother, you have a good idea. Let's go."

When they arrived at Jim's home, they saw another old vehicle in his driveway, a restored Carryall like Jim's, but it looked a few years newer. After they knocked on the door, Jim opened and seeing the boy's he quickly invited them into his home.

Jim asked, "Do you guys think an EMP has struck the US?"

Justin answered, "Maybe…it seems like it did, but what should we do?"

Jim then turned to another man standing nearby and introduced the boys to him. "This is Tim, the guy who drives the other old truck parked in the driveway."

Tim told the brothers, "Jim and I worked together at the SO and were both SWAT team members for many years. Your dad used to call us the Jimmy and Timmy SWAT team. Like Jim, I have retired from the SO. I was also a K9 deputy for most of my working years. I now have another dog, a dog I paid for and trained. His name is Ike, a German Shepherd. He is an attack and tracking dog."

Jim said, "We are making plans to get out of the area ASAP with our families and head east into the mountains somewhere, but so far we don't know where to go. We were thinking of going to Timothy Lake on Mt. Hood. Check out how bad things get then go somewhere else if needed."

At that point, Justin said, "Mom and Dad are up at the ranch near Enterprise along with some of the retired OSP SWAT guys. How about we get together and all go there?"

Jim replied, "That's a better idea, I have been there before. Kyle and I hunted elk in the area. They have room for us to camp, unlimited clean water and together we will be safer than alone."

Justin said, "We need to go back to our apartment for more clothes and camp gear. We can get food, water, guns and ammo from Dad's stash. When should we leave?"

"Tomorrow just before daybreak," replied Jim.

Justin said, "We will be ready in the morning at Dad's house. We had better get going now. See you guys in the morning."

Jim said, "See you guys in the morning." And the brothers left.

Just before dark, Eddy heard a helicopter and went outside to see it. It was a military helicopter, and as it passed over paper sheets were being tossed out of it. Eddy found a piece of paper and read it.

It read, "The People's Liberation Army of China and Korean People's Army now have full control of this area. All people must give up all firearms or will be put into prison. Anyone that resists will be shot. The army will be in the neighborhood soon to pick up all firearms."

CHAPTER EIGHT

Both Eddy and Justin never slept during the night. They were afraid that the Chinese army or looters would come to their parents' home. Suddenly Eddy sat up and said, "I hear someone outside. What should we do if they break in?" and he shook his brother.

Justin said, "I think I heard it, too. Sounds like someone is trying the doors and windows to break into the house."

CHAPTER 9

Kyle's group of Mac, Lonnie, Lenny and Rick left the meeting. They rode in Rick's truck to La Grande Oregon. The city is just over sixty miles away from Enterprise. During the whole trip Lonnie and Lenny kept talking about what each other knew about the situation. Everyone mentioned others they knew who were still in the Willamette Valley and asked each other if any could still be alive. If so, could they even do anything to help them at this time?

They arrived at the armory and met a Guard Sergeant. The Sergeant pointed to where two Humvees were parked, each with a military utility trailer attached. He told them they were to take them back to Wallowa County. He handed Lonnie some inventory documents to sign. They listed the equipment loaded in the Humvees and trailers.

The Sergeant told them, "These are new up-armored Humvee's. They can stop most rifle bullets shot at the engine compartment, all windows and passenger compartment. The tires are run flats. They do not have gun turrets, but if we come across any extra turrets, they can be mounted on the top hatch. The Captain said some of these items are for you guys only. The items are ten M-4A1 rifles with suppressors, two cases of grenades, one smoke and one frag. I suspect you guys know how to use them."

All of them at once said, "YES."

Mac told the guys "Those guns are the newer M-4s. The main difference is the old style had 3 shot burst and full auto. The M-4A1s have semi-auto and full-auto, a much better trigger and other small changes that make it a better gun. Just call them M-4s."

The Sergeant continued, "The Captain wants to talk to you guys before you leave."

Mac said, "Okay, let's go there now. Thanks for all this stuff."

"You're welcome. I will take you to the Captain's office."

Captain Westbrook was also a lifelong Oregonian. His family owned a working cattle ranch about fifty miles west of La Grande in the Starkey area. After he graduated at OSU, he joined the US Army as a commissioned officer, rank of Lieutenant. Being in an infantry unit, he had seen combat in the Middle East. After that, he joined the Oregon National Guard. Most soldiers spoke highly of him when his name was mentioned.

The group went inside to the waiting room. After about ten minutes, the Captain had them enter his office. He introduced himself as Captain Westbrook with the 3-116 Cavalry, National Guard, assigned to La Grande Oregon. The guys all introduced themselves and shook hands with him.

Capt. Westbrook asked that they all be seated. He then updated them with the latest news. "This morning the meeting in Bend was attacked. A Black Hawk helicopter from Idaho had been enroute. In that chopper was my Lt Colonel, Major and others. They radioed that they saw smoke coming from the area where the meeting was taking place. The Black Hawk's last transmission was the building had been blown up and vehicles in the parking lot were destroyed. We believe at that point the chopper was shot down. At the same time, Bend went black. No radios or phones in the area are working. We guess another EMP type weapon was fired along with other missiles."

He paused for a moment and then continued.

"We have not had contact with anyone from the Governor's office since before this war started. Those elected state leaders, State Police command, National Guard command and most central and eastern Oregon Sheriffs who fled to Bend are considered KIA or prisoners at this time. My other Major lived in Portland, and we have not had any contact since last week. As far as I know, at this time I am the ranking guard officer left in Oregon. The remaining OSP offices have a few Sergeants and the troopers. I have asked them to work with the local Sheriffs and city police."

The Captain continued speaking, "Tons of supplies are being trucked into Oregon from Idaho. As of now, Idaho's Governor is allowing his National Guard to assist with supplies. So, equipment and aid are coming from both the Guard and private businesses. They will deliver those supplies to Baker City, La Grande and Pendleton. The guard is currently short on personnel, but our main mission is to get people fleeing from the Willamette Valley to Idaho as safe as possible. The largest amount of people are expected to be traveling on I-84. The city of Pendleton will be the first holding place for them."

Lastly the Captain said, "I am going to have soldiers stationed at the Highway 3 roadblock and use the Bradford Ranch as a base for the roadblock soldiers and bug out place in case the Guard needs to retreat from La Grande. I am going to get men and equipment up there ASAP. Any questions?"

None of the group had any questions.

Mac said, "Here is a portable police radio with a charger," and handed them to the Captain. "We and the rest of Wallowa SO are on net #1, Union County SO on net #2 along with La Grande City PD. We are call sign Ghost Team. To speak to the Sheriff, ask for him by name and ID yourself. Radio us anytime, we have radios with us always and will be ready to assist."

They shook hands and left.

As they left the office, Rick said to the group, "I guess that means there is no State Police command to activate us reserves."

Mac replied, "No, there is not…working for Wallowa County is the right thing to do, at least for now."

On the drive back to Enterprise, Lonnie looked through the documents of the equipment that they had been given. He found twenty-four M-16A2 rifles, twenty-four Berretta M9A1 semi-auto pistols with holsters, cases of 5.56 and 9mm ammunition, cases of MREs and medical supplies. When they arrived back at the SO, they removed their M-4s and 2 cases of 5.56 and one case of 9mm ammo from the supplies.

The Sheriff and Lt came out to meet them.

The Sheriff told the group, "Leave the Humvee's at the county shop. The shop guys will install a county radio, blue lights on the roof and the SO badge decal on the front doors of each vehicle. Pick them up in the afternoon tomorrow. One vehicle is for the team, the other for the Lt."

Lonnie said, "Lenny flew his plane here. It's parked at the airport. I think we will be using it. Can we get a SO radio installed in it?"

The Sheriff said, "That's a great idea. It will be done. Now take the Lt back to the ranch and you guys get some sleep; tomorrow will be another long day. The roadblocks are going to be set up by tomorrow night."

Kyle radioed the ranch. "Kyle to Bradford ranch, Kyle to ranch, do you copy?"

"Yes, this is Mary."

"Let everyone know we are all fine, headed home now. We are all hungry, Kyle out."

"Oh, thank God. See you guys soon, dinner will be ready."

When they got into Rick's truck to leave, it was already dark. They all talked about what had happened and what they should and could do at this point. It was mostly still unanswered questions.

CHAPTER 10

Sunday morning at the ranch. Everyone had a job to do before breakfast. The guys cleaned the bathrooms and main room in the meeting hall as the wives got breakfast cooking. There was still a lot of talk about the whole situation. Many more questions without any answers. All were sad as they mentioned people they knew back in the Willamette Valley. Not knowing if any of them were alive or dead was heartbreaking.

The men decided they would clean up the kitchen and dishes as their wives made lists of items they needed to buy in town. Today everyone would go to Enterprise. It might be the break they needed; just seeing other people in the city.

After cleaning up, the guys opened the wooden crates containing the M-4s. It was just like Christmas morning to a child, but even better. The guys found each rifle had a close quarters scope, a tactical light, a vertical forehand grip, flash hider and suppressor, tactical sling and eight thirty round magazines. All top end equipment.

Lonnie asked, "What's up with these flash hiders? They are way different than we had before."

"They are a newer, better style," said Kyle. "The flash hider stays on the barrel, we screw the suppressor on over it. They may be YHM products made for the military. We need to shoot these with the suppressor on and off to see if impact changes. It might change at 100 yards."

Mac said, "I think we should keep all the M-4s for the team. That way we have spares or could loan a few out if needed. Now, let's grab a case of ammo and get to the gun range."

Off to the range they went, and they fired with the suppressors on and off. They fired on both semi and full auto at ranges from 25 yards to 100 yards just to be sure the guns worked as they should.

Later as they got into Enterprise, Claudia was the first to notice the electrical power was on. She said, "Hey guys, it looks like power is back on. I'm going to try my cell phone, it has a signal. I will phone the boys back home."

She told the others in the vehicle, "Oh, the phone is working, but it will not connect."

She phoned Kyle's cell phone and the call connected.

"Well that's weird, I can call local but not to the valley."

Kyle said, "They likely fried all the valley towers with the EMPs."

The Lt went to the command center at the SO, to meet and be briefed by the Sheriff.

The rest of the guys went to pick up the Humvees. The women loaded into two trucks and headed to the stores.

Lenny asked the shop guys, "Did you guys get the radio installed in my plane?"

"Yeah, and even a new GPS unit."

"Good deal, thanks guys," replied Lenny.

The shop guy tells the group, "We mounted four big blue LED lights on the roof, two facing forward and two backwards. Police sirens and PA systems were added.

They each got extra off-road lights mounted to the front grill guard. Each front door now proudly displays the Shcriff's Office name and badge decal. We also installed GPS units in them."

Kyle said, "Thanks, you guys did a great job. Especially thanks for thinking about the GPS units and for working all night to have the vehicles ready."

"You're all welcome, we need to go home and get some sleep. Later we need to help get vehicle's set up at the roadblocks," said the shop supervisor.

The group went to the SO and were briefed for the day. Again, it was good news, bad news.

"The good news," the Sheriff said, "as you can see the power company got the grid figured out and bypassed the Bonneville dam power lines. So far, eastern Oregon has electrical power, cell and landline phones. There is no phone service to or from the western parts of Oregon and likely will not be for a long time."

The Lt said, "We are working on details to get the roadblocks into place today before dark. We will use a regular deputy at each roadblock with four of the newly deputized Search and Rescue personnel. The Oregon Dept. of Transportation put snowplows onto their 10-yard dump trucks and filled the beds with sand. The plows will stop nearly any rifle rounds. With sand added, they were made into 80,000lb bulletproof, unmovable barriers. Each roadblock would have four dump trucks and one SO marked vehicle blocking the road."

The Sheriff said, "Now, the bad news. A rancher from up in the Imnada area had come into town shot, but he will be okay. He was interviewed at the hospital by a deputy. He told the deputy as he was riding his horse and had just gotten into the public lands on a road next to his ranch. When he rode around a corner, four guys were standing in the road. He thought they were all Mexican because he heard them speak Spanish. They all had handguns and three of them had rifles. One of them took a shot at him, the shot just nicked his arm. He spun his horse around and rode as fast as he could away from the area. He did not think he had ever seen them in town before, but he is not sure. Looks like we may have another Mexican Cartel marijuana grow operation."

Lastly, the Sheriff said, "You guys have handled this stuff up in the National Forest before. What do you think?"

Mac looked over at Rick and said, "Rick, you're the expert with the Cartel grows and you speak Spanish, give us a plan for a mission."

Rick said, "Sheriff, show us on the map where this happened, the grow will be close to where they were seen."

The Sheriff went over to the wall map and pointed out the location.

Rick then said, "It is the start of the growing season. They are just getting set up and starting to plant the marijuana at this time. They will live at the site and be supplied by a weekly drop off of gear and food. They will not have any vehicles at or near the grow site. That is how we find them. We find the suppliers and get all the information we need from them. The suppliers will be two Hispanic males renting a home in Enterprise. Their vehicle will be a van of some type or another, used and beat-up. They would have moved into the house within the last two months.

All workers will be armed, even the guys in the house. Until I interview the guys in the house, we will not know how many workers they have at the grow site or even the site lay out. The number of workers depends on how big of an operation they have set up. What I have found out from past interviews is that they are like forced labor. The Cartel brought them here to work; they did not have a choice. The workers are supposed to shoot anyone, including police, who interferes with the grow. If they do not fight or abandon the grow site, the Cartel will kill their family members back in Mexico. So far, no Oregon police have been shot in grow sites, but in California several cops have been shot and killed.

"The Cartel will send another team to take the harvested marijuana after these guys cut it down around September. At that time, these workers get to go home to Mexico and will get paid."

After a pause Rick said, "I need to phone the OSP office in Pendleton. They have a V-150 armored vehicle stored there for use of the SWAT team on eastern Oregon SWAT call-outs. We will need it. Lonnie, Lenny and I will fly to Pendleton and I will drive the V-150 back here. If we leave soon, we can be back by nightfall."

So, at that point, Rick stepped away to make phone calls.

Mac told the Sheriff, "Get all your deputies here for a meeting. I need to tell them to check with everyone they know who rents out homes in the city and tell them to ask the landlords about who we are looking for right away."

Kyle stepped outside to phone Claudia.

"Honey, how's the shopping going?"

"The store is crowded, but people are not in a panic-buying mode. Good thing we shopped today because tomorrow or the next day most items on the shelves will be gone."

Kyle said, "Please get a case of Snicker bars or two if you can and any power bars. You know how the guys and I like to eat them on long missions. I hope we will be home by dinner."

"Okay, I will get some. See you tonight, bye."

Rick got the okay from the OSP Pendleton Sergeant to take the V-150. The three of them took off to the airport and flew Lonnie's Cessna to Pendleton.

Kyle called in all the new deputized men to meet at the county gun range. Since the M-16s and 9mm handguns would be the weapons used at the roadblocks, he wanted to be sure the men knew the weapons. Each man practiced with a rifle and handgun.

After Kyle returned, Mac asked, "How did it go at the range?"

"Just as we thought, these guys know how to shoot. Most have AR-15s or have been in the military, so they will not have any problems using the guns when needed," replied Kyle.

Mac then told Kyle, "We have located the cartel house. I have the address and the landlord gave me the layout of the house. We need to do a drive by to get more intel before we hit the place."

"Okay, get an SO undercover vehicle, that way no one will know we're the coppers and let's take a look," responded Kyle.

Mac drove the "plain jane" car while Kyle drew outlines of the house, doors, windows and out buildings. After that was done, they went back to the SO to plan the raid for the next morning.

Kyle asked the Sheriff, "Could you give us the best four deputies you have for this raid? We will do practice runs and go over the whole raid tomorrow morning."

"Yes, I know the four who will work out great. You will not have any problems with them. They just need to learn some tactical moves," said the Sheriff.

"Okay, have them here at 8:00am. I am going to phone the three local state troopers. Thanks Sheriff," said Kyle.

Rick returned a few hours later and told them, "I had taken that V-150 to Pendleton just before I retired. It still has a new engine, transmission and tires. The front blade and ram I put on it are still unused. The SWAT team had never deployed the vehicle since I had delivered it. We should not have any issues with the V-150 for a long time. No one at the Pendleton office even knows how to start it, much less use it. I got the okay to keep it here."

"Wow, that's a fantastic deal," said Mac.

CHAPTER 11

On that same Sunday morning just before daylight, Tim and Jim drove their old vehicles loaded with cargo, family and pulling utility trailers to the Morris home right on time.

Eddy asked them, "Did you guys read the leaflets the helicopter tossed out?"

Jim and Tim looked at each other and shook their heads. Jim asked Eddy, "What leaflets?"

Eddy told them, "A Chinese army helicopter dropped these all over near here last night," while holding the paper in his hand. He handed the leaflet to Jim. "We think we heard someone outside during the night trying to open the windows and doors. They never got in the house. Man, were we scared."

Jim read the leaflet and shouted, "Oh...shit!" he handed the leaflet to Tim.

After Tim read it he said, "More than oh shit Jim. This means we must get out of here now. If not, we might never be able to leave. Everyone in the trucks must be armed and ready for trouble."

Justin and Eddy tossed their gear into a utility trailer. The boys then split up with one of them going into each of the two vehicles.

Jim thought for a second about the need to not be seen as they traveled in the dark. He quickly pulled out a screwdriver, removed the taillight bulbs in both vehicles and pulled the wire harnesses that connected the trailers.

As Jim was getting that done, he told Justin and Eddy, "You guys need to take off the trucks inside dome light covers and pull the bulbs out in each truck. If we need to bailout while it's dark, we don't want to light ourselves up as an easy target."

Tim told him, "That is smart, and we should not use the head lights unless they are really needed. Let's keep the windows open and guns in our hands. No stopping unless we are forced to. Since I am following you guys, put your arm out showing me you're stopping or slowing so I do not run into your trailer."

"Will do. I'm done here. Let's go. We will need to drive slower without headlights on, but I think it will be safer," replied Jim.

Nothing was said in either vehicle since everyone was really scared. Each one of them had a holstered handgun and either an AR-15 or shotgun sitting in their lap. They all hoped that they would not need to shoot…if they ran into the Chinese Army, they figured they might all be killed just for trying to escape with guns.

Jim and Tim had planned out the route during the last evening. As they left the city, they drove onto the first major road, the I-205 freeway north from Oregon City. So far, no other traffic or people were spotted.

At the city of Gladstone, they turned off the freeway and headed east, then onto highway 212 toward Mt. Hood. The route they took bypassed all large cities in the metro area. They never saw other headlights or any other vehicles traveling on the roads before daybreak. After daybreak, they saw a few people on bicycles all going east as they entered highway 26. An hour later, Jim stuck his arm out the window and pointed it downward; he was stopping. They stopped both trucks near the small city of Government Camp on Mt Hood. By now everyone had to go to the bathroom, including Ike.

Jim walked back to Tim and told him, "This stop is for a bathroom break. We need to post one armed person in front of my vehicle, and you post someone behind yours, so we don't get any company when our pants are down."

"Funny," said Tim. "But, really it's not. We all know it is needed."

The bathroom was alongside the roadway in the heavy brush of the Mt. Hood National Forest. So far, the trip was going fine. A few miles later they left Highway 26 going onto Highway 35 north toward the City of Hood River. They saw only a few stalled vehicles and no people for the entire way into Hood River. At Hood River they turned east again and entered I-84. Now they started seeing people. People were walking and carrying backpacks or bicycling, all of them traveling on the roadway shoulders headed east. No one looked up at the trucks as they passed. They all seemed to be moving as fast as possible and looked really scared. Several old classic cars passed by them at high speed.

Near the city of The Dalles, they came across the big wreck and needed to drive on the shoulder to get past it. At The Dalles, they could see police on the westbound side of the freeway. All vehicles were exiting the freeway in the westbound lanes and driving into the city.

Tim spoke up to his wife, "Look at those vehicles coming from the east, they are all newer and should not be running."

His wife said, "Maybe the EMP did not affect this area?"

"That could be the reason, but at this point who knows," replied Tim.

As they passed The Dalles, vehicles were entering the freeway also eastbound. Because Jim's and Tim's trucks were loaded with cargo and passengers and had small engines compared to modern vehicles, they could only travel about 45 mph top speed on the flat land. Most other vehicles were disregarding the 65mph speed limit and traveled much faster.

Jim said to everyone in his vehicle, "Remember, we do not stop for anyone out here. We go around any stopped vehicle or people blocking the road."

Jim's wife asked, "What if they will not get out of the way?"

"That means the area is likely a trap. We first shoot over their heads. After that, if they do not get out of the roadway, we must fire at them," Jim replied.

"No way, that's killing people."

"Sorry, but it's them or us. If we stop they could and would likely try to kill us, then take all of our stuff. Is that something we should risk?" asked Jim.

"Okay, I get your point," his wife answered.

They continued seeing people walking and bicycling with a vehicle passing them every once in a while. Westbound traffic was clearly less than normal for the interstate. A couple more hours passed without any incidents.

Both vehicles were low on gas nearing the city of Pendleton. Once they were in an area without anyone on the shoulder, Jim signaled that they were stopping.

Justin offered up, "I will get the extra gas cans out and fill both trucks gas tanks."

Tim said, "Okay, we should be traveling again in about twenty minutes and everyone needs to take a potty break. Use the stand of trees just off the freeway."

They took turns standing guard holding rifles, just in case of an attack.

After they finished fueling and using the bathroom, Tim and Jim got together and walked away from the others. They stopped at some shade off the roadway behind the trucks to talk privately.

Jim asked, "How's everyone in your truck holding up?"

"All scared, this is the first road trip that my wife or daughter have not wanted to stop every two hours to use a restroom. I told them to each take turns sleeping for an hour. That seems to help them, but not me," replied Tim.

"Well, it's about the same in our truck, and I am getting burned out being on 110% alert all the time. I am not scared, but having the family on a mission is taking its toll."

Tim replied, "I hear ya, it seems like we are on a mission and having our loved ones with us is way more stressful than any normal SWAT mission."

Jim asked, "What do you think this freeway will look like in the coming days?"

"Bad guys killing good guys just to take bottles of water is my guess."

At that point Jim said, "I think we have been really lucky. Let's hope our luck holds out and we make it without shooting anyone. HEY! Wait a minute, I see vehicle movement several miles behind us."

Tim used his binoculars to look and said, "OH CRAP! I see two motorcycles stopped in the travel lanes. The lead guy is checking us out with binoculars. Each motorcycle has a passenger. The motorcycles look like smaller road bikes, they might be dirt bikes, certainly not hogs. They all have red bandanas around their heads. Each driver may have a rifle across his lap. But, for sure the guys on the rear have some kind of long gun pointed up. I can see the barrels."

Jim said, "We can't let them follow us or force us into a trap or attack when they want."

"No, we cannot."

"If they drive at us, they're likely to attack us. Otherwise, they will stay away," said Jim.

"I agree, go get more mags and prepare the others. I will keep watch with the binoculars."

While Jim was getting more AR mags, he told the women to lay on the floor and the young men to get ready for a shootout.

Tim yelled, "Here they come, and they're moving fast! Let's get behind those big ass trees over there." He pointed to several trees near the outer freeway shoulder.

"We still have a few minutes before they get here. If they point guns at us or the vehicles, we shoot."

"Roger that!"

Jim had an AR-15 with a scope, Tim had an AR-15 with an optic sight. One motorcycle was following the other, still at high speed.

Jim said, "If I shoot, I will take the rear bike."

"Okay."

As the motorcycles got close, they slowed down to about 20mph. The lead motorcycle rider picked up a long gun off his lap and laid it on the handlebars, pointing it at the parked vehicles. His passenger leaned over, aiming a long gun toward the vehicles. Then the trailing bike riders did the same.

Jim yelled out to Tim, “They don’t see us over here! Let me take out the rear bike first.”

“Okay.”

Jim lined up his scope on the trailing motorcycle driver. He could see the guy smiling as if he was enjoying the chance to shoot someone.

As they got about 100 yards away, Jim heard a gunshot.

Tim yelled, “They’re shooting at the trucks!”

After hearing Tim, Jim immediately fired a shot. The driver was shot just below his neck and was tossed back into the passenger. His blood sprayed all over both. They were knocked off the motorcycle. The driver’s head slammed onto the pavement, bouncing several times before he stopped. The passenger rolled across the road, their motorcycle tipping over and crashed on the freeway. The other motorcycle continued since its riders could not hear the shot over their loud engine noise and were focused on the parked vehicles ahead of them. The two riders were experiencing what happens to untrained people in stressful events. They had tunnel vision; they only see their target.

Tim did not hesitate any longer. He fired his rifle at the other motorcycle driver. The driver was hit and leaned away, causing the motorcycle to go left. Tim shot again and hit the passenger. That guy flew off the back as the motorcycle went off the roadway and crashed.

Jim saw the rear passenger of the motorcycle he shot stand up and look around. The guy walked toward a gun lying nearby and bent down to pick it up. As he stood up, Jim shot him three times in the center of his chest.

Tim yelled out, "Are any moving!?"

"My two are for sure dead. The driver may have lived after the shot, but not after his head hit the pavement. Let me scope your two."

"I cannot see either of your guys breathing, but the bullets are cheap. I will shoot each again," said Jim.

"Hold on a minute," replied Tim. In Tim's truck, Ike had watched everything and was now barking to be released and assist his partner.

Tim yelled to Justin, "Let Ike out, we need him!"

Ike ran over to Tim and laid down, waiting for commands.

"Let's move the bodies and motorcycles off the road. Destroy their weapons and take any ammo," said Jim.

"First, cover us. I want Ike to bite each one to make sure they are really dead and not playing possum," replied Tim.

Within a couple of minutes, Ike had approached each body with Tim right behind him. On command, Ike barked and was directed to bite each man in a leg. None reacted.

Jim ran over to the trucks and asked, "Is everyone in the trucks okay?"

Justin said, "The guy who shot missed us."

All the others told Jim they were okay.

"Stay in the trucks. We will be back in a few minutes. You can get the trucks started. Honk the trucks horn if you see anyone approach from either direction," said Jim. He then walked back to the dead guys and motorcycles where Tim and Ike were waiting.

"Jim, these guys were certainly some type of gang or wannabe gang. Look at the tattoos; my guess is they were from the Tri-Cities Washington area."

"Yeah, good bet, lots of gangsters up there."

Together they pulled each guy into the center ditch. They laid the dirt bikes on the outside shoulder. Then rounded up all the guns. There were four 12-gauge pump cheapo shotguns with sawed off barrels. The ammo was a mix of ten rounds of old birdshot.

Tim looked through all of the dead guys' pockets, then said to Jim, "Good news, they do not have any radios or phones. Maybe they do not have any other friends nearby. They had Washington State prisoner ID cards." He tossed their wallets near the bodies.

"Hey, let's leave the ammo, it ain't any good. Take the shotguns and remove the barrels. We take the magazine end screwcaps and barrels off. We toss each part out the window into the ditch every few miles. That way, there's no connection to us and no bad guys will ever use those guns again," said Jim.

"Yeah, okay that sounds good," replied Tim.

No one in the trucks said a word to each other or asked Tim and Jim questions.

Jim finally broke the ice in his truck by saying, "Okay, next stop in about an hour is La Grande, or we blow through it if it looks bad."

All he got in return were head nods, up and down.

When the vehicles exited I-84 at the Highway 82 off ramp into La Grande, they were stopped at a roadblock manned by a State Police Trooper and a National Guard Soldier. Nearby were other soldiers, all armed with M-16s standing in the ready position. The State Trooper walked up to Jim's vehicle, and upon seeing all the guns they had in the vehicle he said, "Get out, leave the guns inside the vehicles."

They all complied and got out.

The trooper asked, "Are you traveling with the other truck?"

Jim said, "Yes, we are traveling with our families."

"Okay, everyone out of that other vehicle, too. Leave all guns inside the truck and stand over there." The trooper pointed at the grassy area next to the ramp.

The trooper asked Jim, "Where are you guys going? This area beyond the freeway is off limits to everyone unless you live nearby or have family around here. Travelers need to stay on the freeway and head to Idaho. I need to see everyone's identification."

Tim and Jim handed the trooper their SO badges. Everyone else gave the trooper their driver's licenses.

The trooper said, "If you would sign on to work with the city police, you could stay in La Grande. We need more police. If you do not, then you cannot stay. It's really not safe around here, anyway. You will get aid and be safe in Idaho."

Justin heard what the trooper had said. He then said, "Trooper, please let me explain." The trooper was silent and listening, but ready to tell them to hit the road to Idaho. Justin explained, "We are going to the Bradford ranch; our parents are waiting for us there."

The trooper was holding everyone's ID and read the names again.

He asked, "What ranch?"

Justin repeated, "The Bradford Ranch near Enterprise."

"Who are your parents?" the trooper asked.

"Kyle and Claudia Morris, we are from the Portland area."

"No kidding, Kyle's sons…hell, if I don't let you guys through, Kyle would come here and shoot me from a ½ mile away." The trooper continued, "Everyone at OSP knows him. He is talked about regularly. One of the best, if not *the* best, rifle shooters in any police department in the USA. We have, I mean had, training classes based on some of his missions. What do you guys need from me?"

"Just let us get to the ranch," replied Tim.

After the short break, they were ready to hit the road again.

The trooper told them, "I will radio the ranch that you guys are coming. You might get there in less than two hours. Good luck."

"Great, thanks trooper," Jim said. "Okay guys, let's get going. Maybe we can get to the ranch before dark."

As the vehicles left, the trooper switched his radio channel to Wallowa SO net #1. He transmitted, "La Grande OSP to Ghost Team."

A couple seconds pass and Mac replied, "Ghost Team, go ahead La Grande OSP."

"Morris sons leaving La Grande headed to ranch along with two CCSO retired SWAT team men. Jim and Tim with their families and a working police K9."

"Ghost Team copy, thanks trooper. We know every one of them," replied Mac.

Normally the drive from Portland to the ranch would have taken eight hours, but today it took twelve. When the vehicles arrived at the ranch gate, Kyle and Claudia with their yellow Labrador Dacoda were parked there waiting.

Lots of tears were seen among the women and even the men as they shook hands and shared hugs.

Kyle asked Tim, "Should we introduce the dogs to each other?"

Tim answered, "Yeah, there shouldn't be any problem, but out here away from others and away from their normal living area is easier."

Kyle said, "Let's take a walk with the dogs."

Kyle, Tim and Jim walked along the ranch road with the dogs as the others continued talking and hugging one another.

Kyle said, "Both of your families should stay in the lookout. There are two rooms with enough beds. Not as much privacy as home, but a lot better than a tent and outhouse."

Jim asked, "Is Bill going to be okay with us living at the ranch for a while?"

"Yes of course, we already discussed it," Kyle answered. "I have an offer to make you two."

"Okay, what?" asked Jim.

"Sheriff McCabe needs our help. He does not even have enough deputies to work 24/7 in the county, now we have this war or invasion. None of the SO deputies have done any serious police work, just arrested drunks and wrote tickets. They have no tactical training."

"Okay, we got that last stuff covered," said Tim.

Kyle continued, "The Sheriff swore us in today, and we are getting gear from the National Guard. Likely, we will not get paid a dime. You guys want in?"

"Hell yeah!" said Jim.

Tim said, "Me too, as long as Ike is invited."

"Okay, let's get back to the vehicles. The dogs are playing like they are best friends. Oh, by the way, we have a mission in the morning. We are going to do a raid on a Cartel house in Enterprise. Get your stuff unpacked at the lookout and meet at the meeting hall. Dinner will be ready. I have a gift for each of you guys," said Kyle.

"Kyle, our wives will be mad about the mission since we are also retired, but they will understand. We might not have been alive much longer if we stayed in the valley. Here, we have a chance," replied Jim.

Tim asked Kyle, "You think we will ever get out of police work? You know, we're not getting any younger."

"Certainly not for a while. But, I have hope we all will enjoy retirement someday."

On the drive back to the meeting hall, Justin and Eddy told Kyle and Claudia how they met up with Jim and Tim and the shootout with the bikers.

"I am really proud of you guys for thinking through all that mess. I think that after what has happened in the valley, few families will still be together. We are blessed, but cannot forget the suffering of many people we know still in the valley," said Kyle.

Later at the meeting hall after the new arrivals ate a late dinner, Kyle asked Jim and Tim, "What kind of SWAT gear did you bring?"

Tim said, "We each brought tactical vests with bulletproof panels, Glock 17s and AR-15s."

Jim added, "And lots of other guns and ammo. I even have two sniper rifles. I built one in .308, the other is untested in 6.5 Creedmoor."

Kyle said, "I got a custom Ruger, the 'FTW' model in the 6.5 Creedmoor. Man, does it shoot straight."

"Okay, Kyle when we have time, we have a shoot off with our 6.5s. Maybe I can win this time," replied Jim.

"Well Jim, there is a first for everything. Maybe you will win."

All the guys started laughing at Kyle's and Jim's comments.

Just then, Mac walked into the room holding two M-4s. He told the guys, "Brand new from the National Guard and already sighted in." He handed Tim and Jim each an M-4 then said, "They're yours."

Jim said, "Great, but what about the machine gun and suppressor laws? We aren't real cops anymore."

"You guys don't know there is no working state government. They and the leaders of the State Police and many Sheriff's departments, along with most Guard leadership, are dead. Right now, it looks like the highest-ranking Guard officer left in Oregon is a Captain in La Grande. No gun laws will be enforced unless we do it. The President said no US military can assist Oregon or Washington," replied Mac.

"No, we missed that stuff," replied Jim.

Kyle told everyone, "Let's get some sleep and meet back here at 6:00am for breakfast. We need to be at the SO by 8:00am. Besides planning the raid, we have to give the deputies and local troopers some tactical training. Mac needs to get a warrant for the raid."

CHAPTER 12

Monday morning after breakfast, the group of men at the ranch, along with Ike, got into the Humvees and V-150 then headed for the SO. When they arrived, all others involved in the raid were waiting.

"We have two new Ghost Team guys from Clackamas County Sheriff's Office, both retired SWAT. Jim and Tim. Tim has a working assault dog. Jim is the best firearms instructor that I know. We trained and worked together for many years in the metro area. I trust them with my life on any mission or radio call. Before we sit down and go over the raid, we need to get some practice on tactical movements. We can do that here in the SO parking lot. Okay men, circle around me," said Kyle.

Kyle led the familiarization to show the deputies and local troopers the tactical movements they needed to learn.

"Who knows these terms: Groucho walk, moon walk, slice the pie, stack, cover, concealment, police key."

No one raised a hand.

Kyle said, "Okay, we will teach you guys, no problem, but this will be very basic today. Also, today Tim will introduce you guys to his dog and explain what to do and what to never do when the dog is working. We only want him biting bad guys. Rick will show you how to load and unass yourselves from the V-150."

After a short time going over the details of tactical movements and communication while working as a team, Kyle told them, "Mac needs to go prepare an affidavit to get the search warrant. I will draw up the house layout and raid assignments in the briefing room. You guys keep working on what we were doing with the Ghost Team."

After years of writing affidavits for warrants on gangsters, Mac had an easy job of preparing one today. He took off and met with the Circuit Court Judge in Enterprise. The Judge quickly reviewed the documents and signed the warrant. Mac was back at the SO within an hour.

Kyle had the house layout drawn on the grease board. Along with each person was their assignment and vehicle they would ride into the raid. All the others had finished practicing tactical movements with the Ghost Team members. They all came in and were seated in the briefing room in front of Mac and Kyle. Mac explained the raid and went over each man's assignment. After Mac, Kyle explained the layout inside of the house.

Mac picked up the briefing again. "A city ambulance is on standby now and will follow us to the target. It will park two blocks away and be listening to our radio. If any one of us gets wounded, we do whatever is needed to get that person to the ambulance. The Lt is in command and will remain so at the SO. Let's meet at the vehicles in five minutes. Double check your gear."

In this small eastern Oregon town, the drive from the SO was a short distance to the target house. #2 Humvee got into position first.

The V-150 and #1 Humvee arrived a second later and stopped at their assigned locations. Each unit radioed that they were in position.

Mac radioed, "GHOST COMMAND, GHOST TEAM moving to the target."

Mac, Kyle, Lonnie, Jim and two troopers jumped from the rear door of the V-150 and walked with weapons drawn to the front door. Lonnie uses the police key, a handheld door ram, and in one blow the door busted open. He stepped aside as the rest of the team moved past him entering the house. The team split up going to their assigned spots. Mac and his cover trooper walked quickly to bedroom #1. Kyle with his cover trooper went to bedroom #2. Lonnie and Jim cleared the living room and kitchen. The rest of the team took up cover positions around the outside of the house.

Seconds after the door was smashed, Mac and Kyle quickly located both bad guys inside the bedrooms; they were still in bed. They were hardly awake since it was only moments after they heard the front door smashed open. Both Mac and Kyle point the M-4s at the bad guys and yell, "POLICE! HANDS UP, NOW, OR I WILL SHOOT!" Both guys complied, putting their hands up as high as they could. They just got a wakeup call from the Ghost Team. The cover troopers now stepped up and handcuffed the bad guys while being covered by Mac and Kyle. Within minutes of entering the house, finding the bad guys and handcuffing them, the raid was over.

Back in the living room, all were gathered up, bad guys seated on the floor. Mac looked over at Kyle and gave him a nod. Kyle responded by nodding his head. Kyle then said, "Hey we were a little slow, but we still got it."

Mac said, "We're older, but we still got what it takes."

Mac radioed, "Target secured, two in custody."

Each team member radioed the Ghost Command, Code 4: All OKAY.

At that point, Rick came in to interview the bad guys. The deputies came in and searched the house. Mac and Kyle followed them to give advice as they searched. When done, they found twenty-five thousand dollars in a closet and two 9mm pistols; one was near each bed. The guns and money would be given to the Sheriff's office.

From the interviews, Rick learned that the two spoke good English. It was the typical Cartel marijuana grow on public land. The two informed Rick that there were four guys at the grow site. They resupplied the site every Thursday, all the money was cartel drug money for living expenses. The site was near where the rancher was shot.

Of the four at the site, the one who shot the rancher was the only one who would want a shootout with police. He was a member of the Cartel and was the boss for this grow. He bragged about wanting to shoot Americans. The others were just afraid; they never wanted to do this work. The drug Cartel ordered them to work at this grow or else family members back home in Mexico would be killed. The guys at the grow site did not have any contact with anyone except the supply guys when they took food to meet them.

Rick informed them about the war going on in Oregon. Rick told them, "You are under arrest and will be held at the SO's jail, at least until after the raid on the grow site. After that, I don't know what will happen to you guys."

One of the two was so scared, he pooped his pants.

Rick then told the team of what he learned and thought the two they got from the house were being truth-ful.

Mac told the troopers and deputies that assisted them today, “You guys all did a great job. We want you guys to help us to hit the grow site.”

Every one of them sat up a little straighter with pride. All of them said they would help.

Mac finished by saying, “We need to plan the grow site raid for tomorrow. We will do that at the ranch. It is time for a beer. See you guys tomorrow morning.”

Lonnie said, “I don’t trust what those guys told Rick. I think this raid may be different from the past raids. I have a feeling if these guys know about what’s going on now, they will have traps set up to hurt us and want to shoot it out to the last man. Think about it, they have nothing to lose.”

CHAPTER 13

The Ghost Team left the ranch again after breakfast and headed to the SO to attend the daily briefing with the Sheriff and pick up the others.

At the SO, the Sheriff reported he had good news today. "We have semi-trucks with loaded trailers of food and other supplies coming into town today. Since the roadblocks have been in place, only a few people have come though Highway 82 to live in their vacation homes around Wallowa Lake or to live with relatives. Hwy 3 is only having residents coming and going to Lewison, Idaho for goods they needed to buy there.

"Reports from La Grande are that things are getting bad due to lack of supplies. Crime is way up in the city. The RV trailer company in La Grande is giving the city many RV's to house new residents. They will send some trailers here later this week. Let me know how many you want at the ranch."

Mac and Kyle had planned the grow site raid to be around noon. That time will have the least amount of shadows cast that can interfere with visibility while searching through the brush and timber. Also, the bad guys should be in the camp site area eating lunch or resting, not out working the land.

Mac explained to the raid team. "Both Humvees will go along with the V-150. A city ambulance will follow them. Lenny and Lonnie will be flying over the site just before the raid to provide any other intel they might need. They will then circle around the area as long as the team needs them watching from the sky. The Lt will ride passenger with Rick. Tim with Ike will also remain at the V-150 unless needed to track a runner. The four deputies need to space out along the road to watch for runners. Kyle, Jim and I will be the assault team. The three troopers will follow us in as cover and will be the arrest team again.

"The vehicles will park about ½ mile from the trail to the grow site and walk in from there. The camp site is only about two hundred yards up a trail from the road. According to those interviewed by Rick, they did not put any traps out on the trails like some marijuana grows. Any questions?"

No one raised a hand.

"Okay, let's mount up."

After about a forty-five-minute drive, the vehicles stopped at the area ½ mile from the trail.

The Lt radioed, "Ghost Team air unit, proceed to target."

Lenny replied, "Ghost Team air unit enroute, ETA ten minutes."

Mac led the team and set the pace. All remained silent as they walked. At the trail head, Mac signaled for the last two deputies to continue further up the road.

Mac said to the team, "Make sure none of you move off the trail or road unless I direct you to.

If this turns into a gun fight, anyone moving away from their assigned area could be mistaken as bad guys and get shot."

They all nodded their heads.

Mac radioed, “Ghost Team moving onto the trail.” The six slowly walked up the trail.

They approached the covered area of the camp kitchen, then waited and listened. Mac signaled the others with four fingers to signal that there were four bad guys at the site and pointed to where he could hear men talking. They were about fifteen yards from the camp kitchen area. Mac signaled Kyle and Jim to move alongside of him, and they approached abreast of each other, Kyle on the left and Jim to the right. The troopers followed behind them.

As the team stepped into the clearing, Mac yelled, “POLICE! HANDS IN THE AIR!” The three Ghost Team guys pointed the M-4s at the bad guys. The team then walked toward them.

Three bad guys were seated facing them on a bench. The one on Kyle’s end grabbed a rifle off the table. He yelled, “Kill the American pigs!” and started to stand up.

Kyle shot three times; all bullets hit the guy in the center of his chest. The rifle flew into the air as the bad guy rocketed backwards to the ground. The other two raised their arms into the air. One of them shouted in English, “Please don’t shoot us!”

Jim suddenly saw movement through the brush and yelled, “POLICE, STOP!” But, the guy kept running away.

Jim said, “I couldn’t get a shot, unknown if he has a gun.”

Mac radioed, “GHOST TEAM, Kyle fired, we have one EKIA (enemy killed in action), we have two held at gunpoint. We have a runner headed toward the road, unknown if armed or not.”

The Lt told Rick, “Floor it, get the vehicle up to that trail head. Tim, get ready with Ike.”

As the V-150 neared the trail, Rick stopped. Tim with Ike, on a leash, jumped out through the rear door.

Mac learned that the runner was not armed and radioed, "Runner is unarmed. Repeat, unarmed. We are Code 4 at the site."

Tim met the nearest deputy and said, "Follow us as cover while Ike works on the track."

After just a few minutes of Tim looking and Ike smelling for the runner's path through the brush, Ike alerted Tim. He had found the track. Tim radioed, "Ghost Team K9 tracking." He unleashed Ike and commanded, "Hunt."

Within seconds, Ike was tracking near the trail and then back across the road. Within five minutes, Ike was barking; he found the runner. Lucky for the runner, he stopped when the dog caught up to him.

Tim said, "Don't move, or you will get bit." The guy stood still. Tim handcuffed him as the deputy held him at gunpoint.

Tim radioed, "Ghost Team K9 Code 4. One in custody, returning to the road."

Mac radioed, "Have a deputy bring a body bag to the site."

Lonnie radioed the team, "You guys did a great job. Looked like you knew what you were doing down there. See you later. We got it all on film. Ghost air unit clear."

Kyle looks over at Mac and said, "What did he expect? A bunch of green cops out here tripping over our boots?"

Mac answered, "Yeah, Lonnie had the easy job today. What a clown."

Within ten minutes the deputy arrived with a body bag.

"Roll the bag out next to the dead guy," said Kyle. He pointed at the two in custody and said, "You guys pick up your friend and put him into the bag."

One of them said, "No disrespect to you officer, but he was not our friend. He was a bad man and mean to us. We will do as you say."

Kyle responded, "And none of us is here to disrespect you guys. We won't harm you as long as you do as we say. You two will carry him out to our vehicles. No questions. I have someone who needs to talk to you guys. He will answer any questions, and I advise you to tell him the truth."

"Yes, thank you. We are glad to not be working for this man any longer. I speak some English, the others not much."

"Troopers, escort the prisoners back to the road. After there, place them into handcuffs unless Rick says different. He will be in charge of them at that point," said Mac.

Mac, Kyle, Jim and the deputy checked everything out around the campsite. They decided to take the guns and ammo, but left everything else. There was no manpower that could be spared to come back to pull the marijuana and remove all the trash.

Rick met the three in custody and handed each a bottle of cold water. Rick started talking to the three, "I need to ask you guys questions. I will know if you're lying to me. So, if you wish to be treated well and not harmed, tell me the truth."

One guy said, "We have nothing to lie about. Please don't hurt us, we all have family and children back home. We were forced to be here."

Rick then interviewed the three and found their stories to be the same as the other two from the house. He ended by telling them about the war/ invasion in Oregon and Washington.

The guy who had run said, “Sorry I ran. I was peeing when I heard someone shout police. I thought you guys were bandits and here to steal the marijuana and shoot us. Once the dog caught me, I then believed you were the real police. Bandits do not use dogs, just guns.”

The team drove into Enterprise and first stopped at the Medical Examiner’s office. Kyle explained the shooting to the doctor and handed him the dead guy’s Oregon identification. He continued, “Others at the site said this address they have on their IDs is a Mexican drug cartel house in Beaverton. They never lived there, they are all Mexican citizens. All their families are in Mexico.”

“Okay, thanks. I will contact the Mexican Embassy in California and give them the details of the death and send them copies of the fingerprints. Likely, this is not his real name. They may or may not attempt contact with family, but for sure they will not pay for his transport to Mexico. He will be buried here.”

“Okay, bye Doc.”

All the guys that were involved in the raid, including the Sheriff, were in the SO briefing room to debrief about the raid. The Lt stepped out of the raid debriefing and phoned Mary. “Tell everyone at the ranch that the raid went fine. No good guys were hurt, one bad guy KIA. It was Kyle that shot, but don’t tell anyone who did it. Kyle needs to tell his family his way first.”

“Okay, but it’s sad that someone died.”

"Yes, if it could have been prevented, it would have been. Better them than one of us. Hey, I need to find out if you gals could get together enough food so we could invite the Sheriff, all the men that helped with the mission and their families to the ranch tonight for a big dinner."

"Let me call you back in a few minutes."

"Okay, bye."

Mary phoned back a few minutes later. "Yes, dinner will be ready about 6:00pm for around forty people at the meeting hall. You guys need to buy more beer before coming home."

"Great, love you. Be home soon."

The Lt stepped back into the debrief and realized it was finished. He said, "Everyone, give me your attention for just one minute. Great job today and yesterday. Everyone in here, including Sheriff McCabe, be at the ranch at 6:00 pm. Bring your wives, girlfriends and kids. Dinner and beer are on the Ghost Team. The gate will be open, drive to the meeting hall."

Sheriff McCabe said, "I'm in, be there with my wife. By the way, I spoke with the guys in custody and the Judge. We got a deal, they will plead guilty to the illegal marijuana. The Judge will sentence them to probation. They don't want to go back to Mexico. They really seem to be victims in this case and appear to be good men. They want to stay here at the jail and be trustees working for the county. They asked to be able to go to church on Sundays. Who knows, they might get released to help out in other areas besides the jail. The Judge is turning the drug money back over to the SO since there is no state of Oregon to transfer the money too."

CHAPTER 14

The next day was a day off to rest at the ranch from police work. But, everyone went to the SO to visit the Sheriff.

Sheriff McCabe announced, "Everyone from the ranch, please meet in the briefing room." The group walked in and saw most of the deputies already waiting. They sat down in the back rows.

The Sheriff came into the room and said, "The Lt reminded me last night I have some work to do. Would Jim, Tim with Ike, Jimmy, Justin and Eddy please come up here? If you guys are going to be doing police work, I must swear you in as official law officers in this county. Although you will not be wearing the SO uniforms, you will be police officers. The Lt wants you guys in blue like the rest of the team.

"This group represents several firsts in this county. They are the first County SWAT team. They have the first County K9 team. They have the first aircraft to be used by and for police work. They have the first armored vehicles ever used by the SO. In these troubled times, we are damned lucky to have them working here. Some wear baseball caps from the Oregon State Police, two wear the Clackamas County Sheriff's Office baseball caps, and the youngest among them will wear Wallowa County Sheriff's Office baseball caps. All wear the badge of this county,

Wallowa County. I guess that, like in baseball, they are the All-Star Team. They are the Wallowa County All Stars Team."

All attending stood up and applauded the group. The Sheriff walked over to the group and shook the hands of each new member of the Ghost Team.

The Lt stepped forward and said, "Because of my long days traveling throughout the county going to daily meetings, talking on the phone almost nonstop, and at times talking on the police radio, I really need a driver for the Humvee before I get into a crash. Would Jimmy and Eddy take that job offer?"

Both young men looked at each other and said nearly at the same time, "Yes Sir."

"Great! I would like you guys to rotate the job so that you each will work as my driver every other day." Lt then said, "Let's get back to the ranch...as my dad used to say, 'We're burning daylight'."

At the ranch, Mary brought up, "We really need to have a bigger garden put in since we have more folks here, and who can guess what the food supply will become at the store. Now is the time to get started expanding it and planting. Any volunteers?"

All of the wives and the Lt raised their hands.

The Lt said, "I will get the tractor down there and show you ladies how to drive and work the garden with it. We will also need to expand the game fence around the garden if we want to eat the food we plant. Also, could some guys check the fence lines around the cattle fields? If you guys take the side-by-sides, you'll be gone the rest of today. That should be done weekly, but I don't think we'll be able to keep that schedule."

Mac said, "I'll go, and how about Lenny with me? He has never been all around the ranch."

Lenny responded, "Sounds good. I'll go."

Rick said, "I had better not go. My back is feeling beat from spending too many miles in that V-150 over the last few days. You know it wasn't made to be comfortable, just to stop bullets."

Lonnie said, "Kyle and I should go in another UTV. Jim and Tim still need to get a lot of their stuff unpacked."

Everyone was busy getting some type of work done around the ranch. In the afternoon, a guy called the ranch house from the front gate intercom, and Mary answered it.

"Hello. The Sheriff told me to drop off a truck at the ranch," said an unknown person.

Mary replied, "Okay. It will take a few minutes to get down there. You're just short of a mile from me."

"Ok. I'll be waiting here."

Mary then called the Lt through the police radio. The Lt along with Jim and Tim were in the barn. "Someone is at the gate wanting to drop off a truck. He said the Sheriff told him to bring it here."

"Guys, grab your rifles. I don't know what this is about. Let's take a side-by-side to the front gate," the Lt said to them.

As they approached the gate, they could see a convoy of vehicles parked outside of it. Six men stood at the gate and yelled, "SURPRISE!" One man stepped forward, "Sheriff McCabe said to bring these vehicles up here and drop them off."

The ranch guys see a 3,700-gallon fuel truck full of diesel fuel and five brand-new travel trailers from the RV dealer in La Grande. "The Sheriff told me that he wanted a supply of fuel for county use kept here since none is available for miles in this area. He also said that we should get some RV's up here donated to the ranch. I didn't know they would all be brand-new, or that they would be here today."

"Come on in, we'll show you were to park them," said the Lt.

The delivery guys got the RVs parked and leveled near the other RVs next to the meeting hall. The fuel truck was parked safely away from them near the shop.

The Lt told Jim and Tim, "You guys had better get your wives over here and pick out which ones to live in. It will give you a lot more privacy and room than in the lookout."

Jim said, "Maybe tomorrow we can go into town and get what's needed to get the trailers hooked up to the sewer. The electrical and water stuff will be easy to do once we have the parts."

"Yeah, let's get enough stuff to have them all hooked up. Maybe more friends from the valley will make it here," said Tim.

Later that night at dinner, Mac told the group about their travels around the ranch. "We saw lots of deer grazing. Many had newborns with them. There also were a few groups of elk and many with newborns, too. The cattle and fences were good."

Kyle said, "We saw lots of deer, too. Looks like a good year for the deer. We saw only one herd of elk, but it had well over eighty head in it. It seemed to have younger and nicer bulls than some past springs. We saw one cougar but could not get a shot at it. There were no dead cattle from a cougar kill found, but that could change any day. The fences and cattle were fine."

Lenny said to the Lt and Mary, "Now that Jim and Tim made new homes in two RVs, the boys and I were talking about moving into the lookout. Their parents might enjoy the privacy, and we would still have someone to listen to the radio."

The Lt said, "That makes sense, but you guys can't treat it like a college dorm. You must pick up after yourselves and keep it clean."

Lenny looked at the boys and said, "You heard the man."

Justin replied, "We can do it."

Mac mentioned, "After the daily briefing tomorrow with the Sheriff, some of us should make a trip to La Grande to visit the OSP office and get any other gear they might be able to spare for the new guys."

The Lt replied, "That's another good idea. Take a case of 5.56 ammo and a case of MRE's for trade to help seal a deal."

The group had planned on all going into town the next morning. The wives would buy more food, if available. Lenny, Jim and Tim would go to the hardware store to get RV supplies for hooking up the new trailers. Justin said, "Jimmy and I want to stay at the ranch because we want to hunt for that cougar."

Kyle told the boys, "That is a good idea. Take the electronic game call along with my 'FTW' rifle in 6.5 Creedmoor caliber. The 140 grain bullets I loaded will take care of that cat out to 600 yards."

Jim senior agreed, "Take my 6.5CM rifle also. That is the best caliber we have for long-range against a cougar."

When the men got to the SO, the Sheriff started the morning briefing. "You guys going to La Grande today, get up-to-date information from the OSP Sergeant and ask him about La Grande PD and Union County SO. I hear that crime is beyond anything they ever imaged in La Grande. Also, stop by the National Guard armory and see if they will talk about any of their future plans."

Mac replied, "Will do."

Sheriff McCabe continued, "Word is that nothing was settled at the meeting between the US and China. The President has ordered all federal employees and their families to get out of Oregon and Washington, including all personnel and equipment from Fairchild Air Force base in Spokane and the Army training base in Yakima, WA. So far, the only people showing up at the Highway 82 roadblock, besides delivery trucks from outside the county, have been family or local homeowners. That could change at any time and we need to be ready for trouble from outsiders.

"The Highway 3 roadblock has not had anyone trying to get into the county as expected due to being real remote. Only delivery trucks and county residents have been traveling for supplies to and from Idaho and Washington."

After the briefing was over, Mac, Kyle, Lonnie and Rick took off for La Grande. Just two miles past the county roadblock, they saw a stopped pickup on the highway shoulder with an older man working on the engine.

Mac said, "This could be a trap, guys. Get ready!"

"Guys be careful about any gunfire. There is a young boy standing near the truck," warned Kyle.

Mac stopped the Humvee about fifty feet from the truck. Kyle turned on the blue police lights. The guys jumped out of the Humvee and scanned the area while holding their rifles in the ready position. The old man turned upon seeing the guys. He waved at them and walked toward the Humvee.

He said, "Boy, I am glad you guys stopped…. my truck just quit. I think the battery or cables failed."

Kyle yelled, "Stop where you are! Who else is with you?"

The old man said, "Just my grandson Johnny over there," motioning toward Johnny. "He is just twelve years old. What's wrong and why the guns?"

"Sir, we cannot be too careful, we need to check your truck," said Kyle. "Rick and Lonnie, go and check it out." Rick and Lonnie cautiously approached the truck.

Rick yelled back, "No one else here."

"Okay guys, lower the guns," said Mac. "The area is safe."

Kyle asked the old man, "Sir, what's your name and where do you live?"

"My name is Wally Smith. I live in a cabin by the Joso Ranch up near the city of Wallowa."

"Which cabin?"

"Up near the end of Grossman Rd. near the gate."

Kyle said, "Sorry about the guns, Mr. Smith. Nowadays, we must be careful when meeting anyone we don't know. By the way, you sure get some nice elk in your meadow."

Mr. Smith smiled and said, "Yes, I do. So, you know the place. I understand your concern. People in La Grande are acting crazy. I cut firewood to make extra money. I was supposed to get paid two hundred bucks and only got fifty.

Hey, aren't you the retired OSP guys working for the Sheriff?"

Lonnie said, "Yeah. How do you know about that?"

"Everyone in Enterprise calls you guys the old men in blue because you wear blue instead of the Sheriff's Office brown. Besides that, all you guys have gray hair," chided Smith.

All the guys cracked up laughing. Kyle told Mr. Smith, "No one has said that to us, but it's all true. Several of us have driven by your place while elk hunting, outside of your gate of course. Since you got 'Keep Out' posted on your land, we never tried to hunt there. We never wanted to bother you."

Mac spoke up, "Maybe we can get your truck running. Rick, take a look since you know how to fix anything with an engine." Young Johnny had drifted toward the Humvee and seemed really interested in it. Kyle and Lonnie offered him a tour.

Kyle told Johnny, "Go ahead, get in and check it out. Get some cans of coke from the cooler in the back if you want. We also have snacks back there…. grab something for you and your grandfather."

Johnny came out handing each man a can of soda and had a big bag of potato chips. He said, "Man, that's a cool army truck."

Mr. Smith's eyes welled up. He said, "I learned about what happened in the valley. I am really worried about my only daughter. She works at the Denny's in Clackamas near Portland. I hope she can find a way to get here. She has an old 1968 Jeep. It should run fine."

At that statement, all the guys turned to look at each other.

Kyle asked, "What is her name?"

"Linda Smith. She moved to Portland years ago with a boyfriend. Once Johnny was born, the bum left them."

"Wow, what a small world. We all know her. We used to go there and have coffee nearly every week. She is a really nice person. She got good tips from us. Be sure to give the roadblock guys her name and your phone number so they will let her into the county if she does make it here."

Wally replied, "Good idea, I will do that."

Rick walked up to the group, wiping off his hands on a rag, and said, "I got the truck running, but it needs a new battery."

Mac asked Mr. Smith, "Could you pick up stuff we have waiting for us at the NAPA store and take it to the Bradford ranch? Also, please stop by the Highway 3 roadblock and determine what it would take you to cut trees down out in front of the area. We need the area cleared. For that, we will pay for a new truck battery at NAPA. The county will pay you for your work cutting trees."

"Yes, of course. Thanks guys," said Wally. "Oh, by the way, you can hunt on my land anytime. I own a whole section of land there. There's good deer and elk hunting. Johnny and I had better get going."

Kyle said, "Thanks for the offer, Mr. Smith. I will phone the NAPA store and the ranch so they know you're coming. We need to get going also. Nice to meet you."

Kyle then shook hands with both Johnny and Wally Smith. He handed Johnny a Snickers bar and said, "Share this with your grandpa. See you guys later."

CHAPTER 15

As Mac drove the Humvee through La Grande, the guys noticed vehicle and pedestrian traffic seemed about normal, except most people had their heads on a swivel looking around like they're afraid of getting attacked. All eyes followed the Humvee as it passed them. At the OSP office, they met with the station Sergeant. The Sergeant looked like he had not slept in a week.

As the group walked into the station, Mac called out, "Hi Sergeant Anderson".

Sgt. Anderson looked up at the guys. "Hey, I haven't seen some of you in years. I wish you would come and work for me."

"We got hooked up with Sheriff McCabe. Wallowa County doesn't have enough cops to patrol one city, much less the county," said Mac.

"Yeah, I understand. I heard about the Cartel grow you guys took out. By the way, good job on that mission," said Anderson.

"Thanks. Tell us about the city. We understand your troopers are not going outside the city due to all the violence here," said Mac.

"Yeah, real dangerous around here after dark. Not so good in the daytime either, all the troops are working two-man cars for their safety. Most troops have been shot at already, so far just the patrol cars took hits. The troops and city officers have killed three bad guys so far. No time to write reports. Actually, there's no one to give any reports to anyways."

"The big box stores are getting shipments of goods, and so far, have most items stocked. Donated goods are being handed out at the high school. Everywhere that a line forms, to get or buy goods, people fight or shoot each other. The biggest worry I have is the fact that no one gets paid from the State of Oregon. From us cops to welfare, people aren't getting any paychecks. That means many of the people who live in the city."

Lonnie said, "That's worse than I would have expected for a small city like La Grande. The reason we stopped by is about some new equipment. Do you have a good supply in the stock room to help us out? We're mostly in need of uniforms and web gear."

"Oh, yeah. My guys already took anything they might need, and we had it well stocked. Let's go check it out." The Sergeant took the guys to the stock room and they got everything they needed plus extra uniforms. Mac offered the cases of 5.56 ammo and MREs in exchange.

Sgt. Anderson said, "We will need the ammo and MRE's, thanks. We may need your help at some point, let's keep in touch."

"Yes, we will. We need to get going. Good luck here," replied Kyle.

Over at the National Guard Armory the group met with Capt. Westbrook and the Captain informed the group about the information he had on the areas controlled by the Chinese. Westbrook reported, "The Chinese are allowing most people to flee to the east. Public schools are being used as holding areas or prisons for whoever they take hostage. They have started going into the neighborhoods and to every store that sold guns. They get the federal gun purchase forms, you know the 4473s, and then go to those listed addresses to seize the guns.

"Anyone who resists is being shot, anyone who shoots at the APCs or soldiers on the city streets gets shot. Some people have formed into groups to fight back, but they are overwhelmed by the Chinese and North Koreans. Chinese ships are taking all the grain stored at the elevators and logs at the export docks on the Columbia River, new ships are bringing in more soldiers.

"For several days, people were escaping in older vehicles and older light aircraft. Now, mostly only on foot. Reports from the Seattle area are the same. The good news is the Guard is helping to get those fleeing into buses at The Dalles and taken through Oregon to Idaho. They have holding and temporary housing in Pendleton. People with needed skills are asked to stay at one of the cities along I-84. The best news is the Idaho Governor signed the documents to allow Idaho Guard personnel to help in Oregon and Washington."

The Captain paused for a moment, then said, "Come back tomorrow. I can have one Humvee fitted with a gun ring and the V-150, mounting the 7.62 caliber, 240B machine guns on each vehicle. Because we are really short of manpower, I will ask that you escort a convoy back to the ranch. Next week, I may need you for another escort on a convoy."

Mac asked the Captain, "Could you spare fifteen sets of night vision goggles for the team and for the men staffing the roadblock? And how about a pair of binoculars that have stabilized imaging for use in the plane?"

The Captain scribbled in a notebook and replied, "They will be here tomorrow. Anything else?"

Mac said, "We can always use more of 5.56 ammo"

"No problem, ammo, we at least for now have plenty."

"We will be here around 9am," said Mac.

That evening at the ranch, Jimmy told the group about his and Justin's hunting trip. "We never saw a cougar, but shot five coyotes throughout the day while using the game call."

"That's some good shooting, guys. Without hunting coyotes on a random basis, their numbers will get to be too many and cause problems with the cattle," replied Kyle.

Mary told the men, "Wally Smith dropped off the cases of motor oil and stuff from the NAPA store. He had looked at the trees that need cut down at the roadblock and will start tomorrow. He thinks he will be done in two to three days."

"Well, I don't know about the rest of you guys, but I'm going to bed. Tomorrow is going to be another long day," said Lonnie.

All the guys going on the trip in the morning agreed and said goodnight to each other.

CHAPTER 16

The following morning, a few of the guys drove out of the ranch gate at 7:00am and headed for La Grande. Mac drove the Humvee with Kyle and Lonnie as passengers. The V-150 followed with Rick teaching Justin how to drive the massive beast of a vehicle. Eddy was wearing goggles and rode in the open top hatch. The others stayed at the ranch to help with whatever work needed to be done. When the vehicles approached the roadblock, they stopped for a break and an update on any activity.

A roadblock deputy told them, “No one came through overnight, but we expect a bunch of delivery trucks coming through late this morning and afternoon.”

The guys used the stop to get in a bathroom break while Kyle checked out the deputies’ positions to make sure they had proper and safe shooting lanes. “The roadblock looks well set up. We hope to get you guys NVGs soon,” said Kyle. "Guys, let’s hit the road!"

The Humvee approached the same spot where Mr. Smith had broken down. There, the guys noticed a parked pickup with a travel trailer attached facing them. Three men wearing black leather jackets were standing near the front of the pickup. They turned and looked at the Humvee.

Mac yelled, “Get ready guys!” He applied the brakes hard as one of the men at the pickup pointed to the other two men. The two other men turned around and ran toward the rear of the pickup. At that moment, the man still at the front of the pickup bent down and grabbed a rifle. Up to that point, the rifle had been unnoticed by the guys in the Humvee. The man levered the rifle action and fired. The bullet struck the passenger side windshield right in front of Kyle's face. Luckily for Kyle, the bullet ricocheted off the bulletproof glass.

As Mac stopped the Humvee, Kyle shouted, "I got that son of a bitch!” Kyle opened the door and continued holding it open with his foot. He leaned out and fired from between the Humvee body and open door while remaining seated in the Humvee for protection. Kyle fired his M-4 on full auto. He emptied the thirty rounds in the magazine in less than two seconds into the man as he tried to lever the action and shoot again. The man never got the rifle raised for another shot. The rifle he was holding splintered into pieces and flew out of his hands. He had been struck multiple times and fell backward, landing on the ground behind the front fender.

Kyle yelled out, “Reloading!” and had another thirty-round magazine in his rifle in less than three seconds. He then scanned the scene for more threats.

The V-150 was 1/2 mile behind the Humvee when Rick heard the gunfire and yelled into the V-150's intercom at Eddy, “Get inside and close the hatch!" Then he said, “Justin, stop the vehicle and get out of the driver’s seat. The Humvee may be under attack. That was an M-4 and some other rifle firing. No one fires off a whole mag in one burst unless there is big trouble.” Rick then climbed into the driver seat and drove the V-150 as fast as it would travel to close the distance that had grown between them and the Humvee. Justin was watching as a lookout through the front passenger side bulletproof hatch glass. Eddy got strapped into a rear seat, an area without any windows.

Back at the shootout, Lonnie yelled, “One guy ran to the right! He has a handgun and got behind some large boulders.”

Kyle responded, “Copy.”

Mac saw the third man come out from behind the passenger side of the pickup firing another lever-action rifle at them. A bullet flew above Mac’s head, missing him by only inches. Mac aimed and fired three shots. The man was knocked backward as his rifle fell to the ground. Mac fired three more times and the man flopped to the ground face first.

Lonnie had opened the rear driver side door and pointed his M-4 out, scanning for more threats. Moments later, Rick drove the V-150 up along the right side of the Humvee and stopped. Eddy and Justin could hear the pinging of bullets bouncing off the armored vehicle as the guy with the handgun shot the V-150.

Rick said, “We can’t see who is shooting. Do you know where the shooter is?”

Lonnie ran to the V-150 rear door and pounded on it. “Eddy, open up the rear door!" yelled Rick. Lonnie got inside and plugged into the intercom. Eddy closed the rear door. Lonnie told Rick, “The shooter is hiding behind the boulders just to the right about 30 yards away.”

The man raised up and fired his handgun again. Two more bullets bounce off the V-150. “Now I see the SOB,” said Rick.

At that point Rick radioed to the Humvee. “Let me handle that guy." Rick lowered the blade on the front of the V-150 and drove toward the boulder where the dirt-bag was hiding. The V-150 would push the boulder to crush the bad guy unless he gave up.

Mac said to Kyle, “Keep scanning for more threats and stay behind cover.”

The V-150 continued toward the boulder. As the V-150 got about ten yards away from the boulder, the man suddenly jumped up, turning and running away. Both Rick and Justin noticed a Diamond Back rattlesnake hanging on the man’s right arm. The snake looked like it was over five feet long. “Damn, look at that!” shouted Rick.

Kyle saw the man running, still holding a handgun. He lined up the scope dot and fired one shot. The man dropped to the ground with the handgun still in his right hand. The snake coiled back and struck the guy in his neck. Then the snake calmly slithered back into the boulders after injecting a second full load of venom into him. The man kicked his legs into the air and rolled side to side screaming. He fired his handgun into the air until it was empty. Seconds later, the man just stopped moving. His arms dropped to the ground.

The guys kept scanning the area with their rifles looking for any more threats while remaining behind the cover of the vehicles.

Mac told everyone, “Hold for a couple minutes. Let’s catch our breath and standby.” He then requested, “Status check, everyone.”

All reply Code 4.

Mac asked Rick, “What can you guys see from the V-150?”

Rick answered, "The guy laying by the front fender is not breathing and clearly has been shot.... a bunch of times. The guy that ran from behind the boulders has not moved. You guys won't believe this; that guy was bit by a giant rattlesnake… then Kyle shot him… the guy, not the snake. We're not sure who killed the guy, the snake or Kyle."

Mac reported, "The man lying near the rear of the pickup has been still for several minutes." He then told Rick, "Get on the PA and callout to anyone in the truck and trailer to come out."

Rick spoke into the PA's microphone. "This is the police, you in the truck and trailer come out NOW! Unarmed, with your hands up, or you will be shot."

They all now hear women screaming from inside the trailer. One of the women is shouting, "Don't shoot us! We are chained-up and cannot get out of the trailer, PLEASE… HELP… US!"

Lonnie had gotten out of the V-150 and told Mac and Kyle, "I will cover your approach."

Mac and Kyle moved forward to check the men near the truck. As they check the bodies, they see the motorcycle patches on their jackets. At that point, they realized the dead are members of the motorcycle gang "Snake Heads" based in Portland, and they also own a farm outside of La Grande. The two moved on toward the trailer.

Mac shouted to the women in the trailer, "Quit screaming!" Then they were silent.

"Who's in the trailer?" Mac asked.

The same woman's voice replied, "Just us two, no one else. We were kidnapped. The motorcycle guys chained us to a bench."

Mac slowly entered the trailer with Kyle covering him. Mac saw two young women seated on the bench. They were only wearing bras and panties. The two were dirty and looked like they had been treated roughly. Both were handcuffed and chained to the floor. The trailer was quickly checked for any other threats and none were found.

Standing in front of the women, Mac asked them, "How many men were traveling with you?"

"Three."

Mac, looking at them, thought they might be only teenagers and had likely suffered unspeakable things from the men. He then felt good about him and Kyle shooting the men. Mac said, "You're safe now, but we need to deal with the bodies outside. I promise you, I will unlock the handcuffs, and we will get some clothes for you in just a couple minutes."

Both women started crying and said, "Thank you, we have been beaten and raped by those guys for several days."

Mac met up with all the guys and asked, "Did anyone use net #1 or call this in to the SO?"

All reply, "No."

Rick said, "We were all on the open net, just car to car. It is only good for a short distance, no one heard us talking."

"Good, we can't use the radio to report or even talk to others about this incident. I am glad we stayed on the open net so no one else beyond us heard the gun battle. I will phone the Lt in a few minutes about the incident. Rick, you can help me interview the women. We have a big problem."

Kyle said, "Yeah, we do. We visited the Snake Heads farm about ten years ago, and I shot and killed one of them. Some members still want a piece of me."

Rick said, "Only because he came out of the house shooting at the trooper, who by the way froze. If you didn't shoot that Snake Head member, he would have killed the trooper."

Lonnie asked Kyle, "Did you tell your sons about that incident?"

Both Justin and Eddy were still in a bit of shock standing nearby. They had never seen their dad or any other SWAT guys in action. Add to that, they had never seen anyone shot.

Kyle told Lonnie, "No," and looked over to his sons. "Sons, I need to tell you about that incident in a few minutes."

Mac and Rick took bottles of water into the trailer and unlocked the handcuffs holding the women to the chains. They found some clothing in the closet and allowed the women to get dressed and cleaned up. Rick then interviewed the two.

Kyle told his sons, "The Snake Heads are a small motorcycle gang that sells drugs in Portland. Their motorcycle patch has the head of a rattle snake, ready to strike. At one time, OSP had an informant in the gang that knew they were growing marijuana and making Meth on a farm up near La Grande and Elgin. The OSP dope cops got a warrant and the SWAT team made the raid on the farm. I was the over watch sniper positioned behind the house. Up until that incident, we had used local troopers to help the team. But, never after that time. The local troopers set up outside near the rear of the house. As Mac went in the front door with the assault team, one guy fired a handgun at the team several times while running out the back door. He stopped and fired the gun again as he was standing on the porch. That time when he shot, he was not aiming at anyone.

"One of the local troopers was nearby behind cover. When he saw the Snake Head gang guy come through the doorway, he stood up holding an AR-15. But, he had exposed himself.

"The Snake Head member scanned the area with the handgun and saw the trooper just standing there, not even aiming his rifle at the thug. He swung the handgun toward the trooper. I had to shoot that gang member; he was a Prospect for the gang. That means he was a new guy to the gang. The new guys need to wear that name on the back of their jacket or vest like two of these guys here are wearing. As the guy lay on the porch dying, the trooper started giving him aid to stop the bleeding. He told the trooper he was sorry and passed away without saying another word. That trooper resigned from OSP the following week. He never returned to police work.

"Prospects tend to be the most dangerous guys in the gang toward police because they need to prove how tough and loyal they are to become full members. It may take them over a year to ask for and get voted into the club as full members. That day, none of the rest of the gang members in the house were any problem. But, one member was Ralph Stoner. He was the Sergeant at Arms for the gang at that time. He is now the club President. We learned that back then Ralph tried to talk the club president into killing me, your mom, and you two guys. The club members took a vote and the hit was denied. They realized what the police would do to them. Their club might not exist any longer, and they would get killed in any shootout with the police. Needless to say, Ralph doesn't like me. Also, I knew Ralph as a kid. He lived 3 blocks away from me. We used to hang out together. He became a bully back then and grew up being in and out of prison most of his life. He is one really bad guy. Since I got into police work and he into the biker gang, I guess you could say we are arch enemies."

"Dad, we never knew about that or what you really did on the SWAT missions. We asked Mom a few times, but she wouldn't tell us anything," Justin said.

"Boys, doing my job was nothing to brag about to family. The SWAT missions were really tough and at times disgusting work. Stuff that should not be talked about at home with the family. Now that you guys are men and that part of my life is over, we can talk about it from time to time."

Mac walked up to the group who were still standing next to the V-150. He said, "I have a plan worked out and the Lt agreed. We will put the dead guys into body bags and into the pickup bed. Then we'll clean up this area of all evidence of a shootout. After that, we will drive the pickup with the trailer up the county dirt road nearby. We will find a spot to stage it to look like someone robbed and killed the gang guys and took the women.

"I phoned Lenny. He's going to fly out here and take the women back to their homes in Mosier Oregon. No one can say anything to anyone, even at the ranch, at all about this incident today. It is for our safety. Only us, the Lt and

Sheriff will know about it. If the gang learns about what happened here, they will want a war against us. They might even try to attack the ranch. Well, we need to get to work before someone drives by here."

It took an hour to clean up the site. They then drove to a location, four miles from the highway on the dirt road. They took the dead guys out of the body bags and laid them out near the truck and trailer to create a scene that looked like the gang guys were at a camp spot and an ambush took place. About that time, Lenny landed his plane in a nearby field.

Mac made a phone call to OSP office at The Dalles requesting they assist with taking the freed women back to their homes. Lonnie flew with Lenny and the two women. As they got close to the city of The Dalles, Lenny radioed the troopers. "Could you guys block all eastbound lanes near mile marker 95? After the freeway shuts down, I will land in the eastbound lanes."

"OSP Dalles copy."

After the plane rolled to a stop. The local troopers were briefed on the incident. They took the women and they were back at their homes with their parents a short time later.

The others had continued into La Grande to the Guard Armory.

On the way, Mac told Kyle the whole story about the women and the Snake Heads. "The two women are actually teenagers, they just graduated school. They said that they are best friends and live in Mosier right off I-84. The three gang members broke into their homes last Sunday night. They beat up their parents and kidnapped the two of them. The truck and trailer belonged to other neighbors. The gang had killed those neighbors, took the truck, trailer and the old rifles they used to shoot at us.

"The women were taken to the gang's farm and forced to eat some pills until they nearly passed out. Then, they were raped by these three guys every night since. Today, they were being taken on a drive up into the Wallowa Lake area. The gang guys were going to break into the empty vacation homes and look for food, supplies and drugs. The gang guys had stopped to pee where the shootout occurred. As they were stopped, the women heard two of the Snake Heads say that they were getting tired of the girls and should kill them at Wallowa Lake and dump their bodies into the water then find other fresh sex slaves. They also said there are other women being held at the farm, some might have been kidnapped from La Grande at night during the last week. The two were kept away from the other women, so they don't know much else."

Kyle told Mac, "This type of activity has been the norm for the lowlifes in the gang. Remember, Ralph finally got convicted of a rape some years ago. The judge gave him three years, he was out in two. The Snake Heads gang are going to be a bigger problem sooner or later that we will need to deal with. No one else can do it."

"Yeah, I know. And we will need more guys than just the team when that day arrives," said Mac.

CHAPTER 17

They arrived in La Grande later than expected, and Mac explained to Captain Westbrook that they had an incident on the way. "We need a replacement passenger side windshield in the Humvee." When the Captain asked for details, Mac said, "I can't discuss it at this time, but I will as soon as possible."

Captain Westbrook was slightly upset, but did not ask any other questions.

As the day progressed, they met the soldiers that were going to the ranch, led by Sergeant Best. The Sgt. explained, "We are all volunteers to help out Oregon from the Idaho National Guard. I brought my wife and two young sons with me to live in La Grande, but it is not safe to leave them in the city."

Rick spoke up. "Sgt. Best, maybe we can help out. We know of a house in Enterprise that is now empty."

"That would be great if I can get them out of here. Is Enterprise having problems like La Grande?" asked Sgt. Best.

"No, and I doubt it will. It is really small-town USA. Everyone helps their neighbors type of town," said Kyle.

Mac then phoned the Lt and asked him to check with the landlord of the house they removed the Cartel from and to find out if Sgt. Best's family could live in it. Lt phoned Mac a short time later and said, "The landlord wants the family to stay at the house as long as they need it. He is repairing the front door today."

Mac told Sgt. Best of the good news.

"Thanks a lot guys, that's great news. I need to get to the motel and get my family packed up and into our pickup to travel with the convoy to Enterprise," said Sgt. Best.

By 3:00pm, the vehicles had guns installed and a new bulletproof right-side windshield in the Humvee. Sgt. Best instructed all the guys how to operate the 240B machine guns. He also handed the guys the NVGs, image stabilizing binoculars and ammo they requested. After that, the convoy got ready to leave and all the soldiers finished last minute inspections of gear and vehicles.

The convoy contained nine vehicles. The Bradley and ACP are tracked vehicles, so the top speed of the convoy would be under 40mph. Mac pulled out ahead and turned on the blue police lights to get any other vehicles they met to pull over to allow the convoy to pass on the curvy, narrow, two-lane highway.

Kyle radioed the roadblock. "Ghost Team and convoy are enroute and we expect to be in Enterprise in ninety minutes."

As the convoy passed the roadblock, all present waved and shouted out. Just before entering Enterprise, The Lt's Humvee and Sheriff's marked SUV pulled in front of Mac and Kyle with their police lights on. Mac and Kyle then noticed the people lined up on the sidewalks holding US flags and waving at them.

Kyle said, "I guess the Lt set us up as a parade through town."

Mac answered back, "Yeah, I wish people in Portland had supported their police and military like in this town."

An hour later, the convoy made it to the ranch to a smaller, but happy crowd. The wives had dinner almost ready for the whole group. It was a great time to meet each other and have a few beers after dinner.

The next morning was the seventh day since the takeover of western Oregon and Washington by the Chinese. Sgt. Best was instructing his men where to set up the tents they would be living in and arrange all of their gear. After he was finished, Sgt. Best took the Guard Humvee to Enterprise and his family followed in their pickup. He told Mac, "I will be back by night fall."

The next morning during breakfast at the meeting hall, Sgt. Best came over and sat next to the Lt., Mac and Kyle. Claudia got the Sgt. a cup of coffee and said, "We have fresh eggs, bacon and hash browns. I can get you a plate as you men talk if you want breakfast."

"Please do, I would like a good breakfast," replied Sgt. Best. After she left, Sgt. Best told the guys, "We will take over the roadblock on Highway 3 by 10:00am. I want to keep the ODOT 10-yard dump trucks with snowplows blocking most of the roadway. I will use one of the military trucks in the center of the road. It will be the only vehicle moved to open a lane so vehicles can pass. The Bradley and ACP will be parked in fighting positions nearby in case of an attack. After we get completely set up. I will keep eight soldiers at the roadblock working twelve-hour shifts. The guys not there will be at the ranch sleeping and helping with any ranch work you guys need. At the roadblock, we eat MREs. While at the ranch, could we use the meeting hall kitchen? We have fresh food and will be resupplied weekly."

The Lt said, "Of course, and tell the men to use the bathrooms and showers as needed."

Sgt. Best thanked the Lt and continued, "You know, one of the reasons we set up here is in case the Guard retreats from La Grande. So, there will be trucks coming to the ranch to stockpile military supplies. But, another reason we are here is due to the increasing violence in La Grande and on I-84. The Captain wants Wallowa County supplies to come into Washington and down Highway 3, bypassing I-84 and La Grande. Trucks on I-84 have already been attacked by citizens. All military supplies for La Grande and Pendleton will be coming from Highway 3 then to the cities starting on Monday or Tuesday."

Sgt. Best finished his fine country breakfast and after cleaning up the table he said, "I need to get my men to the roadblock and had better get going. See everyone back here at dinner."

The very next day at about noon, the Ghost Team received a radio call from the Highway 3 roadblock. Sgt. Best told them a truck had just come through from Washington, and the driver reported that about twenty miles north on Washington Highway 129 he passed a shot-up truck on the side of the road. The driver was lying dead nearby. The truck had been carrying food and it appeared the food was all gone.

"Could the team drive up there and check it out?" asked Sgt. Best.

The Lt replied, "I will send the team ASAP. It might take an hour or longer before they arrive."

All the team men gathered in the meeting hall and listened as the Lt went over his plan. "This sounds like someone in that area did this because that place is really remote. Highway 3 in Oregon becomes Highway 129 in Washington and ends in Lewiston, Idaho about forty miles from Oregon. Not much at all between our roadblock and Lewiston, but miles of timber. I want Lenny, Lonnie and Jimmy to fly over the highway all the way to Lewiston and back. They need to look for evidence of people living off the highway, likely they will be in tents and RVs."

"Mac and the rest of the team, take the V-150 and the gun Humvee. Check out the truck for evidence and bring back the body. If the plane finds a camp, Mac will decide if it should be checked out now or later with more men. There are not any Washington police at that area at all, but I might be able to get help from Lewiston. Guys, load up and get going; I will be phoning Lewiston PD."

The two vehicles stopped at the roadblock and spoke with Sgt. Best before continuing. He told them, "Earlier, a local guy drove back from Lewiston, and he said the only people he saw were in two pickups. They were parked on the roadside and those guys looked him over really good as they passed. The local had three others in his truck, all pointing rifles out through the windows. Those parked pickup guys might be who killed the truck driver."

Mac said, "Thanks for the information, it could be who we want."

The Lt phoned Mac. "Lewiston PD will come and recover the body. The driver worked and lived in their city. They will not investigate the crime, but said they will assist us if needed."

"Okay, we're leaving the roadblock now," replied Mac.

They decided to travel at slower speeds than normal in case they came across an ambush site. They finally arrived at the shot-up truck and were looking over the crime scene. Some of the guys placed the driver's body into a body bag. Kyle noticed that the truck had skidded to a stop in the roadway, and he found glass on the road where the windshield had been shot. Mac and Rick went through the truck and they discovered bullet holes in the windshield and blood on the driver's seat and door. At the rear of the truck, they found the cargo doors left open, and the rear bumper had been bent from another vehicle pushing it off the road. Inside the cargo area were a few racks of bread left, but nothing else.

Lonnie radioed the Ghost Team. "We are about ten miles north of you guys. There is a roadblock of two pickups, there are five armed men. The guys have a small delivery truck stopped—HURRY UP! They have the driver out of the truck."

Mac replied, "COPY, ENROUTE!" then yelled, "Let's go guys, full speed, lock and load all guns!"

Lonnie radioed Mac again. "They just shot the driver! We are circling a wider and higher pattern so they don't shoot us down! So far, they don't know we're up here. It's a liquor truck from Lewiston. Three men are taking cases of booze out the rear doors while the other two stand guard. All five have AR-15 or AK type rifles."

"Copy, we are pedal to the metal, maybe two or three minutes out! Tell us when we are at the last curve before them!" said Kyle.

"Will do, you will be about one hundred fifty yards away from the bad guys after the last curve," replied Lonnie.

Mac told the team, "As we clear the last curve, I want both vehicles to slow down to a walk speed and V-150 at the right side of us. We approach side by side, taking up the full width of the highway. Rick, call out on the PA to try and get them to surrender. If they will not comply, Tim and Jim open up on them with those big 240Bs."

"SLOW DOWN!" shouted Lonnie. "You guys are in the last curve now!"

At that point, the V-150 got right alongside the Humvee as they came out of the curve. Rick quickly turned the siren on then off to get their attention. Before Rick could key the PA's microphone and speaker, the V-150 had become a bullet magnet again. One of the lookouts started firing, then both were bouncing bullets off the armor. Another second later, the other three started shooting. Now their bullets were hitting both vehicles, mostly in the gun turrets.

Mac yelled, "OPEN FIRE!"

Both machine guns opened up, spraying bullets all over the bad guys and their pickups. Three of them went down with multiple hits as the last two retreated to behind the pickups. Tim and Jim stopped shooting for a moment, then one guy stood up and ducked back down. The other stood up and fired a round and ducked again. Then the first guy stood up and fired and ducked down.

Jim shouted, "Like the game whack a mole, but this is whack a bad guy with bullets!?"

Mac replied, "They think so. Hose down both pickups, they won't last long. Empty the ammo cans."

Each 240B was fired in several quick bursts and the bad guys did not stand up any longer.

Lonnie said, "All bad guys are down and not moving."

The Ghost Team drove up and looked through the bulletproof glass in each vehicle.

Rick said, "It's over, all clear."

Lonnie advised, "Jimmy spotted a campsite maybe a mile back toward the other truck, off to the right. He thought there was a green army type tent near some big trees. We will fly over low and check it out."

On the ground, the guys found a bloody mess near the pickups, which were shot-up enough that they would never run again. They placed the truck driver into a body bag and laid him near his truck. They carried the bad guys over to the roadside ditch and dropped them into it, then pushed the pickups off the road with the V-150. The guys found that each bad guy had an AR-15 and a handgun along with ammo for both in their vest pouches. They took all the guns and ammo. They all wore older style army clothing.

Kyle said, "Looks like these guys were a bad guy prepper group."

Mac said, "Yeah, let's hope there ain't any more at the campsite."

At that moment, the plane flew back overhead. Lonnie said, "The camp has a large old army surplus type tent, also two small cargo trailers. We didn't see anyone; it is the second dirt road on your right."

"Okay, we will check it out shortly," said Kyle.

A few minutes later, both team vehicles drove into the campsite as the plane circled overhead. They had Tim and Jim stay in the gun turrets to cover the others as they cleared the area and the tent. They quickly realized the camp was empty. Mac told Lonnie, "The camp is clear, there are five sleeping cots set up in the tent. You can head back home, see you guys later." Lenny flew over, tipped the plane's wings and left.

Mac then phoned the Lt. "The five guys in the pickups came from Wenatchee, Washington according to their driver's licenses, and their vehicle registrations showed they owned the pickups. We picked up all the guns and ammo they had, they have a really well stocked campsite with lots of MREs and other food. We do not have room to take that stuff."

The Lt replied. "I will send some rapid response men up there tomorrow and have them salvage what they can. Sheriff McCabe will phone the Sheriff of the county and inform him about the mission. Lewiston PD should meet you guys in an hour at the trucks. See you guys tonight, good job."

"Copy, thanks."

The next morning, Lt told the Ghost Team, "I have come up with a plan for daily patrols. I want the gun Humvee and a two-man deputy vehicle to patrol as a team throughout the county every day that there is no mission planned. The reason is to be seen by the citizens. I want them to know we are here and protecting them and do police work when and where needed. Stop in each community and talk to people, let the kids check out the Humvee, kind of like community policing. The team schedules will be a day on, a day off. Team #:1 Mac, Kyle, Rick and Justin. Team #2: Lonnie, Jim, Tim and Ike. Air Team: Lenny with either Eddy or Jimmy, and from now on we keep the plane here at the ranch. All we need is an aviation fuel truck and a hanger, and I have those coming. Any questions?"

Kyle asked, "Which team starts tomorrow and what time?"

Lt responded, "Tomorrow Team #1 is up. Meet the deputies at the SO at 9am each morning. For the rest of today, let's get done at the ranch what did not get done since we have been too damn busy doing police work."

CHAPTER 18

The Lt with Eddy as his driver, along with Team #1 in the gun Humvee, arrived at the SO just before 9:00am. The guys decided to take some needed supplies and the NVGs to the Highway 82 roadblock and stop in the small communities along the way. In the afternoon, they would take county roads back through the northern parts of the county to the ranch. The trip would take all day.

While they were stopped in the city of Wallowa, Kyle heard a roadblock deputy radio the SO dispatch. The deputy asked for advice about a woman stopped at the roadblock wanting to get into the county. The deputy said, "She is alone, her driver's license shows she is from Clackamas, Oregon. She says her father lives in the county. We have phoned him, but the phone call is not getting through. She says her father is Wally Smith. Her name is Linda Smith."

Kyle keyed his radio mike. "Ghost Team to Highway 82 roadblock. Ask that person who tips her the best of any retired state trooper she knows."

The deputy radioed back, "Ah.... she says you do, sir."

Kyle replied, "That's Linda Smith, tell her we will be there in 15 minutes."

"Copy, sir. She is in really bad shape, a real mess—she may have had a nervous breakdown."

Kyle asked, "Does she need any medical attention?"

The deputy said, "No, she is just really upset."

Kyle told the deputy, "Allow her through the roadblock and take her into the travel trailer. Get her water or anything she needs. We are on the way."

All the guys high-five each other.

"Unbelievable," says Rick. "I bet she has an interesting story to tell about how the heck she got here."

Both the Humvee and the SO marked vehicle arrived and Kyle got out first. Linda saw him through a window in the RV. The RV door flew open and she ran out toward the Humvee. By then all the guys were out of the Humvee, and she stopped and looked them over. "What are you guys? Did you join the army? You're driving an army truck, and do you have machine guns?" She started crying and gave Kyle and big hug. The guys noticed she was a mess; her jeep was dirty and it had dried blood on the outside of the driver's plastic door.

Between wiping her eyes and runny nose, Linda quickly spoke of trying to tell the guys she was attempting to get to her son and dad. She hardly took a breath of air.

Kyle told her, "Slow down a little, you're now safe. I know about your son and dad and they are fine. I will take you to them." All Linda could do is cry more and give all the guys a big hug.

Kyle walked over to Mac and told him, "Go ahead and continue the patrol. I will drive Linda in her jeep to the Highway 3 roadblock where Mr. Smith is cutting trees down. I will see you guys at the ranch later tonight."

"Okay, let's give the deputies the stuff we brought and split," said Mac.

Before they leave, a deputy informs the guys that four members of the Snake Heads gang came by on their motorcycles earlier and wanted to get into the county. "They were rightly refused and real mad, but they saw the deputies pointing the M-16s at them. So, they u-turned and left."

Mac told him, "Make sure everyone knows that gang is big trouble. Never let any of them into the county. I bet they will be back."

Kyle got into the driver's seat of the jeep and looked closely at a bullet hole and the dried blood on the plastic door. Linda was still talking nonstop. Kyle told her, "Please be quiet for a couple minutes and listen. We met your son and dad. I know where they are now. You're a big mess, let's stop at the SO. There you can take a shower and put on clean clothes before you see your son. Then, let's stop at the restaurant and get some lunch. When was the last time you ate?"

Linda said, "Two days ago, I'm starved." She then leaned over and gave Kyle another hug and kiss on his cheek. Kyle's face turned red. Linda said, "I could just fall in love with you. You're my hero."

Kyle's face turned even redder. He replied, "There must be others in this county to fall in love with. Heck, I'm married and fifty-two. And you're what, thirty-five?

"Yea, so what."

To change the subject, Kyle asked Linda to tell him about what happened to her during the last week as they took off toward Enterprise. Linda said, "I had lived in an apartment not far from the restaurant. Like everyone else on Saturday, I woke up without power and no cell phone service or a working computer. I asked my neighbors at the apartment building if they knew what was going on. All said they didn't know, but also said none of their cars would start. I noticed that there were no cars traveling anywhere. For once, the freeway was quiet. I never checked my old jeep and left it parked in the garage. I ended up cooking food on the Bar-B-Q that day and several days after that. The second night, I started hearing gun fire around the area. Each day I heard more and more shots being fired. Then, the water stopped running in the apartment. Everyone was getting worried, but no one knew what to do but wait for help.

"At night, I finally went to the jeep and tried to start it. It started right up and then I worried that someone might hear it and steal it. So, I shut the engine off right away. At that point, I decided to drive to Wallowa County to Dad's cabin. I had sent Johnny over here the weekend before so he could spend the summer with his grandpa. The next day, my friend Kim from the restaurant rode her bicycle over to my apartment. We ending up making a plan to meet the next day at my apartment, and together we would drive the jeep to Wallowa County. So that night, I went around to some of the cars in the apartment parking lot and siphoned gas until my jeep tank and the extra gas can were full. I put some camping gear and clothes into the jeep.

"I waited for Kim the next day, but she never came. By then I was running out of food and bottled water. I finally decided to leave by myself that night. I drove on the county back roads until I got to I-84 near the Corbett on ramp. On I-84, I saw dead people along the roadside and a few other people walking east bound. At The Dalles, I talked with state troopers who informed me for my safety that I needed to follow one of the buses headed east to

Pendleton. I followed a bus until I got real sleepy, then I drove off a freeway ramp and parked a little ways from freeway. It was out in the middle of nowhere. I felt safe, so I fell asleep while sitting in the driver's seat.

"Then, the scariest thing happened. I woke up hearing a man saying, 'Let's get her.' Luckily, I had an old .357 revolver that Dad gave me sitting in my lap. The guy was trying to open my door. I was so scared, but I raised the gun, pointed at him and cocked the hammer back. He just kept pulling on the door handle and laughing at me. He looked like a monster; all dirty, hair everywhere, a long greasy beard and his teeth were rotten. I pulled the trigger and shot him. He spit blood out his mouth and all over the door, then he fell against the door and onto the ground. I got the jeep started and took off as fast as I could drive it. I then spotted another man standing near the jeep on the other side, and I fired a shot at him through the passenger side door as I was driving away. I never looked to see if I hit him or not.

"After I reached the freeway I stopped, opened the door and threw up. I realized I had peed my pants. I just sat there and cried a few minutes until I saw a bus driving east, and I followed it until near Pendleton. I got to the La Grande exit near dark, and the police there wouldn't let me travel on Highway 82 because I didn't have an address on my driver's license in Union or Wallowa Counties. But, I knew I could drive on old gravel and dirt logging roads back over Mt. Emily into Wallowa County as I had done with dad many times in the past. So, I turned around and exited onto the Mt. Emily gravel road. I made it over half of the way before I needed to stop again and sleep.

"That night, I slept in the jeep with the gun on my lap. After daylight, I started driving again. It still took hours and most of my gas to get to the roadblock. When I arrived at the Highway 82 roadblock and couldn't continue, I just lost it and broke down."

"Well, I'm glad you made it here. That took a lot of courage," said Kyle.

Kyle and Linda arrived at the SO, and Linda showered and changed into clean clothes. Kyle filled her jeep with gas, washed it and patched the bullet holes in the plastic doors with duct tape. When Linda came out of the locker room, Kyle's head quickly turned to take a long second look. Linda was wearing tight-fitting jeans and a T-shirt that showed off her figure, and she did have a nice figure.

"Wow," Kyle said to her. "That's the Linda I know. You sure are pretty all cleaned up, and you smell good, too."

"I don't even have any makeup on, Kyle."

"Linda, you don't need makeup on to look great."

They then went to the Big Bear restaurant to eat lunch. While there eating, the owner Flo walked over to their table to talk with Kyle. Flo then noticed he was with Linda and said, "Hi Linda, I haven't seen you in a few years."

Linda explained, "Since I moved to Portland, I haven't gotten back here very much. It just took two days to get here. I'm going to live with Dad and my son here now. The metro area is crazy bad, I didn't know what happened until I got to The Dallas."

Flo replied, "If you're wanting a waitress job, I really need someone."

"Yes, I do need a job badly. When could I start?"

"How about get a full day's rest with your family and start in two days. Work from noon to close at 8pm."

"Thanks so much, I won't let you down. See you then."

After eating, Kyle and Linda drove on Highway 3 from the restaurant toward the Bradford Ranch and the roadblock near there. Linda said, "I feel much better and am relaxed enough, I think I need a nap. You know, the last few days I haven't slept much." She placed her head against Kyle's shoulder and quickly fell asleep.

They arrived at the roadblock about forty-five minutes later. Kyle parked the jeep behind another vehicle near the site's RV.

Linda woke up. "Why are we stopping here?"

"This is where your dad and son are working today. Let's surprise them," replied Kyle.

They went into the RV and met Sgt. Best. Kyle asked him, "Could you send a soldier to get Linda's dad and son without saying anything except that the Sgt. needs to talk to them?"

"Yes.... I will. Sounds like they will be getting a big surprise."

"Yep," replied Kyle.

A few minutes later, Wally and Johnny walked into the RV and Linda stepped around the corner to see them. "Hi Johnny, hi Dad," she nearly yelled. Johnny rushed to his mom. They hugged, then Wally got to hug Linda. Lots of hugs and tears flowed as they met, even from Wally.

Kyle told them, "I need to get to the ranch and can drive Linda's jeep. Could the three of you follow in Wally's truck?"

Wally said, "Let's go, we got to get home and bake a big dinner tonight."

When they arrived at the ranch, Mary asked them to stay for dinner. Everyone in the meeting hall wanted Linda to tell them about Portland since the war started and about her trip to get to Wallowa County. Linda did not leave any details out of her trip, until the point she made Kyle's face turn red several times. She left those details out of her story.

After dinner, Kyle took Mr. Smith aside and asked, "What weapons do you have in case you need to fight bad guys in these troubled times?"

"Well, I have an old 30-30 rifle, but little ammo. I could not find any during the last trip to La Grande and Linda has my old Ruger .357."

"Well, I have a lot of ammo," replied Kyle. "And I picked up a nice old 30-30 that I should give to Linda. I will go get those."

"We don't have any money to pay you, we can't accept them," said Wally.

"Oh, BS. I am only offering these to you because we need firewood here at the ranch and don't have time to cut it. You get the guns and ammo in exchange for working here."

"Okay, deal. Thanks a lot. I owe you much more just for getting Linda here safe and sound."

"Mr. Smith, she got here almost all by herself. We are all happy she made it. You should be real proud of her."

"I am very proud of her. One thing for sure, she is not a metro snowflake. And quit calling me Mr. Smith, my name is Wally."

Everyone nearby laughed at Wally's remark.

Kyle left and retrieved some ammo and two rifles. He returned shortly with armloads of stuff. He said, “Here, all this is for you guys.” He then put the cleaned up 30-30 rifle from the last shootout on the table, along with eight boxes of 30-30 ammo. He turned to Johnny and said, “This bolt action .22 rifle is for you. Your grandpa will teach you how to shoot it and how to do it safely. This is a five hundred round brick of ammo. Before you use it up, I expect to hear about some nice fat squirrels you shot for dinner. Lastly, Linda here’s two boxes of ammo for that trusty .357.”

Linda and Johnny gave Kyle hugs and Wally shook his hand.

Wally said, “We’ll be here next week to get that firewood cut for you guys. Thanks for everything. We need to get home to the cabin. You know it will take an hour just to get on the other side of your ranch on the gravel road.”

Everyone walked outside and waved bye.

CHAPTER 19

Salem Oregon: Governor's office a few months before the Chinese invasion, late afternoon on a Friday, only three men were in the office.

Governor Arnold Olson was seated behind his desk. Secretary of State Jack Madison (the #2 man in state government) was seated on the nearby couch. Standing near the Governor was a state trooper. He was one of six troopers assigned to the dignitary protection unit (bodyguards for the Governor). He would drive the Governor home to Portland after this meeting. His name was Chao Wang.

Mr. Madison told the Governor, "I have decided to go on a two-week camping trip the week after the Memorial holiday weekend."

"Oh, what are you going to do? More checking out old gold mines and ghost towns?"

"Yeah, my only hobby these days. I am taking my pickup with the travel trailer and the ATV. I will be checking out the area around a ghost town named Whitney and old homesteads off Highway 7 east of Baker City."

"Your wife is staying home again I imagine?"

"Yeah, she won't go camping any longer. When we travel, if there's not a hotel to sleep in, she stays home."

"Okay, I think Chao and I had better hit the road, the I-5 traffic to Portland can be bad if we wait much longer. Jack, I will see you Monday morning."

"Bye Governor, see you Monday," said Jack.

Senior Trooper Chao Wang was married to a Chinese born woman who he grew up with near his home town and had three children. He was hired by OSP at the age of twenty-three, coming into the department as the first Chinese-American state trooper. He had a bachelor's degree and spoke excellent Mandarin Chinese along with several other Asian languages. His family had lived in the San Francisco Bay area for several generations.

Just two months later, Chao Wang visited the Secretary of State's Office.

"Hi, Chao, have a seat. My secretary said you wanted to talk to me," said Jack.

"Yes Sir, I have a question to ask of you. I remember you and the Governor were talking about you going on a camping trip by yourself. I have vacation time I need to use up and was wondering if I could go with you. I have never been to any of the mountains or woods in Oregon and have never looked for gold or seen a ghost town."

"Well yeah.... sure. I have a travel trailer that has several beds. It carries the ATV in the back area. The ATV I travel around on is made for two people seated side by side with room for gear in the back. But, what about your family?"

"They are spending that time visiting my wife's family in San Francisco, and I really don't want to go. I do not get along with her parents," said Chao.

"I understand, let's get together in a few weeks and plan out what gear you need to bring and food to eat. I think we would both enjoy the trip."

"Thank you so much." Then, Chao said, "I need to get back to work."

Thursday morning before the invasion, Jack drove his truck with the travel trailer into the OSP Salem office to pick up Chao. Chao said, "That's a nice old truck. What year is it, and did you restore it? It looks showroom new."

"Thanks, it's a 1969 Ford F350, 1ton 4x4 with the big old 460 v-8 engine. I had it restored a while back. It was a lot more money than I wanted to spend, but in the end, I think it was worth it. At about five mpg fuel usage, I just use it to pull the RV. Let's put your bags in the trailer and I can show you the inside."

"Wow Jack, this is a big trailer."

"Yeah, it's 30 ft long. The back area is just ATV storage. But, you can sleep on the couch, it folds out into a bed. I get the bedroom. Let's hit the road."

While driving to the camping area, Chao said, "Jack, I have heard stories that you were a badass army guy back in your younger days. I would like to hear the story if you want to tell it."

"Well, I bet most of the stories are just BS, but I will tell you the truth," replied Jack. "I grew up on a farm near Albany, and we mainly grew sod. I went to OSU and back then the war in Vietnam was hot, lots of GIs being killed. After college, the Army was in real need of helicopter pilots, and me being young thought that would be fun. It was hell over there; not fun at all. I flew gunships called 'Cobras' and after my first tour was finished, the Army couldn't get enough pilots to fly the unarmed medical choppers. I got paid more and stayed flying the Dust-Offs. I lost crew members and one co-pilot, but survived through all that. Back home things changed a lot with new laws about farming, so my folks sold the farm. It is now several subdivisions. I then got into politics and worked my way up from that point. Now, I work side by side with many who protested what I did during the war. It's been said that I bring some reason to the state government when others ask for unicorns and fairy dust."

Chao said, "I was told you saved many men and got lots of medals."

"Well, I suppose I did but.... I don't like to talk about the war much. It was really hell. I lost some good friends," replied Jack.

"Okay, I won't bring it up again."

About three hours later, Jack pulled off the highway and parked in a large pull-out area next to the highway. The area was large enough to camp at and had been used by others. That day, they were the only vehicles parked there.

"We're here," said Jack. "Let's get the ATV unloaded from the trailer and packed up with our gear. I plan on camping out in the woods til Monday. After that, we will move to another area. We have about another two hours of ATV travel before we get to the spot where I want to set up the camp site."

"Is it okay to leave the truck and trailer here? Won't someone steal them?" asked Chao.

"It should be safe. Funny though, do you know Kyle Morris?

"Yeah, I know him along with everyone else at OSP. He retired not long ago," replied Chao.

"Well, he once told me that I needed to get a club for the steering wheel or someone would steal the truck. I never got around to getting one. Oh, he retired. What's he doing now?"

"I have not heard. Hey, I brought my service pistol and two extra magazines. Should I wear them? And what about cell phones?" asked Chao.

"I would bring the gun to have it just in case. I am carry-ing my trusty 1911 .45 auto also with two spare mags. The cell phones may work, but I doubt it. I also doubt we will even see another person up there, but there are bears and a few cougars."

"Okay Jack, I am ready."

"Me too, let's go. I will drive."

From Friday morning through Sunday night, all the two did was hike up or down a few creeks and pan for gold all day. Each day, Jack got some small flakes of gold. Monday around noon, the two were returning to the truck. As the two had gotten back near the highway, they were engaged in small talk.

"Ya know Jack, not having cell service for a few days seemed hard, but actually, it was nice."

"Yea, real peaceful up here. I do not like hearing the damn phones ring every day."

"Hey, what the heck, Jack.... your truck is missing!"

As they approached the parking area they saw that the trailer was still there, but no truck. No other vehicles were parked anywhere in the area.

"Crap... Chao, the trailer door is open. I bet they ransacked it. We had better stop here, and slowly walk up to the trailer and check it out. There could be someone still inside."

"Jack, you cover me and I will clear the trailer."

"Okay."

After a minute inside the trailer, Chao yelled, "All clear! They took nearly everything, come on inside."

"Chao, don't you have a satellite phone?"

"Yes, I did. I left it in the trailer, and it's gone too. It seems the cell phones still do not work around here."

"Well Chao, on this highway there should be some people in trucks or cars coming by here soon. I guess we just sit and wait."

The pair sat near the highway for an hour and never saw a single vehicle. Then they heard voices on the road far away from the pullout. Soon after that, a pair of young adults riding bicycles came into view. It was a man and woman, both with packs attached to their bikes and on their backs. They peddled at a slow pace toward the two of them. As the bicycling pair got close, Chao and Jack could see both riders were armed with handguns in holsters on their belts.

Chao and Jack stood, walked into the roadway and raised their arms and waved. Chao said, "We are stuck here, someone stole our truck. Do you guys have a working phone?"

The man stopped close to them, and the woman stopped further back and remained behind the man. They both dismounted their bicycles.

The man said, "The cell phones we had were fried like everyone else's phones back in Bend."

Jack asked, "What do you mean fried like everyone's phones? We have been in the mountains for four days. This is just a dead zone for cell service."

The man asked, "Have you guys had contact with anyone since Friday?"

"No," said Jack. Chao and Jack turned their heads and looked at each other.

The man continued, "Well then, let me tell you what happened. Saturday night Oregon and Washington were invaded. We don't know much, but the Willamette Valley is blacked out. No one has had any contact from anyone west of the Cascade Mountain range. We lived just outside of Bend, and on Saturday morning Bend was attacked. We were told what was left of the state leaders had fled to Bend and were targeted in the attack. They were all at a meeting at the Bend Police Department. It was hit with missiles or bombs. As of that time, nothing electrical has worked. That's why the bicycles. We're headed to Baker City, but we don't know if it was attacked or not.

"Oh shit, this is bad, really bad," said Jack as he turned to Chao.

Chao replied, "Yea, looks like no help is coming for us here."

The man said, "Good luck guys, we need to get going. See ya."

"Good luck to you also," said Jack.

A couple minutes passed before either said a word.

"Hey, Chao. Let's figure out a way to drive the ATV to Baker City on back roads. We need to avoid this highway. It will attract both the good and bad people. I have food for one more day and water is not a problem since I have a life straw. It will give us clean drinking water when water is drawn through it from a stream and there are many streams in these mountains. We should have enough gas to make the trip if the trailer still has fuel. The trailer has an ATV fuel station. We need to check it and find out if that got stolen or not."

Jack went over and turned on the gas pump, hooked up the gas hose and fuel pumped out. "We can top off the ATV gas tank and the spare can. I have a map that shows the back roads. Let's get busy. We need to stop and pick out a camp spot before dark, maybe we will get to Baker City by noon tomorrow."

"Okay, I think when we get near Baker City, you should stay hidden. I will go and visit the OSP office and get intel on what the heck is going on. Let's keep your identity a secret," replied Chao.

During the next two days, the pair traveled to Baker City. They found a good location to keep Jack secretly hidden outside the city until Chao found that the city and the OSP office were safe. Only the station Sergeant knew the truth about who Jack really was, just in case there might be an attack to kill him. Jack had been in phone contact with the governor of Idaho and a few people in Washington DC, and he had learned about everything that had happened. He mainly wanted to get a working state government again. Chao had been in phone contact with his family in San Francisco ensuring them that he was okay and safe in eastern Oregon with the Secretary of the State.

It was decided to move Jack to a personal friend's farm outside of La Grande. There, he would be hard at work attempting to set up the new state government with help of the National Guard. Still all in secret with his OSP bodyguard Chao Wang near him at all times.

Chao went outside away from all the others and made a call to his wife back in California.

CHAPTER 20

Back in Wallowa County, the next several days of police patrols were routine with no incidents requiring any arrests. Sgt. Best was sending out Guard patrols north to Lewiston and back to protect the trucks and traveling citizens. If you exclude the marijuana raid and biker gang incident, the Wallowa County reported crime rate had not even gone up since the war had started. Most of the food and other aid coming into the county was donated. Those items were handed out free in limited amounts. As before, the people in this county helped each other out more than most cities or communities. To live in the county, because of the lack of services of a big city and the remoteness, required a person to learn to be self-sufficient.

At the morning SO briefing, the group learned that the Oregon Secretary of State Jack Madison was alive and in La Grande. He had been secretly sworn in as Governor. Only a few key people knew at the time for his protection. He had been busy working with other states and the US government in getting aid to Oregonians and building up the Oregon National Guard. The US military was still not assisting the state at all.

Only two things were settled between the Chinese and Washington DC at the second meeting. 1: The Chinese would not move forces east of the Cascade Mountain range at this time. 2: The Chinese would allow Red Cross flights with food and medical supplies into the airports they controlled. The Chinese claimed that they had restored power to many hospitals by stationing working generators at them and will have the public water plants running again soon.

The following morning was the day of what is now named the Wallowa Vacation Home Battle. The entire assault was broadcast over the normal SO net #1, so everyone in the county with any county radio could hear the mission. All county employees stopped their work to listen.

After the Lt radioed that the officers were okay, the wives and off duty soldiers that were gathered around the radio in the meeting hall all jumped up shouting praises of thanks. Mary yelled out, "Thank God, our men are okay!"

Then, everyone on the radio net started hearing the radios clicking. This went on for nearly a minute. Each person who was listening outside of the assault team pushed the transmit buttons on and off once without speaking. Each person clicking their radios was giving the assault team members the highest praise of all, the police radio salute for a job well done. The Ghost air unit cleared and flew toward the ranch. Lenny told the group Eddy had the whole battle on tape.

Sheriff McCabe arrived and was walked through the house with the Lt and Mac. Mac pointed out how the assault went down as they walked through the entire house. They finished and walked back outside, and the Sheriff told the team, "I am real proud of you guys, every one of you here today. Those four SOBs got just what they had coming. Because of those lowlife scumbags inside that house, the county lost two good men. The county ME will document their deaths and their ashes will be dumped at the county landfill." The Sheriff, with tears running down his face, shook the hands of the deputies, troopers and Ghost Team members. The Sheriff then left and headed to the hospital to talk with the woman who had been held hostage.

The Lt asked the fire department crew to help place all dead into body bags. He said, "Put the dumb ass losers into a SO pickup bed. Let's get the funeral home up here so they can take the victim's body."

Mac told the Lt, "Let's get everyone else here to go through the house and bring out anything that has value. We will take the stuff to the donation center."

Kyle and Jim met with their sons and told them they do not need to go inside. What they would see inside the house may cause them some trouble to deal with. Justin asked his father, "Dad, did I kill any of them? I feel sick." He started shaking and crying.

Kyle quickly grabbed Justin by the shoulder and walked him away from the house. After several steps, Justin bent over and vomited. Kyle handed Justin a bottle of water. He said, "Son, it doesn't matter at all who shot them. What is important is that you did exactly what the Lt told you to do, fire the machine gun. And you did it without delay or question. Your actions likely saved some of our lives. What you're feeling is normal for anyone who has a moral compass. I am very proud of you, and I understand your feelings. It's okay to be upset. I have a question; do you want me to tell your mom what happened here, or do you want to talk to her first?"

"Dad, I want to tell her about it."

"Okay son, she is a good listener. Let's walk around the area and look away from that house of horrors. See how beautiful this area around the lake is at this time of year? We need to do some fishing as soon as we have the time. I didn't bring the boat for nothing. Remember the last time you caught those big trout?"

"Yeah, Dad. They made a great dinner that night. I'm going to get Jimmy and we will be down by the lake for a while."

Mac and Lonnie found 18,000 dollars in cash. They suggest that the money be split between the deputy's widow and the hostage. The Lt agreed, took the money and then left to meet the Sheriff at the hospital.

Before the guys left, they had filled two pickup trucks with food and clothing to go to the donation center. The county ME had arrived and taken the four to be cremated. The funeral home had removed the woman's dead husband. The group made it back to the ranch late again, but their wives had dinner and cold beer waiting for them.

After they ate, the Lt told the group, "The Sheriff told all of us to stand down for 1 full day tomorrow. He said we are not to do any police work at all and no going to the SO. He also has a doctor in town to see each of us for a physical. Anyone who wants to visit an acupuncture/ chiropractor, the best guy in town cleared all other clients to see you guys. You know we have been working hard and nearly nonstop. Even more than in the old days when we were a lot younger. The doctor visit is not optional."

CHAPTER 21

At the meeting hall during breakfast, when most were finished eating, Sgt. Best stood and said, "Can I have everyone's attention for just a couple of minutes? First off, the Oregon National Guard wants to give the Ghost Team a toast for yesterday's mission. JOB WELL DONE, GUYS!" All raised their coffee cups or glass of milk to the toast. "Second, really good news for the meeting hall today, we are getting a refrigerated trailer that has its own propane power supply. We will be adding more soldiers, and one of them is a cook assigned here fulltime to lead or assist with meals at the meeting hall. Okay folks, enjoy the rest of your breakfast before it gets cold." He then sat down.

Everyone gave a quick round of applause.

The Lt then stood and added, "When the Ghost Team and families go into town today, we will be going off in different directions. How about I phone the Big Bear restaurant to reserve their meeting room and we all meet there for lunch around 1:00pm? The meal will be on me."

Everyone gave the Lt thumbs up and left the meeting hall to prepare to head into Enterprise.

Kyle's family and Rick and his wife left about the same time in their own trucks.

Kyle phoned Rick, "Let's get to the chiropractor first. The medical doctor after that."

"Okay, sounds good. We'll meet there," replied Rick.

When they got in town, they drove right to Dr. Yan Chen's office. The guys went inside while their families left to visit the market. Once inside, they met Dr. Chens' wife at the front desk. Kyle introduced them to her and said, "I think we both need some adjusting and acupuncture. We have been beating up these old bodies lately."

She said, "We have heard about your work, thanks for visiting us. I will have the doctor meet with you in a couple minutes."

Dr. Chen entered the lobby. "Hello, Mr. Morris and Mr. Barnes." Kyle and Rick stood and shook the doctor's hand. "I am honored that you have come to see me. Please let me introduce myself. I came to the United States from China as a child with my parents. At that time, I only spoke Chinese. I quickly learned English in a public school. I was taught the Chinese methods of Acupuncture and Chiropractic care from the very best. I was also taught EMS medical care. I moved my family here from Portland about fifteen years ago. We love this place. This is the best city in Oregon to live in and raise my family. Sheriff McCabe has asked me to be part of the county rapid response team as an EMS responder. If called, I have a large medical bag ready to go along with my gun. Today, I promise you guys you will feel better after my treatment."

The guys left the doctor's office a couple hours later.

Rick said, "I feel ten years younger."

Kyle replied, "Me too, let's see him once a week."

"Yes, let's do that. If we get the time," said Rick.

Kyle and Rick had some extra time before the lunch meeting at Big Bear and decided to visit the gun shop/sporting goods store. As they were picking out some gun maintenance and cleaning stuff, the store owner, Shorty, saw the two and walked over to say hello. He asked them to come over to the gun counter; he wanted to show them something before they left. Shorty stood there with a big grin on his face. He said, "Look at these cases of ammo and the prices."

"Wow, I haven't seen that much ammo in a long time! And what's up with the prices? You're giving the stuff away," said Kyle.

"Boys, one of the big three US ammo companies decided they would sell as much ammo to the Oregon and Washington gun shops that are still in business for only the cost of shipping it. The other two ammo companies, not to be outdone, did the same. I am only making .25 cents a box."

"Is that to anyone?" Rick asked Shorty.

"No, any police and rapid response team folks get two boxes free. What do you guys want?"

Kyle said, "Thanks, but we have enough, and we get supplied the main ammo we need from the Guard. Does the Sheriff know about this deal?"

"No, this all came in this morning with a letter explaining the deal. The letter also said to reorder as needed. And wished us luck fighting the invaders."

"Okay, I will let the Lt know about this deal at your store. Did you know Sheriff McCabe and the Lt have gotten just over two hundred county residents signed up to fight against any bad guys coming here, be it Chinese, NK or others?" asked Kyle.

"Yeah, I know. I am one of them. My job is to resupply them in the field."

Rick spoke up, “We had better pay for this stuff and get to lunch.”

“I won’t take any of your money,” Shorty held his hands up.

“Well, okay. How about I start a donation? Here’s twenty. Set up a donation jar to help those injured while fighting. I think sooner or later we will be in deep shit here unless the President helps us,” Rick said to Shorty.

The two guys had arrived at the restaurant early and were the first from the ranch in the door. Flo and Linda saw them enter and came over to escort the two to the meeting room. Flo said, “This meal is on us. Well, actually, the beef came from your ranch, anyway. All the ranches are donating an animal a week to help keep the cost of beef down. Most other fresh foods are being donated in limited amounts. Our prices have been able to drop here and also at the butcher shop. I was told in Pendleton and La Grande most food products costs skyrocketed and are in short supply.”

Rick replied, “Being in a smaller community like here has some good points. It seems like around here more people help each other instead of only themselves.”

The guys sat down, and Linda sat next to Kyle. She said to him, “I need your help.”

“Sure, Linda. Anything. What’s up?”

Under the table, Linda put her hand on his leg and Kyle’s face started to turn red again.

“Well, next week Dad will be at the ranch cutting your firewood. If I show up, could you take me to the gun range and show me how to shoot better?”

“Yes, of course. But, you did damn good shooting on the way here.”

"Thanks, but I want to be better. And, this will be just the two of us."

"Okay, no problem," replied Kyle.

Linda stood up and asked, "Do you guys want to order now? I recommend hamburgers or any of the steaks. I know where the beef came from; it's the best beef in the county." She made a quick laugh.

"Yeah, let's eat now. I will have a burger, fries and a cold bottle of beer," said Kyle.

Rick said, "Make mine the same."

After Linda walked away, Rick leaned over to Kyle. "What's this about going to the range.... just the two of you?"

"She wants help to shoot better," said Kyle.

"Yeah right, Kyle. I think you're missing some signs."

"Oh, crap, do you really think.... she means... adult alone time?"

"Well.... yeah, I think so," said Rick.

Kyle replied, "Oh, NO." and shook his head.

The Lt and Mary arrived as the guys were finishing their meal.

Kyle told the Lt about the ammo deal at the gun shop. The Lt got up and went outside to phone the Sheriff with the good news. It was almost 1:00pm and all the others arrived. They were all engaged in small talk during the meal. The talk was about shopping or the visits to the doctor. At the stores they got nearly everything that was on their lists from food to ranch supplies.

After everyone had eaten, the Lt stood. "The funeral for Deputy Jones will be in two days at 10:00am. We need to be at the SO at 6:00am. The funeral procession will start at the SO and loop through the city, then end at the high school gym. Guys, this will be the biggest funeral this city has ever seen. Deputy Jones was the first law officer ever killed in the line of duty in this county. Even back in the Wild West days, no one killed a lawman here. We'll take both Humvees and V-150. Since we do not have class A uniforms, let's wear our same utility uniform with tactical gear, minus the helmet and remember. Polish your boots.

"Team #2 is up for patrol tomorrow. The Sheriff told me that Westbrook wants a meeting with me in the morning. I want Kyle, Mac and Lonnie to go with me in my Humvee. Normal mission gear for that trip. Nothing is expected to happen, but who knows. By the way, Westbrook is now Major Westbrook." He sat back down.

Lenny stood up and told the group, "I will need to fly to Pendleton tomorrow in the afternoon. They have some parts I need for the plane's engine. Jimmy and Eddy could fly with me. It would get them some more ground spotter time."

Eddy said, "Cool, I'm in."

"Me too," said Jimmy.

The Lt looked at Kyle and said, "You're up for the next doctor visit along with Rick, Eddy and Justin. See you guys later at the ranch."

Everyone went their own way; either to do more shopping, drive back to the ranch or to see the doctor and hopefully get a clean bill of health.

CHAPTER 22

The four men in the Humvee made it to the Guard HQ without any incidents on the way. They had been seated in Major Westbrook's reception room for only a few minutes. This time, the Major opened his own office door and invited them inside. "Hello men, I have been told you guys have put the equipment I gave you to good use."

"Yes, we have and thanks again," replied the Lt.

"Well, as you have seen by the military vehicles passing through your county, the Army is growing in size. Now that there is an official Oregon Governor in place, Idaho's Governor and Governor Madison got together and signed some documents. The Idaho National Guard General will take command of what's left of our Guard in Oregon. I am now the Operations Major. Please keep me as your contact here at HQ. We now have several new officers, including another Major and Lt Colonel stationed in La Grande.

"We have moved scout units into hiding places near several highways and the I-84 freeway. Each unit has an M-1 tank, two Stryker's and an APC or two besides the supply vehicles. Those Stryker's with the 30mm bushmaster guns will shoot down anything the Chinese might fly at us. They are in place as an early warning in case the Chinese attempt to come through to Eastern Oregon. They will engage the enemy and retreat. Lots of soldiers and fighting equipment are building up in Idaho for use in Oregon.

Get this, the Texas Governor signed over about 5,000 soldiers from the Texas National Guard who by the way, all volunteered to come here. They and their equipment will be used in both Oregon and Washington. It will take a while to get them all here and deployed to fight. The President is pissed; he doesn't want us to fight. He said us standing up to the Chinese Army on our own soil will hurt the peace talks. He is spending more time trying to stop us than stopping the Chinese. We will start flying Blackhawk choppers along I-84 from Idaho to Pendleton. You might see some above Highway 82 and Highway 3."

"Sgt. Best was promoted to Platoon Sgt. and there will be a full platoon of soldiers for the roadblock, ranch and patrol. That means a few more soldiers will be staying at the ranch. More soldiers will be kept at the roadblock as a fast action team if needed to fight in the area. The roadblock will become a normal stopping point for military vehicles that need fuel or a rest for the soldiers. I am sending two female soldiers to the ranch. One is a cook to help out at the meeting hall. The other is a SWAT cop from Houston PD. in real life. Could you put her into the team?"

Lt said, "Hell yes. Is that her only assignment?"

"Yes, and with her I am sending a M107 .50 caliber sniper rifle, a Barrett semi auto; it's one badass sniper rifle. Also, she brought her M2010 in .300 win. mag. caliber. It's a Remington bolt action gun and an M-4 like yours. Oh, I almost forgot. I am also giving you two-night vision FLRs rifle scopes. I was told they mount on any rifle with a rail and they are the latest thermal vision. Your newest team member will arrive at the ranch with all the gear tomorrow."

"That's all great news. We were told about the cook from Sgt. Best," said the Lt.

Major Westbrook continued, "Governor Madison wants to talk with you guys at his hideout. I have an SUV for you to drive there with. I think it is best not to drive over there in the Humvee. We don't want people to think the Governor or anyone important is at the ranch. Just follow the lead SUV. It's about a ten-minute drive from here. Sorry guys, but I got a war to help plan. Good luck, see you again."

The men remained all geared up in their load carrying ballistic vests, handguns and M-4s with SO badges attached to the front left panel and State Trooper baseball caps on their heads. They were led out to another parking lot with non-military vehicles.

In the lot they saw two guys in civilian clothes standing next to two plain Jane SUVs. One of the guys said, "Hey, you four. Follow us, but not too close. That's your ride over there." He pointed at a blue, full size, real dirty SUV.

Mac said, "Get in, I'm driving, I don't trust any of you guys."

Kyle told the Lt, "I think the reason the Major asked us here was just to send us to the Governor."

Lt said, "Yeah, I got the same feeling. I suspect the Governor wants us to leave the county and work for OSP again."

"Well, he can ask, but I'm saying no. Hell no," said Lonnie.

Kyle added, "If we were not available the other day, those guys at Wallowa Lake would have not been stopped from killing anyone they wanted. Heck, they may have taken over the city of Joseph. The best use of us is in Wallowa County."

"Guys, we just need to listen to what the Governor has to say and each one of us will make up his own mind if it comes to that," replied the Lt.

A few minutes later they pulled up to a gated driveway. A guy in civilian clothes came out of a small guard shack and opened the gate. The ranch house was around 100 yards further up the driveway. Only a single vehicle was seen parked in front of the house. Cattle and horses were in the fields around the house. The men followed the SUV around to the back side and then noticed several Humvees parked there and a couple more SUVs.

Mac parked and all the guys got out carrying their M-4s. They walked over to the two guys who led them.

The Lt asked, "Who are you guys? I don't know you from OSP."

"Oh, we're Oregon Guard assigned to the Governor. Our job is security at the house or any other off-site location."

"Okay, you know who we are, right?"

"Of course, everyone in the Guard knows the Ghost Team."

Another man opened the back door of the house and looked around at everyone standing in the parking area. He then shouted, "You guys can't bring those machine guns into the house! The Governor is inside."

The four looked around at each other and Lonnie said, "WHAT?"

Mac looked at the man standing in the doorway and yelled, “Knock off the gun safe zone crap. We carry these inside, or the Governor comes out to talk.” All eyes were on Mac.

Lt said, “Hold it down Mac.”

Out from Kyle’s mouth everyone heard, “Good one, Mac.”

There was a stare down with the guy in the door. He just stood there looking at the Ghost Team like a grade school teacher at misbehaving children.

Lonnie said, “Hey guys, let’s get the hell out of here. We have real police work to do.”

They all turned and walked back toward the SUV.

As they stepped into the SUV, they heard a voice shout, “Hey Bill, hold on! Get in here and keep your tactical gear on, including the guns.”

They turned and saw the new Oregon Governor Jack Madison standing in the doorway. He walked out toward them at a fast pace. They also noticed all the Guard guys running around the Governor, anticipating an attack.

The Governor said, “Men, let’s get inside where we can talk.” Then, he raised his voice so everyone nearby could hear him. “Hell, I need more men around me who know not to leave their guns in a vehicle!” He looked around at the others. “You guys need to learn fast who is a good guy or a bad guy.”

The Guard men were standing around looking at the ground. Several shook their heads.

The Ghost Team followed the Governor into a dining room with a large table that could seat all of them. Four other Guard men in civilian clothes followed them into the room.

The Governor turned to his Guard security team. "It's okay guys. I am in good hands here." He pointed at Kyle and Mac. "Those two have been by my side before. Don't piss them off. I think even at their age, they can kick your ass or stab you before you have time to react, or just shoot you from ½ mile away. Please leave us.... go take a break. I will let you know when we're done."

The Governor asked the Ghost Team to be seated. "I am really sorry about your greeting. They do mean well but, they need training."

"Yeah, we noticed," said Mac.

The Governor continued, "None of us have much time for idle talk nowadays. So, I will get right to my point. My main goal as Governor is to have police deal with all civilian issues and let the National Guard take the fight to the invaders. As of now, nearly all the duties of the National Guard has been protecting and assisting getting those that fled from the valley out of Oregon. The number of those fleeing should drop to almost none in about another week. Then, we will have a massive Guard buildup to prepare for war. The new Governor's Mansion is going to be the Wallowa Lake Hotel. It's just too dangerous here and in any other Oregon city at this time. We will be moving over there next week."

"I can understand, that place is easy to defend and real remote. It has its own power generator in case of grid failure," said the Lt.

"And you guys are close to it," added the Governor. He pointed around to each man seated at the table.

Mac asked, "Governor, what do you need from us?"

"Well, if you guys would work for me fulltime that would be a big help. But, I was told by Sheriff McCabe that is not likely to happen."

"Not now, anyway. If we weren't working for Sheriff McCabe, there might not even be a hotel there right now," said the Lt.

"Guys, here's my plan. Speak up at any time you think I am wrong. I am taking the La Grande OSP office, the Sgt. and the eight troopers with their families to live at the hotel. That makes eleven troopers and Sgt. Anderson, if I also have the Enterprise troopers working there. Their only job will be protection of me and the other state leaders. There will also be some Guard soldiers living there, and their main job is to help me with military issues. We will have a chopper pad put in and have armored SUVs and Humvees. The state had 90 members in the legislative branch. We only know of ten of the sixty State House Representatives and six of the thirty from the Senate are safe. They will be moving to the hotel and continue to work for the state. On the federal side, both Senators are safe in DC along with three of the five Representatives. None of the top state judges have shown up safe anywhere, but then they all lived in the Willamette Valley. Right now, we have the eastern Oregon circuit court judges able to work. I know some in the legislation got scared and fled Oregon. I say abandoned Oregon. Those in DC are staying in DC, we think they can help Oregon best there."

"Actually, that sounds like a good plan so far. But, those troopers need training to protect you properly," Mac pointed out.

"Well, I also have trooper Chao Wang who can help with that stuff," said the Governor.

Kyle leaned toward the Governor and said, “We know him. He had just gotten fully trained for the dignitary unit when I retired. So, he has only been on the job a short time. How did he get here, anyways? Any others from the unit alive?”

“I do not think any others are alive, or if they are their likely to be in a Chinese prison or fighting over a bottle of water.”

Kyle said, “I know Sgt. Anderson is up to getting the troopers to work as a team or get any normal police stuff taken care of. Your protection is completely different; it’s specialized police work.”

The Governor said, “I think Chao is up to getting them trained.” He then told the guys the full story about how Chao wanted to go with him on the vacation and the difficult time they had to get to La Grande. Following that he said, “So, guys, mainly what I am asking is that you help lead my vehicle through the county or even on to other cities when I travel if we think it might be too dangerous for my normal security. Also, most of the security team will need to remain at the hotel to keep it and the others safe. After a couple of weeks, I want all of you guys to come and take a close look at the whole security operation and see what changes are needed.”

Lt said, “We can do all that. By the way, you are the man we need to lead the state.”

“Thanks for the comment, it does mean a lot coming from you. I have way too much other stuff to get done today. You guys grab some bottles of water and any snacks you want before you head home. When possible, I really do want to meet your families and visit the ranch. Thanks for coming here today.”

They all stood and shook the Governor's hand before leaving. They walked past the Guard guys and noticed that none of them would even look up at the Ghost Team.

The Lt said, "I don't get it. That Wang guy was written up to be fired when he was new. I even backed up the Sergeant who wrote him up. He was not cut out to be a cop, much less an OSP trooper. I was told that a Major in Salem said he needed to stay, and they would find a position for him."

Kyle said, "After hearing the story about how Chao and the Governor made it to here…it all stinks."

The Lt replied, "Guys, we need to tell Major Westbrook about Chao Wang and only just the other team guys for now. That means not even any of our wives. We could be all wrong about Chao. But, I really agree with Kyle; his story stinks. I sure hope Chao is not a Chinese spy. Mac, next stop, Guard HQ."

That evening at the ranch the Lt told the guys, "The doc phoned me today and said everyone passed the physical. He did say we are all pushing our bodies too hard and should take more time off. He said Aspirin and Advil are our friends, take when you need them."

CHAPTER 23

The Ghost Team was at the SO around 6:00am except Lenny, Justin, Eddy and Jimmy. Lenny with the other three would fly low over the gravesite and he would tip the air craft wings before the gun salute. The Lt had a list of all personnel who informed the SO that they were coming and would be involved in the funeral procession. This list of names included OSP Troopers and SO Deputies from other areas in eastern Oregon. Also, the Wallowa County Fire Department and EMS units along with the Idaho State Police would be in attendance. The ISP had sent their honor guard to perform the gun salute. The Guard soldiers that were off duty volunteered to man the Highway 82 roadblock for the day. All members of the Wallowa county SO would be attending the funeral.

Lt stood in the bed of a pickup in the parking area of the SO and shouted to everyone to gather around. He gave those involved in the procession a few instructions. "I know most here have never been in a police funeral, so this is how we do it. All emergency vehicles, police, fire and EMS units will turn on all emergency lights before you leave this lot and turn them off after parked at the gym. Do the same for the route to the gravesite. The gym cannot hold half the people that are showing up. Folks are being told to stand along the roadside of the route we take.

Sheriff McCabe told me to thank each and every one of you who showed up today; your support means a lot to him and the SO. You each have a sheet of paper listing your position in the procession, try to stick with that. The SO will make the standard announcement as we start on net #1. Let's roll."

After all emergency vehicles had their lights on, Sheriff McCabe pulled out onto the roadway first in his marked SO SUV, then behind him, the hearse. The SO dispatcher made a radio call that was played in the gym loud speakers and heard on all police radios. "Wallowa County Sheriff's Office calling Deputy Donald A. Jones…. Deputy Donald A. Jones…. Deputy Donald A. Jones."

Then the county Chaplin responded over through the radio, "Deputy Donald A. Jones is not present; he has been called by his maker to a higher duty."

As the procession made its way through the city, hundreds of people lined the streets, some waving US flags, others saluting the hearse and procession. All members of the rapid response team were wearing blue arm bands on their left arm and stood at attention with their personal rifles as the procession passed.

About 2 hours later, after the funeral service and grave site burial had finished, a member of the Idaho Honor Guard found Kyle. Kyle knew him from his past; it was Sgt. Burris. They shook hands as Sgt. Burris told Kyle, "We have been told you guys are kicking bad guy ass over here."

"Yeah, nice to see you. It's been a couple years. You placed second right behind me in that last SWAT rifle competition. That was the last match I shot before re-tiring."

"Hey, now that you're retired, maybe I'll win at the next match. But, on a serious note, I need to give you some good news. I got the boss and the new Oregon Governor to sign an agreement. It allows us to assist you if you call us for any help, any time. We have a Bearcat and can send one or two teams. The National Guard loaned us a gun turret and 240B like yours. We just got it installed and tested."

"That's cool, give me your card. If we get in it deep, I know we can count on your team."

"Just remember it will take us up to six hours to get here," said Sgt. Burris.

"I will call you if we get any big missions, or if we get a competition shoot going at the ranch."

"Okay, see ya."

"Thanks for showing up, see ya," replied Kyle.

That afternoon Lenny walked over to the ranch house to speak to the Lt about something strange they had spotted from his plane. Lenny told the Lt as they were flying back to the ranch, "We flew low over the ranch two ridgelines west of yours. The one that has a long air strip. Eddy noticed a tall antenna near the house and a green tent set up next to the antenna. Those were not there the last time I flew over the area. That was the day of the assault on the vacation house. I thought the ranch was only used during the big game hunting seasons."

The Lt walked over to a large wall map in his office. "Show me where you saw it."

Lenny looked at the map and found the Bradford Ranch. Then, he ran his finger directly west about ten miles and two ridges tops over. He pointed and said, "Right here, there is a house, barn and hanger with a few smaller buildings on top of the ridge along with a really long air strip."

"Yeah, that's a ranch owned by a Hollywood star. They visit it during deer and elk seasons. They fly a Beechcraft Super King Air. It's a twin-engine plane that seats ten. They usually have several other planes arrive around the same time and some big expensive motorhomes show up. The rest of the year, only a single caretaker lives there. The SO will know his name and phone number. I will get it and tell you what I find out at dinner tonight."

"Okay, see you." Lenny left.

At the meeting hall as people arrived for dinner, Sgt. Best was standing outside the doorway with the new Ghost Team member waiting to introduce her to the group. "Guys, this is Jeanette Jones, or JJ," said Sgt. Best. Everyone coming by shook her hand and told her their names. The other new soldier was in the kitchen already at work with a few others making the meal.

After everyone was finished with dinner that evening, the Lt stood up near the front area of the meeting hall and said, "I need all the team guys, including our newest team member, along with Sgt. Best to remain in the meeting hall after dinner. We have another mission to plan. The SO will patrol by themselves tomorrow and maybe a few more days after that."

A few minutes later, the guys along with JJ, grabbed a cold beer and sat at a table closest to the 3 ft by 4 ft wall map of Wallowa County in the meeting hall. The Lt started the meeting. "I guess everyone knows about what Lenny reported to me this afternoon."

They all nodded their heads up and down.

"We call this place the Hollywood Ranch." He pointed to it on the map. "Well, I got the caretaker's name and phone number. I felt it better not to phone him. The reason is the guy is a rapid response team member. The SO called him several times about today's service, and he has not returned a single phone call. Another member said he last spoke with him three days ago. Something is wrong at the Hollywood Ranch; there is no reason for anyone to put up an antenna and a green tent. Guys, we need to recon the place and that will not be easy. We need to have support ready to assist the recon team. The recon team will need to plan on spending up to two days in the brush."

"That area is an ass killer, most ground around the ridge is near vertical to vertical," said Kyle.

The Lt replied, "Even the road up the hill side to the top has several switch backs, but it can support trucks. They have propane, fuel trucks and big motorhomes drive up there when it is clear of snow. The road is the easy way to get there, and we cannot go in the easy way. Too big of a chance of tip wires, trail cameras or even lookouts. My idea is to get a heavy armed support team staged where they could be assisting the recon guys in about fifteen minutes and not be seen. Just in case the recon needs help ASAP. The recon team will be Kyle, Rick, Sgt. Best and JJ."

Mac asked, "Sounds like you think this could be Chinese?"

Sgt. Best and the Lt both answered, "Yes we do."

The Lt continued, "But, they could be a gang or another group. We won't know until we have eyes on the place. Think about it guys. That is the high ground, it has a large air strip, the biggest besides the Enterprise Airport in this county. It is very remote and difficult to get to without being seen. Most importantly, it is a ridge that drops down with a view of most of the valley and a clear view to several miles of Highway 82. It is the perfect place to ambush a vehicle on the highway and escape."

"Oh, crap Lt, remember the Governor is coming through there next week," said Lonnie.

"Yeah, I know," replied the Lt. He turned to Sgt. Best, "Check and see what assets you can get to help and standby in the area, maybe a chopper or two and lots of ground guys. Let's finalize the mission plans after break-fast. The recon guys, you also need to help plan this mission. See ya around 6:00am."

CHAPTER 24

After breakfast, Kyle set up his laptop and projector to display it on a wall screen. Sgt. Best had a list of equipment and men that would be available. Kyle turned on the projector and started his presentation. "I have a Google Earth map for an overview of the area." He displayed it so all could easily see the details. He looked back toward the kitchen and saw all the wives stop working and walk back into the room to watch. Kyle thought for a moment. That was okay; they needed to know about some things the team does and see a mission planned out.

Kyle continued, "My plan is about the recon team only. Sgt. Best will cover all the military stuff after I am done. So.... here it is. Recon team drives in Rick's truck, all dressed in regular clothes, guns will be hidden in the cab. Gear and uniforms hidden in the truck bed under his bed cover. We drive by the gated road that leads to the Hollywood Ranch, here." He then pointed out the location. "We stop and pee just to check it out for cameras, then move on. Hopefully, no one is watching the area. If we are seen by locals or the bad guys, we should pass as travelers or tourists. From that gate up to the air strip and ranch is about a fifteen-minute drive on the private road.

"I suggest that the rescue/backup team of the guys and vehicles park on the public road about one mile before the gate at a turn off, here." He again pointed out the location on the map. "Although the road is a public road, it has little traffic. The guys parked there may not even see another vehicle pass by them. Recon stays on the public road which continues around the ridge and parks where the powerlines cross the road going up to the ranch on the west side of the ridge." He again points at the map. "That is about another eight miles from the gate. There, we put on uniforms and gear up. You can see the clear cut through the timber for the powerlines. Now, notice the heavy timber not far from that cut. That timber goes up the entire hillside, making perfect cover for the recon team ascending the hill.

"Recon moves up through that timber for about two miles. Near the top, we move around the north side of the ridge, staying in timber, and go to the east side. Then about where the ranch house is, we set up a hide where we can see the buildings. Of course, we will be on the opposite side of the ranch house across the air strip and open area. We can remain in timber 'til around six hundred yards from all the buildings and the ranch house. Grass should be deep and thick up there this time of year.

"All bring NVGs. We already have ghillie suits made to match the underbrush of the area. We will each take one and wear it when appropriate. We will each have police radios and headsets. Also, we need to take two GPS units, Sgt. Best and I will have them. Sgt. Best will also have a military radio, and we each bring cell phones, but only turn them on to be used for backup if other communications fail. The hike should take up to four hours for us to get into place. I want to move into position during daylight and be out by daylight tomorrow, but we may need to stay until dark on day two before pulling out. We will leave on same route as entered."

"Great job Kyle," said the Lt.

Sgt. Best stood and said, "I have one Bradley and two APCs with soldiers that will stage on that road. And great news; we will have two Blackhawks from Boise here around noon. They will park at the ranch and remain on ground unless needed for evacuation of the recon team or any wounded. Both choppers have side mounted machine guns and will carry medics."

"Great job Sgt. Best. Comments or questions?" asked the Lt.

There were none.

The Lt stood. "Okay, let's get this show on the road. Recon leaves at 11:00am, support at noon."

Kyle went over to JJ and Sgt. Best and told them, "Water will be real important, so fill your hydration bags. Have at least one liter and even take a couple of extra bottles. Pack whatever food you want to eat without cooking. Bring a solid foam pad to lay on at night. Rick and I are going light on ammo to save weight. You choose how much you want to carry. As you know, on this mission we avoid shooting. I know the climb is going to be hard, steep and in warm temperatures, but at night it is cool to cold."

Sgt. Best asked, "I want to be clear about who's in charge."

"Good point," Kyle said. "I will be in charge of the recon team's movements. You, of all support. Our radio call sign is pathfinders: your #1, me #2, Rick #3, JJ #4."

"Sounds good. See you at the vehicle in a couple hours," replied Sgt. Best.

The recon team left the ranch on time. The drive to the gated road at the Hollywood Ranch would take them about an hour, traveling most of the way on a gravel roadbed.

"Hey JJ, tell us about yourself and the SWAT unit at HPD," Rick said.

"Well, I was hired by HPD at nineteen. Dad and my uncle also worked at the PD. I spent 5 years in patrol and then put in for the SWAT team. I hope you notice I work out and can take down bad guys as well as most men cops."

Kyle said, "Yeah, nothing gets past me."

"Anyway, I have been on the SWAT team for three years now. I joined the Texas National Guard a little over a year ago. My main assignment on SWAT is sniper, counter sniper. That's also what I do in the Guard. Can I convince you I spend a lot of time at a gun range? We all train on the SWAT team for each position, and it's a full-time job at Houston."

Rick asked, "You got much time doing this type of mission?"

"Only in the Guard have I hiked, climbed and slept with my sniper rifle. Not too many mountains or tall timber in Houston."

"You fired at any bad guys?" asked Kyle.

"Yeah, and I hit them, too. Two were sniper shots that were not difficult, and once I blasted a guy with an MP 5 in a house. That fool came at me with a hunting knife."

"JJ, we're all okay with you being on the team. But, to get fully accepted, the guys will need to see you work," said Rick.

"I understand, and I will be watching you guys closely for a while. Sgt. Best filled me in about you guys. You sound solid to me, just older than who I normally work with," said JJ.

Rick said, "Funny, we have been getting the age thing mentioned to us from time to time."

"Look, the gate is just ahead; Rick and I will cross over the fence and walk into the road maybe about 100 yards and take a pee. You two just stand around the gate like you're waiting for us. Check it out as closely as you can. Talk like you're tourists just in case someone is listening," Kyle told them before leaving.

The team was done and back on the gravel road in about ten minutes.

Kyle said, "That was a standard cattle gate and fencing you will see used all around here."

"Sgt. Best what did you see?" asked Rick.

"It had a chain and padlock holding it closed. A bolt cutter will have it open in seconds. We did not see wires or alarms or hidden cameras. There wasn't any electric wires near the gate, I will phone the support team and let them know the details."

"Great! We didn't see anything out of place. It appeared the road has not had anyone or any vehicles on it for a while," said Rick.

JJ asked, "What type of big game and other animals will we be around us while on this mission?"

"Deer and elk likely will be seen on the hike and maybe walking around us at night. Along with rattle snakes in the daytime, coyotes, porcupines at any time. There are also a few cougars up there," said Kyle.

"Wait a minute, rattle snakes and cougars? Explain," said JJ.

"The snakes will be out in the open areas mostly around rocks and dirt in the direct sunlight. We will travel in the shadows and grass. Likely, we will not see any snakes. But, I will point them out if we get close to one. The cougars hide in the shadows, grass and sometimes in the trees where we will be walking."

JJ let out a big breath of air and said, "Oh, great. I wish I didn't ask."

"Kyle lost a confirmed kill to a big snake last week. We just do not know if Kyle or the snake killed the bad guy," said Rick, then let out a big laugh.

"Oh, please tell me that story when we're done," replied JJ.

"Okay guys, there's the power lines up ahead. Rick, find a good place to park. He can tell you that story better than me, and I know he wants to. The snake was about five feet long, but he will tell you it was eight feet," said Kyle.

"Knock it off, you guys are scaring me! Rattle snakes five or eight feet long, quit it!" replied JJ.

"Okay, don't say we didn't warn you. They get real big up here," said Rick.

The pathfinder team parked and got their gear on, which included camo face paint. Kyle decided not to have anyone wear the ghillie suits on the climb. It was too warm already and could cause over heating issues. Plus, no one at the top would have ever been able to see them approach due to the steep hillsides and heavy timber. They did a coms check, and Kyle told the support team they were moving on foot.

They started out up the steep hill. Kyle reminded the team no talking unless needed and to walk slow and quiet. They spaced out about every ten yards, with Kyle in the lead. He would check his GPS about every 100 yards to stay exactly on course.

About two and half hours later, the team got to within several hundred yards of the ridge top and the opening to the air strip. At that point, Kyle motioned for Rick and JJ to take point on either side of him. He then motioned for Sgt. Best to approach. Kyle quietly said, "Go to each of them, help them get the ghillie suit on, make sure it's covering them correctly. Then tell them we move in about fifteen minutes. Now we will move around the ridge top, to the left. We need complete silence from here on out. After you're done with them, then you and I put the suits on."

Sgt. Best nodded and completed the task.

Now the terrain they traveled on was mostly flat or just a gentle slope. A short time later, Kyle spotted a doe mule deer and her fawn walking and grazing. Kyle thought, a good sign that meant no other humans were near them or the deer would have been running away. The team sat and waited until the deer grazed down the hillside and were out of view. If they spooked the deer, the deer could run to the air strip. Someone up there on lookout might realize other humans were in the area. Then the pathfinders would become the hunted.

Kyle finally got near where he wanted to approach the edge of the timber and motioned for them to group up.

Kyle said, "Rick and I will go forward as far as safe to set up a hide. Rick and I will leave our packs here, you two remain right here. I will radio further directions when I can. If I cannot talk, I will click the radio two times. If you see anyone, you click the radio two times. You need to stay put unless I say to move or you get attacked."

Both Sgt. Best and JJ nodded their heads.

Rick and Kyle crawled up to an area where they were still in the shadows of the timber and deep grass where they could see the buildings including the green tent and antenna. At that point, they laid still for ten minutes only moving their eyes to be sure no one was watching them. After that time, they did not see or hear anyone.

Kyle told Rick "Set up your scope and check out each building. I will point my rifle on the tent."

Kyle radioed Pathfinder #1 "We're in position, Stay in yours, no enemy near us at this time."

"Copy" was the reply from Sgt. Best.

They did not see anyone or hear any noise caused by humans anywhere for nearly an hour. Then, suddenly right at 4:00pm, men ran out of the house. All were armed with an AK style rifles and wearing military uniforms.

The men stood in line on the sidewalk near the house, then all at once they went to standing at attention.

At that point, another man slowly walked out the same door and stood in front of the other men. He was wearing a clean sharp pressed uniform and had a holstered handgun. An officer of some type, could be Chinese or Korean, they could not tell. Another man ran out of the tent. He turned back into the tent, then ran out again. This time he was holding a rifle similar to the other soldier's rifles and he got in line with the soldiers. Kyle and Rick could then hear shouting. The man standing in front of the other soldiers was shouting and pointing at them. He took out his pistol and waved it at the soldiers.

"Shit, Rick they are for damn sure Chinese or North Korean soldiers."

"Yeah, I count ten soldiers. Before we report this let's see if that officer beats or shoots any of the soldiers. He is surely pissed at the whole bunch," said Rick.

"Copy, wish we knew what he was shouting."

Then, the one soldier ran back into the tent. Four others ran off into the barn, the officer slowly walked back into the house. The rest just stood around, several started smoking cigarettes.

The four came out of the barn driving a UTV that carried four persons. The rear cargo area was loaded with gear. They headed south past the building and out of view driving down the hill side into the timber.

Rick said, "I think that's all the soldiers up here. They do not seem to have anyone set up to watch for trespassers."

"Unless they are well hidden. Scan the area really good! I am going to report to Pathfinder #1. I am going to advise them not to come up here until after dark," said Kyle.

Soon after that the three soldiers that were standing around near the house walked into the barn and came out with shovels. They walked over to a shallow hole, stepped in it and started digging. They got about waist deep and then stopped. The three went into the house and carried out a heavy object wrapped in a blanket.

Rick scoped them out and said, "That's a body in a blanket, I bet it's the ranch care taker."

The soldiers dropped the body into the hole and covered the body with dirt. Then calmly walked back into the house.

Kyle said, "I wish I could shoot each one of them. Right here, right now."

He then reported what they had just seen to Pathfinder #1.

Just before dark the UTV returned, all four soldiers were on it, but the gear was missing.

Rick said, “I bet you they are building a hide to watch the highway.”

“I think so too, until we know something different.”

A full hour after the sunset and no other activity was seen anywhere at the ranch. Kyle radioed Pathfinder #1. “I am returning to your position to guide you forward.”

Then all three pathfinders returned to Rick’s location.

Rick, told them “Get out your foam pads to lay on since the ground will be damn cold.”

Kyle asked Sgt. Best, “Can you two lay and watch here while Rick and I go back to our other position? We have about ten hours before sunrise. Could you two take the first watch, the first six hours? We can take the last four. We really need a break.”

“Yes, sounds good to me,” said Sgt. Best.

“We will go to half watch. One sleeps the other watches,” said Kyle.

“Okay, we will do the same. Unless something happens.”

At the exchange time, Kyle and Rick moved up to the hide. They were informed by Sgt. Best “The soldiers changed the radio/tent guy at 12:00am. No lights have been seen on anywhere except in the tent and no other activity was seen.”

Shortly after sunrise three soldiers came out of the farm house and went into the barn. They then drove the UTV toward the same direction as the day before. The

UTV returned with just one soldier about twenty minutes later.

At 8:00am, the soldiers ran out onto the sidewalk as before. The radio guy ran out and got into line. The officer slowly walked out to them. This time there are eight soldiers. The officer shouts and points at the soldiers in the line. After a few minutes, he returned to the house. The soldiers stood around and smoked for a few minutes then they went back into the house. A different soldier then went into the tent.

Kyle said to Rick "I think we learned enough, time to get out of here."

"I agree. You tell pathfinder #1 we are coming back to him."

When they met up, Kyle briefed Sgt. Best and suggested they leave now. They pulled back and returned on the same route around the ridge and then downhill back to Rick's truck. The Pathfinders met with the support team. The Lt and Sgt. Best talked about standing down for now and returning to the ranch. There they would plan an assault on the Hollywood ranch. The idea was to hit the place around 3:00 or 4:00am and in full force.

Back at the ranch, all involved went to the meeting hall for a meal, it was lunch time anyway.

After everyone ate, the Lt and Sgt. Best walked up into the front area. Lt told them "Sgt. Best and I will be planning the assault. Everyone else rest and get some sleep. Be back here at 6:30pm.

We will then finalize the mission, eat a late meal and head out about 2:00am. Any questions?"

Rick stood up, "LT I have a question and comment. The question is, do we want to take any hostages for intel reasons? And, if so, Dr. Yan Chen might be a good asset to have with us."

"Please explain why Rick," replied the LT.

"Several reasons LT, he is EMS trained and has his gear ready. He is on the county rapid response team and he speaks Chinese. We can trust him, and would not a prisoner be a good thing to have?"

"Great points. I will make sure he is here for the briefing. Okay guys, see you here later," replied the LT.

CHAPTER 25

That night, all the Ghost Team members and soldiers going on the mission were seated waiting for the Lt and Sgt. Best to start the briefing in the meeting hall.

The Lt spoke first. “Okay, guys what we know is this: we have 10 enemy army soldiers at the Hollywood Ranch. Perhaps one is an officer and one is a Sgt., but we do not know for sure. This mission will be a joint police-military assault, likely the first ever in Oregon. The reason is the Ghost Team has the expertise to get in a house and a prisoner out without firing a shot. That’s our mission. The National Guard are well trained soldiers, but none except Sgt. Best have any combat time.

“The recon team found that the enemy did not appear to have any heavy weapons, guards posted or fixed fighting positions. No evidence they have night vision equipment. That could change any day if they get more support. As of now, we guess they were brought in by chopper.”

“The Ghost Team will assault the main house with military support. Mac, Kyle, Lonnie, JJ, Lenny and Jim are the assault team. I know the house layout; I have been in it several times. On the main level there are two bedrooms. Those are the Ghost Team targets, likely the Lt and maybe a Sgt. sleep there. Upstairs is like many cabins out here. It has a bathroom and is mainly a dorm room with many bunkbeds. The rest of the soldiers will be sleeping up there. Other rooms on the main level are a kitchen, living room and a bathroom. We want the one or two soldiers in the bedrooms taken alive as prisoners of war. The others die unless they surrender. We get the two outside hopefully without waking the rest upstairs. The Ghost Team will not shoot at anything outside. The military will not shoot at the house until the team is out unless we order otherwise. That way, we limit any killed or wounded by friendly fire. Tim and Ike will remain outside and will hunt down any runners, but only after daylight. The military takes on the rest. Sgt. Best, you're up."

Sgt. Best said, "Men, we drive up the road to near the top of the ridge. There we dismount and follow the Ghost Team across the air strip and then clear the outer buildings. We follow the Ghost Team to the house and surround it. After the Ghost Team gets out, Dr. Chen calls out on a loud speaker to the rest of the soldiers to surrender. If they fight, we fight back. We can fire a couple grenades in through the windows or even use the Bradley's guns. That should end any gun fight quickly. At daylight, we will search out their set up south of the ranch house on the hillside. Our choppers are on standby to evacuate wounded. Our vehicles will be brought up to take up fighting positions after we are in place and hopefully before any gun fire.

"We stay at the target until Major Westbrook gets his force to occupy the area; that force should arrive around 8:00am by ground vehicles. They will set equipment up to shoot down any Chinese choppers coming to assist or resupply. Until then, it's all us without any backup.

"We move out at 3:00am, hit the house around 4:15am. Daylight is at 6:25am. Let's make the Major proud."

The convoy left the ranch on time, and they stopped near the gate. A Sergeant that was with Sgt. Best used a bolt cutter and removed the lock. He opened the gate and the Bradley followed by two APCs, passed through it. He got back into the Humvee with Sgt. Best and they followed the armor up the road. The police vehicles followed along behind the military.

The convoy stopped one mile from the air strip and the foot soldiers got out of the APCs. The Ghost Team unassed out of the V-150. The Ghost Team turned on their NVGs and took the lead walking toward the air strip and ranch house. They all walked slowly along the tree line, and as they got near the first building, they could see light coming from an open tent flap. It was the radio tent; no other light was seen anywhere around the ranch. At this time of night, no birds or other animals made a sound; the whole area was quiet.

Mac said, "Kyle, cover the tent as the rest of us clear each outer building. Soldiers, stage up in the trees here until we have cleared these buildings."

With the outer buildings easily cleared, the Ghost Team moved on to the front area of the ranch house. The soldiers remained near the outer buildings and in the trees to prove cover for the Ghost Team.

Mac stopped the team. He said, "JJ, take the radio guy. I'll cover you."

"Okay." JJ knew exactly what that entailed.

The rest of the team kept their rifles aimed at the house as Mac and JJ silently walked up to the open tent flap.

From about 25 feet away, JJ stopped and took aim. She fired one round. Her silent shot hit the sleeping radio guy at the base of his head. His body jumped up a little from the impact, but his head remained on the desk, still wearing headphones. The two moved back to the others.

Mac radioed Sgt. Best. "Enemy in radio tent neutral-lized. Slowly and quietly move your men up into positions around the house. We will hold here until you're in position."

Sgt. Best answered, "Copy"

Only a few minutes passed. Sgt. Best radioed, "Guard in position."

The team grouped up. First in line was Lonnie. His first job was to quietly use a lockpick to open the door.

Mac reminded Lonnie, "Check to see if it is even locked before working on it."

"Yes, boss."

The house appeared completely dark from the outside. No noise was heard.

The rest of the Ghost Team slowly walked onto the porch. As they were standing there behind Lonnie, a sound came from inside, and they all froze in place. It was the sound of a door opening, footsteps on the floor, then another door closing.

Lonnie said, "Sounds like someone left a bedroom and went into the bathroom. I can hear him peeing in the toilet."

Mac told Lonnie, "Try the door handle. But, don't go in."

Lonnie grabbed the door knob and turned it. He said, "It's unlocked."

"Copy."

CHAPTER TWENTY-FIVE

Mac now had to make a tough call. He thought for a moment: should they wait until the guy walks back into the bedroom, or go in now? Either way, the element of surprise would be quickly lost. Whoever is in the bathroom was awake. They could back off and wait an hour, but they did not have the time to wait, and anything could go wrong by waiting that long.

Because of Mac's years of doing high risk police work, his mind was used to making fast, possibly life-changing decisions. His mind was made up in mere seconds.

"Guys, we go in as planned. Jim, Lenny and I take the first bedroom. If the door is open, I go in the bathroom. You three do the same at the second bedroom."

"Copy."

"Okay. On three. Best, you copy?"

"Copy."

Holding his fist up. "One, Two, Three, team moving."

Mac entered the living room. He could see light under the bathroom door at the end of the hallway and he heard someone peeing into the toilet. The team moved as slowly and quietly as possible. The first bedroom door was closed, but the second bedroom door was open. Mac listened with his ear near to the first door; he could hear snoring inside. The guy in the bathroom was still peeing.

Mac slowly turned the doorknob and opened the door for his group to walk into the room. He could see a uniform hung up by the closet, a pistol belt on the chair with a hat and tall boots nearby. It appeared to be an officer's room. The other three Ghost Team members walked to the open door at the second bedroom and scanned the area. The room was clear. Inside the first bedroom, Mac motioned for Lenny to taser the sleeping guy. Lenny stepped forward for the shot. He stepped on a loose board and a loud squeak was heard. Everyone in the room froze.

Suddenly, the soldier sat up and yelled something in Chinese.

Lenny shot him with his taser, and the soldier shook and went limp. Jim quickly put duct tape across his mouth, slipped a bag over his head and flex cuffs on his wrists and around his ankles.

Then at the same time, the other team led by JJ reentered the hallway and walked to the bathroom. They all hear the yell from the first bedroom, then from the bathroom they hear movement and a loud thump outside. They stood on either side of the bathroom door and opened it slowly as not to wake the others still upstairs. JJ scans the bathroom, and she saw that the window was open. Who-ever was in the bathroom had jumped out. They turned around and went back to the first bedroom.

JJ radioed Sgt. Best, “We had a guy jump out the bathroom window. Unknown if he is armed or not. He left his clothes and shoes in the house.”

Best replied, “Copy, nothing heard from my men back there.”

Jim entered the hallway with the soldier over his shoulder. JJ’s team then turned around and covered the first team’s exit. No one from upstairs had made any sound. They must exit the house as slowly and quietly as they had entered. There were still eight men upstairs with machine guns, or worse.

Moments later, the two teams were outside and returned to cover around the corner of the barn where Sgt. Best was staged for the assault. Jim laid the prisoner on the ground. Sgt. Best told the Ghost Team, "My men did hear someone hit the ground and run away, but they do not have night vision back there. Actually, I am glad they held their fire. We still hold the element of surprise at the house. We can get the runner at daylight."

JJ said, "Yeah there was an AK rifle in the bedroom, and who takes a gun to pee at 4:00am? I think we will find him unarmed, without pants, shirt and shoes."

"Good news," said Sgt. Best. "Tim and Ike will find him after daylight."

The soldier the team took prisoner started to wake up and moved around, trying to get out of the flexcuffs. Jim punched him in the side of his head hard. At that moment, the soldier quit moving.

Kyle saw the punch and said, "Good one Jim."

Mac told Sgt. Best, "Your show now. This time we'll cover you and keep this guy safe, good luck."

"Copy, thanks."

Sgt. Best radioed, "Okay men, heads up. Dr. Chen will be on the loud speaker in a moment, get ready."

Dr. Chen stepped up to the corner of the barn and said in Chinese, "Enemy soldiers in the house, this is the United States Army. Come out now and surrender, you are surrounded." He then repeated the same thing in English.

At the same time, Sgt. Best radioed the vehicles. "All vehicles proceed to target house."

Seconds later the upper windows on all sides of the house where being broken out and the enemy soldiers inside blindly sprayed bullets out into the darkness around the house with automatic rifle fire.

"Men hold your fire, stay behind cover! Bradley, use the 7.62 gun and return fire to the upper level of the target!" said Sgt. Best.

The Bradley had made it to the house and stopped in just a couple minutes. Gunfire was still coming from the broken-out windows. Now the Bradley was receiving direct gunfire. The 7.62 machine gun on the Bradley started spraying the house. It drove around and stopped to get a different angle into the opposite side. The gun fired on/off for a couple minutes and stopped. Its gun fired all 200 rounds of belted ammo from the ammo box into the house. The enemy gunfire had stopped.

Sgt. Best radioed, "Sergeant, fire a grenade into the upper level, then a second into the main level."

After the two large bright flashes and loud blasts of the grenades went off in the house, Sgt. Best radioed, "Cease fire! Cease fire! All men crease fire! Hold your positions."

CHAPTER 26

Over the loud noise of gunfire from the enemy, the Bradley's gun and grenades were going off. The prisoner was trying to roll around and kick his legs.

Mac told Jim, "You had better remove the hood and sit him up. Let's make sure he can get air okay. For all that work, let's not let him die now."

Kyle shined a light on the prisoner as Jim sat him up. Jim then removed the bag covering his head. The prisoner's eyes were wide open. He was trying to speak with his mouth taped shut.

Kyle asked, "Do you speak English?"

The prisoner nodded his head up and down.

Kyle told the prisoner, "We are American police and United States Army, you are our prisoner. I will remove the tape over your mouth if you will not scream, is that a deal?"

The prisoner nodded his head up and down again.

"Jim, remove the tape from his mouth. If he yells, give him another punch, this time break his nose," said Kyle.

Sgt. Best told the Ghost Team, "The dust and dirt stirred up by the gun and grenades has settled down now. The four men and I that have NVG will clear the house."

Mac replied, "Okay, be careful. Take it slow, no reason to hurry through the house."

In one pull, Jim removed the tape from the prisoner's mouth. He took several deep breaths of air and shook his head. He then asked, "May I speak?" in perfect English.

Kyles said, "Yes. But remember, no yelling or shouting, or you get a broken nose."

The prisoner said, "Thank you for not killing me. I am not a bad man; may I have some water?"

"Yes. Lenny, get a bottle of water and help him drink it. For now, his hands stay behind his back," said Mac. He then leaned over and whispered in Kyle's ear. "Have the doc come over here to watch and listen to this guy. Tell him not to speak to the prisoner or let the prisoner know he speaks Chinese."

"Okay."

The prisoner took a drink of water and his breathing returned to normal.

"Again, thank you for not killing me. I and my family are most grateful. Let me tell you who I am and why I was forced to come here to this dumb war."

"Okay, we got the time. Just don't tell us a bunch of lies and BS," said Kyle.

"Thank you, I have nothing to lie about. My name is Ho Zhang, I am a Lieutenant in the People's Liberation Army. My family owns the Sumitona Corporation, a large tire company in China. We sell millions of dollars of tires here in the US and other countries. My father and uncles who own the company required all of their sons to join the army as officers before allowing us to manage any part of the company. I have lived in China my whole life, but learned English as a small child. I, of course, speak Chinese as well.

"I hate this war, it is wrong. But, I was ordered to come here. I do not want to fight the United States of America or anyone. We make a fine living making and selling tires. This war is going to put many hardships on the business and the workers. Even much of China's export businesses will have hardships trying to sell to the rest of the world. Only a small number of Chinese leaders wanted this war. Even in the army, most do not want this fight. The junior officers have talked in private and it is believed that North Korea is why all this happened. Their leader badly wants to take over the South and remove any outside troops. As you know, he hates the US, and we think he is crazy. We cannot understand why the few leaders of our country allowed it. The Korean people are just savages, thanks to their ruling family. I am sorry to say the Korean troops are committing terrible things to your people. Some Chinese officers have stepped in to stop them, and then they were removed by higher ranking officers."

"Okay then, why did you kill the caretaker of this ranch? He was not a soldier," asked Kyle.

"I am so sorry about his death, I did not kill him. Only I and my Sergeant are Chinese soldiers. The rest here are North Korean. We took the caretaker as prisoner. I made sure he was fed and treated well. I told the Korean soldiers to watch him as the Sergeant and I went to set up an overlook position above the highway. When we returned, they had tied him to a chair, beaten and killed the poor man. I was so mad, I got them outside yesterday and nearly shot the one who did it. I see now I should have shot him, anyway. I told them I would shoot any who did not do exactly as I said from now on. I have written a letter to explain how it happened. I was going to leave it here at the ranch when we left. I have made a cross for his grave and was going to put it up today and say a prayer for him. I left the letter and cross inside the bedroom closet."

"We will turn you over to the US Army later today. I suggest that you answer our and their questions and be truthful. Right now, they want to execute you for the death of a US citizen," replied Kyle.

Lt Zhang hung his head down. "I understand that. But, I did not do it. My letter might help prove that. I vowed to send his family money from my own account once I get back home. Where is my Sgt.? he can confirm everything I just said."

Mac asked, "Was he in the other bedroom?"

"Yes, the Korean soldiers slept in the upper level."

"Well, he jumped out the bathroom window when we got you. We will find him after daylight," replied JJ.

Kyle and Mac then left the barn to meet with Sgt. Best. It was nearly daylight now, and Sgt. Best and his soldiers had just exited the house. When Sgt. Best met with Kyle and Mac, he told them, "Everyone in the house is dead. That 7.62 gun and the rifle fired grenades, sure did the job. Is the prisoner alive?"

Mac said, "Yes, he is. And good news, he is talking."

Kyle and Mac informed Sgt. Best what Lt Zhang had told them.

"Hey, Sgt. Best, we have an idea how to prove 100% if this guy is telling us the truth. You should go and talk with him. Mac and I will go through the bedroom and get all of his stuff."

"Good idea. When you're done, let's go over the idea. Once Ike finds the runner that may also help. I want to leave everything else the way it is until the Major gets here to look it over," replied Sgt. Best.

Mac and Kyle went into the bedroom. There they found the letter and cross. Along with that, they found his personal cell phone and over five thousand dollars hidden in his pack. Kyle pulled Lt Zhang's handgun from the holster. He said, "Mac check out this gun. It must be worth thousands. Look, it's a custom Browning Hi-Power 9mm. Man, it has a gold-plated trigger, gold-plated take down parts, even the sights are gold-plated and some type of Chinese custom engraved grips." He then unloaded all the magazines and cleared the gun of all ammo.

"Wow, this guy does have money. In the letter, he explained how the Koreans killed the caretaker against his orders and wrote he would send a company worker to find the caretaker's next of kin after the war and give them twenty-five thousand dollars. He ended the letter saying the death has shamed him and he asks for forgiveness," said Mac.

"I think our idea will work out great. Let's take this stuff and tell Best."

Back at the barn, Sgt. Best was talking with Lt Zhang as Kyle and Mac walked in. Doc Chen was still standing nearby. Mac pointed at Doc Chen, then outside. The doc then walked outside.

Mac asked Sgt. Best, "Can we talk outside?"

Sgt. Best followed Kyle and Mac outside of the barn away from anyone being able to hear them. Mac told him what they found in the bedroom.

Kyle said, "Sgt. Best, here's our plan. The final test for Lt Zhang is using the Chinese radio and calling in resupply. You guys shoot them down. Give the US newspapers a story, tell them you found these guys up here and killed everyone and then shot down their resupply choppers. You take Lt Zhang and the radio to a safe place and use them as you need to kill more enemies. We will have Doc Chen listen to the radio message. If he says anything, but what we tell him to say, he gets a bullet in his head, right here, by me."

"Yes Kyle, that sounds great and it might work. Would you be able to do that if needed?"

"After what happened to the caretaker, yes," replied Kyle.

"Okay, we will wait 'til the Major gets here, I need to run it by him first. You know how that works."

"Of course, we need to get Tim and Ike on that track. Let's send JJ and Jim with them."

Tim had JJ remove all the clothing that belonged to the Sergeant in the bedroom and tossed them out the bathroom window. He took Ike over to the pile and let him get a good sample scent of the man he was going to track. Then Tim told Ike, "Hunt." By the time JJ walked out and around the house, Ike had found the trail. Together the four of them headed down the steep hillside into the thick timber.

Back in the barn, the guys gave Lt Zhang his uniform and allowed him to put it on. They placed the flex cuffs back on his wrists, but not as tightly as before and now in his front so he could sit without pain to his wrists. Lt Zhang told Sgt. Best about the other secret Chinese outposts and their locations in Oregon.

Kyle searched the phone numbers in Lt Zhang's phone. Kyle was looking for any of the numbers that were special, only given to OSP units, like the dignitary unit. If he found any, it might connect trooper Wang to this outpost and Lt Zhang.

About twenty-five minutes after Ike started his track, Ike found the Sergeant. It looked like he had been running and fell. He was not moving. Jim took a quick look at the body and told the others, “Look out! The man is dead, but this was a cougar kill! The cat will still be close.”

JJ asked, “How the heck can you know that, Jim?”

“This is a classic cougar kill site. The body was dragged from over there.” Jim pointed at the drag marks on the ground. “Also, the Sergeant was killed by the cat grabbing his neck from behind and breaking his neck in its mouth in one quick bite. You can look and see that his neck is broken. They almost always attack from behind, likely the Sergeant ran right past the cougar never knowing it was nearby. The cat chased him down, jumped up on his back and bit down. The body is face down and those rips of removed flesh across the man’s back are where the cat started to eat him.”

“Oh my god!” said JJ. “I didn’t notice until you pointed that out.”

Jim, while explaining the kill site, was turning a circle and looking around the area. He pointed up into a nearby pine tree just 20 yards away. “There it is, the cougar is on that big limb. JJ, shoot the damn thing, NOW!”

The group at the barn heard a faint rifle shot. Then a minute later, another.

Jim radioed Mac, “We found the runner, he was already dead. A cougar had attacked him. JJ shot the cat in a tree near the body. It is her first cougar kill, and a big one at that.”

"Copy, we will send down some soldiers with a body bag. Standby until they get to you."

"Copy."

Major Westbrook arrived with a convoy of military vehicles and soldiers about that same time. Sgt. Best walked the Major through the house and showed him the Chinese radio. He then explained about the prisoner and how Kyle had planned to destroy the resupply choppers.

"I agree, do it," was the answer from Major Westbrook.

Kyle then told Lt Zhang his last test to prove himself enemy or friend. He would make a fake radio call on the Chinese radio.

Lt. Zhang said, "I will do it. That might shorten this war and save lives on both sides."

Kyle and Mac walked beside Lt Zhang with Sgt. Best and Doc Chen following them to the radio tent. The dead Korean soldier had already been removed earlier. Lt Zhang picked up the radio microphone. He looked around and noticed Kyle was holding his Glock along his side. It was pointed at the ground. He looked up at Kyle and straight to his eyes. Lt Zhang was a smart man; he understood what would happen if he was lying to the Ghost Team.

Lt Zhang spoke in Chinese and said, "Please send the resupply tonight. We are running out of food. The radio battery is failing, I might not be able to use the radio again until you bring a new battery."

"Copy, three choppers will be at your site at 1:00am tonight. Same route as before."

"Lt Zhang copy, out."

Doc Chen nodded his head up and down.

Lt Zhang turned to the guys standing around him. After a pause, he said, "Sgt. Best, if you place soldiers on the Interstate 82 Bridge across the Columbia River with missiles by midnight, you will be successful." Then after another long pause, Lt Zhang looked at the ground and back up at Kyle. "Kyle, I trust your word, I see it in your eyes. Will you keep my pistol and return it to my father should anything happen to me? He gave it to me when I received my officer's commission."

"Yes, I promise you I will. Until the war is over, your family will believe you were killed here today."

"Yes, I understand, thank you, I hope we will meet again after this stupid war," replied Lt Zhang.

Major Westbrook had two soldiers walk Lt Zhang to the air strip. The Blackhawks from the ranch were enroute to pick him, his gear and the Chinese radio up. In a few minutes, they would be flying back to Boise, Id.

Sgt. Best told Kyle, "Zhang told me he was sent here to watch for military vehicles and military supply trucks on the highway. He was to record the type, how many, which way and what time they passed. Nothing about civilian vehicles."

"Okay, thanks. I will get a SO truck here to take the bodies to the MEs office and we will dig up the caretaker's body and take it to the funeral home in Enterprise. Sheriff McCabe should know how to contact the ranch owner and the caretaker's next of kin to tell them about this mission and to get the letter to his family."

That evening by phone, the Lt had briefed Sheriff McCabe on the whole mission.

The Sheriff had phoned the only taxidermist in Enterprise about the cougar that JJ shot.

The taxidermist agreed to go and recover the cougar and make it into a full wall mount for JJ. It would be mounted with the fur on the hide, all claws, long tail and a wide-open mouth showing the large teeth. The same teeth that had killed an enemy soldier. Its story would be told in Enterprise for many years to come.

CHAPTER 27

That night Guard soldiers, six shooters and six target spotters, took up firing positions by spreading out across the I-82 Bridge. The six shooters were armed with Stinger handheld missiles that shoot down aircraft up to five miles away. They sat and waited.

Just after midnight, an observer stationed thirty miles west of the bridge radioed the bridge soldiers, "Three choppers in bound at high speed. They're on the deck, without lights."

The helicopters approached fast, just feet above the Columbia River. Flying in a tight formation about a mile away from the bridge, they started upward to fly over it. With their under bellies showing, the order to fire was made. The pilots likely never saw the missiles fired at them. Even if they did, the missiles fly at mach 2.5 and had locked onto their targets. They were hit within mere moments. There was no way for the helicopters to avoid the missiles.

Three big fireballs were seen in the darkened sky followed by three loud explosions. That sound was so loud, workers at a nearby ranch went to the windows, looked into the sky thinking it was thunder. The pieces of the destroyed Chinese transport helicopters with crew and cargo fell into the deep and fast-moving Columbia River where they quickly disappeared, never to be seen again.

Major Westbrook received a phone call a short time later.

"Major, three enemy choppers shot down, unknown number of EKIAs."

"Great news, Sergeant. Notify scout teams #5 and #6 to proceed to the enemy missile sites at Fort Rock and Burns Junction. Have them strike at daylight."

"Yes Sir, the Abrams tanks and Bradley's will quickly and easily destroy them."

"Sergeant, make sure to have the teams get photographs and EKIA numbers. Can we get assault teams to those outpost lookouts on Highway 7 and Highway 244?"

"Yes Sir, both should be destroyed by noon."

"Okay get me the EKIA numbers on those. I want to have a press release by 4:00pm. Americans need to know the Chinese are not staying in the Willamette Valley as they agreed to do with the President last week."

"Copy Sir, I will call ASAP after I get the information."

During breakfast in the meeting hall, the guys were tossing about ideas to get the newer Guard soldiers at the ranch some tactical shooting experience.

Lt said, "Ghost Team, take this day off from patrol. I am going into the SO to get briefed on what's going on today."

"Okay then, let's set up some plywood walls at the range and go through shooting drills with the new Guard guys," replied Kyle. "With their help, it should not take long to set up."

JJ asked, "What's the maximum yardage we can shoot? I want to get all you guys up to speed on the .50 cal. and shoot some rounds."

Mac said, “We can set up to 2000 yards. Let’s get targets set up from 800 to 2000 yards and all fire that rifle.”

“I am also going to pick out two rifles to use those night scopes on and sight them in tonight,” said Kyle.

“Okay, see you guys tonight,” and the Lt took off to town.

The Ghost Team spent all morning and part of the afternoon training the guard soldiers on house clearing as a team and put in some shoot/don’t shoot training with hostage targets. After that, the Ghost Team took turns spotting for a .50 cal. shooter then shooting it themselves. In the end it was realized besides JJ, only Mac, Kyle and Jim could use it and hit man sized targets, most of the time up to 2000 yards.

Near 4:00pm, Mac got a phone call from Major Westbrook. The Major said, “Watch the news at 6:00pm. I am going on live with the results of the missions we have done. I am also going to give the nation some facts about the invasion that the US government has not been willing to tell the media or the people.”

“Great, we will watch it together at the meeting hall,” said Mac.

“Governor Madison wants to get to the new mansion tomorrow. He will be traveling in three unmarked SUVs. La Grande PD will escort him to the city limits at 0900. Could your team lead with the gun Humvee and trail with the V-150 from there to the hotel?” asked the Major.

“Yes, of course we will. Be there at 8:45am.”

“Good, I will let his Zebra team know,” replied the Major. “Thanks, Mac.”

Mac informed the others about the mission the next morning and about the newscast at 6.

The Lt got back to the ranch and met everyone at the meeting hall hanging out cleaning weapons and other gear. He told them, "Sheriff McCabe said La Grande is getting worse. The Snake Heads gang comes into town in groups of four to six and bullies and fights the locals. They have stolen from people coming out of stores with food. It's a guess that most crime at night involves them. The other night a guy who has a large rifle collection had someone breaking into his home. The home owner took a shot at the guy and missed. Right after that, he heard motorcycles startup and take off. He phoned the PD and reported it. The next night, his house was fire bombed. The family was found dead inside by the fire department. The rifles were still locked up inside his gun safe.

"Also, the gang has shown up at the highway road-block several times wanting to drive through the county. When they are told no way, the gang yells, shouts and waves the middle finger salute before leaving."

Mac told the Lt about the team's escort mission for the Governor. He said, "Likely nothing will happen, but let's have everyone on the team involved including the air unit."

"Good idea, plan it just like in the old days when the President came to Portland. Get some SO marked units involved to block a few of the intersections so they get some experience on convoy escort. The air unit could replace the scout vehicle," said the LT.

"Well Lt, great minds think alike. I was going to cover it tonight after the 6:00pm news. I am including Sgt. Best with Guard vehicles to be spaced out and parked in pullouts along the route just as a show of force of what we have here for the Governor."

"Another good idea, Mac," said the Lt. "I know the Governor would like that. Although he might want to stop and shake their hands. That's just the kind of man he is, as you know."

Kyle spoke up, "We are going to need to take out the Snake Heads at their farm someday, likely sooner than later. Not sure we can do it without National Guard assistance."

All heads nodded up and down.

Just before 6:00pm, everyone got popcorn or other snacks and sat around to watch the big screen. Major Westbrook was going to be the main story of the news broadcast.

A voice came on the TV and then a woman. "Hello, I am reporter Sally Page here to broadcast a live message from Major Westbrook of the Oregon National Guard. We are at an undisclosed location for our safety."

The camera panned over to show the Major standing at a podium. Behind him was the United States and Oregon State flags with a large detailed map of Oregon between them.

Major Westbrook began his speech.

"As the world knows, we were invaded several weeks ago, and the United States military has been told to stand down and let it happen. Most believe it has not been a violent invasion. The Federal government has told those that fled not to talk to the media. Those that have tried to tell the truth are being called liars and alarmists. I am here to inform all people of the US what we know. We know this is the truth because it was repeatedly told to my soldiers by the helpless people of Oregon fleeing from the invaders.

"First off, look at this map." He pointed to the Willamette Valley and Oregon coast from Washington State to the California state border. "The area in red was taken over and is controlled by an invading Army. We have assisted the movement of nearly 1.5 million Oregonians who fled the Willamette Valley. These are their words as told to us at the aid stations. Killing and raping is normal by the invaders. They have broken into many homes and killed the residents. Young girls and even boys have been raped in front of their parents. Nearly all persons in public offices have been hunted down and killed or imprisoned. Some are being put into forced labor to work for the enemy. Nearly all persons who needed medical assistance to live have now died, due to no electricity. That is most of the people in nursing homes, hospitals, care centers, etc. People of the United States, those numbers we estimate to be in the tens of thousands of US citizens. Some were your close family or other relatives and friends.

"Some citizens who fled do understand the Chinese language and they reported hearing Chinese talk about Oregon and Washington becoming part of China for the great supply of timber, wheat and other natural resources that are in big demand in Asia. They want to take over all the large grain farms throughout central and eastern Oregon and also the timber harvest in western Oregon. We were told that the Chinese military would not go beyond the Cascade Range into central and eastern Oregon. That they only are here to get what they have paid for already.

That they are treating our citizens good, giving them food, water and aid. Do any of the real facts show that?"

The Major then stepped up to the wall map. "Many of Oregon's leaders that escaped the Willamette valley were meeting in the city of Bend in central Oregon. That is here on the map." The Major pointed to the city. "The building they were in was targeted and destroyed, including a National Guard helicopter that was flying nearby."

He stopped talking for a moment before continuing.

"Our scout teams of Oregon National Guard soldiers have been operating in eastern and central Oregon. We have seen and shot down Chinese military helicopters near the city of Pendleton in eastern Oregon. We located and destroyed Chinese missile sites near Burns and Fort Rock. Today, our teams destroyed three outposts of Chinese and Korean soldiers in eastern Oregon near Highways 7, 82 and 244. At the locations, we asked them to surrender and they shot at us. So far, we have killed every one of them."

The Major then pointed to each area on the map.

"We have killed 78 enemy troops on the ground and an unknown number that were in the choppers. All many miles east of the Willamette Valley."

The Major again paused for a moment.

"I cannot understand why the President of these United States is allowing any of this. This was an invasion of the United States of America and a war against its citizens. I will not tell you when and where we will respond, but I am here to tell you we will respond, just citizen soldiers in Oregon against an invading army. Lastly, in Oregon we have a new Governor. He is operating out of an undisclosed location for his safety. He will broadcast information to America through this same network at some point in the future. I will not take any questions. Thank you, and God Bless the USA."

"Now, for once I really want to see the next White House press briefing," said Lonnie. "That speech should cause the President to do some explaining to the people."

"We cannot do anything about what DC does, good or bad," said Mac before standing up. "Guys, we need to keep OUR heads clear for OUR missions. We have an escort mission to plan. Let's get it done."

CHAPTER 28

The gun Humvee and V-150 arrived on Highway 82 at the La Grande city limits, parked and awaited the Governors convoy. Most of the Ghost Team was on board the two vehicles. The Lt had the command post set up at the SO. Lenny, Eddy with two Guard soldiers were in the air unit. Along the route, Sgt. Best had two spare Bradley/APC teams and support troop trucks stationed. They were parked at pull outs on the highway just in case any help was needed since they found Chinese near the highway just a few days earlier. The SO deployed two marked SUVs with four deputies in each vehicle in the city of Wallowa on the highway to stop any westbound traffic until the convoy passed.

Just before the meet time, Trooper Chao Wang radioed, "Zebra units #1, #2 and #3 enroute with the package."

"SO, command copy," replied the Lt.

"Ghost Teams #1 and #2 copy, in position," replied Mac.

As the city convoy approached the Ghost Team, the city police vehicles pulled over and stopped behind the V-150. At that moment, Mac quickly pulled out onto the road in the gun Humvee to lead the three SUVs. The V-150 drove up and onto the roadway behind them. The SUVs did not even need to stop.

Lenny radioed, "Air unit report: Highway clear to Wallowa City, Guard units are parked in position. Air unit is now headed East again above the route."

A dozen miles from La Grande the convoy approached the small quiet town of Elgin. It's a city that is really just an intersection at Highways 82 and 204 with a population of a couple hundred on a good day. The only bar in the city is near the highway intersection. Eight motorcycles with riders still on them just arrived on Highway 204 and backed their motorcycles into parking spots in front of the bar.

The gun Humvee approached and Mac said, "Look left, Snake Heads at the bar."

Kyle radioed, "Convoy, be advised eight Snake Heads at bar in Elgin."

When the motorcycle gang first heard the big diesel engine of the gun Humvee, all riders sat on the motorcycles and waited before turning to look. Upon seeing the Humvee and the other vehicles following it, all eight raised their right hand and gave the convoy a middle finger salute.

Mac said, "I guess not much has changed with that bunch of lowlifes."

"They're all armed up with rifles and handguns, is that normal?" asked JJ.

"Is now," replied Kyle.

"One of them started talking into a handheld radio," Rick advised as he passed.

Justin swung the gun turret in the V-150 and pointed the machine gun at them. The Ghost Team's V-150 then got a two-handed middle finger salute from each member.

Lenny said, "I will be back over to Elgin in less than five minutes to check them out."

"SO, command copy," said the Lt.

The convoy continued on the highway at a speed of 50 mph to where the convoy was about ten minutes from passing through the roadblock. Lenny got on the radio. "Break! Break! Air unit to command, a large group of Snake Heads gang, high speed east bound on 82 from Elgin headed toward the convoy!"

Lt said, "Confirm their number and type of arms they carry."

"Eddy counts thirty-seven in total; three in the lead, the rest side by side. Most are armed with long guns."

"How long will they take to get to the roadblock?" Lt asked.

"At their speed, fifteen minutes, maybe a couple more."

Mac asked Rick, "Can you step it up to 60 mph?"

"Yes, but no faster than that."

Kyle radioed, "Roadblock, open the through lane. Three SUVs coming through hot!"

"Copy, lane now open."

Trooper Wang shouted in a panicked voice into the radio, "Zebra #1, WHAT SHOULD I DO!?"

"Calm down, breathe, do not shout into the radio," said Kyle in a slow calm voice. "Drive like you trained, do your job. We're here to help. At the roadblock, continue on. The SO will lead you after that. The Humvee and V-150 will stop and deploy to fight."

Kyle continued, "Roadblock, prepare everyone to fight and get a SO marked vehicle to lead the convoy with four deputies."

"Roadblock, copy."

Sgt. Best got on the police radio "Break! Break for National Guard. Bradley and APC with sixteen-foot soldiers enroute to roadblock ETA eight minutes, 2nd team with myself ETA twenty minutes."

"Command, copy."

"Ghost Teams, copy."

"SO, units in Wallowa City, proceed west at code 3 until you meet with convoy. At that point, follow convoy to SO. Convoy lead vehicle, proceed code 3 to bring the package to the SO HQ," said the Lt.

Dispatch to all units: "Signal two! Signal two! This net restricted, no radio traffic unless involved with this emergency until further notice."

The three SUVs passed through the roadblock at 60 mph. The marked SO unit sped away just ahead of them driving with police lights and siren on.

The Ghost Team vehicles had come to a hard stop; every tire skidded as they stopped in front of the roadblock. Lonnie and Jim jumped out from the rear of the V-150 and ran up on the hillside near the road to take up sniper positions. Mac u-turned the Humvee and stopped in the open lane between the ODOT 10-yard dump trucks. Off to the side, Rick had u-turned the V-150 and backed up to the roadblock.

Mac radioed the Bradley, "Gun Humvee blocking road, advise when 1 minute away. Humvee will move to the left. V-150 is parked on your right. Bring Bradley and APC thru, block opening with the troop truck. Deploy troops behind cover."

"National Guard copy, move NOW! We are 1 minute out!"

"Ghost Team, copy."

The Bradley and APC had to slow to a walk speed to drive between the roadblock ODOT trucks and then parked in line with the V-150 and gun Humvee. The troop truck parked in the open slot and the soldiers got out running to find good cover near the armored vehicles. As the last soldier found a fighting position, everyone at the roadblock could hear the roar of thirty-seven high speed street choppers without mufflers headed at them.

JJ manned the gun turret in the Humvee, then without waiting to be told, she locked and loaded the 240B. Justin did the same in the V-150. Mac and Kyle stood behind the opened armored doors of the Humvee with M-4s switched to full auto, no suppressors on them this time. Kyle looked up and gave a head nod to Mac. Mac nodded back, the sign given that each knew they were ready, and this might be the war they had felt was coming. Both also knew that in any gun fight, not everyone comes out alive.

The remaining deputies at the roadblock were standing in the dump truck beds aiming their M-16s over the truck cabs in fighting positions.

At about three hundred yards away from the roadblock, the first of the motorcycles came into view at high speed. When the motorcycle riders saw the roadblock, all three braked hard and started to skid. Then, they proceeded to the roadblock at a cautious low speed. The other thirty-four riders behind them approached and reacted the same. This time, the last four riders crashed into each other.

Mac and Kyle walked forward on the outer edge of the roadway. They knew better than to stand directly in front of their back-up shooters line of fire. As the three motorcycles got up to about twenty-five yards away from Mac and Kyle, Mac raised his left hand and with his index finger drew a line across his throat, signaling the riders to shut off the engines and stop. The three obeyed and stopped on the roadway center line. The Sergeant at Arms was behind the leader. He turned and motioned the others to stop and shut their motorcycles off. All stopped side by side in a nice straight line behind their leaders as they had been trained. The four who crashed were busy picking up their motorcycles.

The lead rider stepped off his motorcycle and yelled, "Is that you Kyle Morris!? So, we meet again. You're kind of old to be playing cop or army guy or whatever, aren't you?"

"No Ralph, I am not too old yet. I am too old to ride a bike like that, though. After seeing your panicked stop, do you need to change your Depends panties?"

"Funny guy, aren't you? You should show some respect to the Snake Head President!" He then pointed at the two behind him. "Also show respect for my Vice President Rogers and Sergeant at Arms Shaw. You guys know Rogers, but Shaw is a new addition to the club. Mr. Kyle Morris, killer of Snake Heads."

"I am showing you respect," said Kyle.

"Okay you guys, cut the crap. Ralph, this is really important if you want to live beyond this moment. Listen, if any one of your guys raises a gun, we will kill every one of you in mere seconds. You first, then use a firehose to clear the road of the bloody mess. Got it?"

"Yeah Mac, you're still an asshole. I can see the machine guns."

"What is it you want Ralph?" asked Mac. "President of the Snake Heads."

"Several things, Mac. We want to look for three club brothers that said they were going to Wallowa Lake, but never returned. We want to use this public road as is our right. We demand respect from you and all police around here. And who the hell gets armed guards to drive around here?"

"Ralph, we do not know anything about any lost gang guys. They never showed up here, and if they did, they would never be allowed past the roadblock. Only residents are allowed beyond here or anywhere in this county. Trespassers will be arrested or shot. Those arrested get to stay in jail as long as the Sheriff says they stay. You know about the war we are in now, don't you?"

"Yes."

"Until you start taking teddy bears to the children at the hospital, quit selling dope and stop acting like bullies to the citizens, then you're getting as much respect from us as possible. What we do, how we do it, and with whom is none of your damn business. If it ever becomes any of your business Ralph, I will come and tell you," said Mac.

"Trust me Mac, if you want people in Wallowa County to continue to live high on the hog like you're doing now, getting all the food and supplies without hardships like the rest of us, you will give us the respect we demand."

"Ralph, we are done here. Time to pick up your injured prospects and leave. You have about five minutes. At that time, the Oregon National Guard lead officer will arrive with lots more army guys. He does not like you, and he makes the rules when he gets here, not me. Every one of you will be arrested. If you do not surrender, believe me they will shoot. They will shoot every one of you," said Mac.

"Yeah, like I said, you're an asshole." Ralph Stoner then turned and walked back to his gang while giving Mac and Kyle the middle finger salute. Within a couple minutes, all of the motorcycles were started and turned around with their president leading the way.

"Well Mac, what you said was BS, but old Ralph bought it. I call that a win," said Kyle.

"From up here, that looked fun," Lenny said. "You guys stay in your positions for a few minutes. We will follow them for a while to make sure they do not turn around and come back."

"Copy," replied Mac. "Roadblock to Command, we are all code 4."

"Dispatch copy, clear signal two. All units back to normal radio traffic," said the dispatcher in a nice, clear, female voice. "Command copy, we will hold the package here at SO HQ until Ghost Team arrives."

Sgt. Best arrived with the 2nd squad just as the gang was riding away. He walked over to Mac and Kyle. "They didn't stay long, what was it all about?" he asked.

Kyle said, "Well Sgt., Mac said a big fat lie. He said once you got here, you would be in charge and that you would shoot every one of them."

"Mac, did you really say that?"

Nodding Mac said, "Yes sir, I did."

Sgt. Best said, "Oh.... good cop, bad cop. I get it, I am the bad cop today."

"Yes sir, that was a snap decision on my part," replied Mac.

"Kyle, what makes you think that was a lie? Maybe I would have had them shot. Those guys are living on borrowed time," said Sgt. Best.

The three of them all had a big laugh. It was the needed release after such a tense moment.

Ten minutes later, while the gang was still heading home, Lenny radioed the Ghost Teams. "Snake Heads still headed towards their farm. Slower now because a couple of the crashed bikes. I am going to clear and return to ranch."

"Okay guys, let's stand down. All Ghost Team members meet up at the rear of V-150," said Mac.

"Well guys, I believe we need to visit the Snake Heads' ranch ASAP. We know they have been kidnapping, beating, robbing, stealing, killing, selling dope and bullying people in La Grande. Let's talk to the Governor about getting the National Guard to help and as many cops as possible," said Mac.

"About time, Mac," said Sgt. Best. "The Guard will help you guys. We just need the Governor's okay. I had hoped to meet him today. He did give us a thumbs-up out his window as we passed each other."

"We need several days to get current intel and plan a mission against them," said Kyle. "There is around 60 total gang members. We have enough evidence to make arrests. But, the gang will not surrender to us. We will need to shoot it out with them."

"We need to get this escort mission finished," said Lonnie. "Let's discuss a mission on the Snake Heads tonight after dinner. Sgt. Best, you be there also."

"I won't miss it. See ya later."

CHAPTER 29

The next afternoon there was a meeting at the Governor's mansion to discuss the Snake Head gang. The Lt, Mac, and Kyle attended along with Sgt. Best and Sheriff Carlson of Union County, where the gang's farm is located.

Governor Madison, after learning of the police resources available, said, "I would really like to keep the National Guard out of the fighting. If needed, just use them for holding and transporting of any prisoners, but I am willing to change my mind. Mac and Kyle, get current intel about the farm and gang then come back to me with a mission plan in a couple days."

On the way back to the ranch, Sgt. Best mentioned that the Guard had several UAVs (unmanned aerial vehicles) in La Grande. He suggested that the next day they fly over the gang's farm to get current intel and photos.

Kyle asked, "Any chance the gang would see or hear the UAVs?"

"None at all, Kyle. It flies too high and cannot be heard from that distance. The camo paint makes it impossible to see from the ground even if you know where to look. We will have real time video here on my computer and can print photos that look as good as your family portraits."

"Wow, that's great. I am going to phone Idaho State Police SWAT and give them a heads up for the mission. We can really use their help this time," replied Kyle.

Lt was having breakfast in his home with Mary. Sheriff McCabe phoned him, and they spoke for several minutes.

Mary asked, "What's up now? That sounded bad."

"Yes dear, it is really bad. We need to get over to the meeting hall and tell the guys. The Snake Heads killed, looted and kidnapped in La Grande last night. They took over the city of Elgin and put up roadblocks on the highways."

The two took off to the meeting hall to inform the team of the new events before anyone left after breakfast.

The Lt came into the meeting hall and raised his hands. "Could everyone please sit down and listen for a couple of minutes? I got some updated information on the Snake Heads." He waited until everyone was seated and he had their attention. "I just got off the phone with Sheriff McCabe. He informed me the gang used stolen cargo trucks last night and broke into the Walmart in La Grande, where they shot and killed the security guard. They stole mostly food and clothing. The whole incident was caught on camera. They also stole school buses from the bus yard, also seen on camera. A young woman went missing after her shift ended at 2am at the 24hr dinner. A cargo truck was seen speeding away just after she went outside. They used the school buses to form roadblocks on the highways at Elgin. Residents were kicked out of their homes, some were shot.

"They claim any vehicle can pass through the city after paying a 50-dollar fee to the gang. Sheriff Carlson went to

Elgin. Shaw came out from the roadblock and told him that any cops coming around their city would be shot on sight. He further said that they are going to hunt down and kill the old OSP guys where ever they find them. Kyle and Mac have bounties on their heads. That was not a threat; that was a promise, he said."

There was compete silence in the meeting hall after the Lt finished.

"How many were killed in Elgin?" asked Mac.

"We believe up to ten. You know the residents are only retired folks, mostly old cowboys, not too many people there who could fight," answered the Lt. "I need to call the Governor. I am going back to the house. You guys start putting together an assault mission."

Mac stood up. "Okay folks, clear the tables, get a cup of whatever your drinking, sit down up front and let's start tossing around ideas. I want Kyle and Sgt. Best up front. Lonnie, could you take notes?"

About five minutes later, the Ghost Team and the two Guard Sergeants with Sgt. Best were seated at the nearest tables to the big screen TV. Sgt. Best stood up first. "I will have the UAV in the air shortly after 9am. I told the controllers to fly over Elgin for now, they will be over the city for most of the day. When it needs refueled, another one will be on station, and they will fly through the darkness if needed. At night the video will be as good as in daylight. We will have a live feed showing on this TV and recording for review at any moment."

Kyle was next. "I got ahold of Sgt. Burris from ISP SWAT yesterday. He and a pilot will be landing an ISP plane here at the ranch around 10am. He will assist us in planning and will explain what resources he can get here to help. They may be here for a day or two, and will be staying in an empty RV."

"Guys, we will need to watch them for a while, maybe even a couple of days to learn of their patterns and their fire power," said Mac. "This sounds like possibly the most dangerous mission we have ever had. We need to get it right!"

Lonnie spoke up. "Yeah, and they will not submit to arrest. We need to plan this as a war battle."

When the UAV started sending a live image of the city, all in the group sat and watched. The Lt was notified and he arrived minutes later. The video showed that the gang looked like a city full of workers throughout the core area. On Highway 82 at both the North and South ends of the city, the gang had placed 3 school buses, making a complete roadblock. It was clear they set up two large buses at each side of the roadway and those were being stock piled with weapons to be used as fighting positions. They had smaller short buses placed in the gap and were moving those to allow vehicles to pass through. Some gang members were in and out of the motel, hardware store and gas station taking what they wanted.

On the Highway 204 roadblock, they had three pickups parked across the road and four gang guys stationed there. That highway always had very little traffic, normally just locals coming into town. Sheriff Carlson had his office phone all the outer area ranches off Highway 204 and told them about the gang takeover of Elgin so they would avoid the city. The gang had cars parked to block the few other small roads that entered the city.

The gang had complete control of Elgin's city core, about eight city blocks. Inside of that area, they had a gas station, a bar, a small grocery store, a small hardware store, two restaurants, and several old homes besides the motel. The motel they controlled was two stories tall and had twelve rooms total. The only motel in the city.

The Lt thought it was a good time to update the group. He stood up near the side of the TV and stated, "La Grande PD is stopping all vehicles on 82 headed toward Elgin and are advising them not to travel through Elgin at this time. They are not allowing any delivery trucks to proceed through Elgin for fear of the drivers getting killed and the trucks being taken by the gang. The trucks are re-routed back through to I-84 to Pendleton into Washington and back south on Highway 3 to Enterprise. That adds a couple hundred miles and many more hours to get to Enterprise from Boise, but at least the drivers and cargo will be safe from the gang.

"Our Highway 82 roadblock near the county line also advised that no one has traveled to Elgin or La Grande, and the few that were going to go smartly turned around. Our roadblock reported that this morning two vehicles came through from La Grande before they knew about the gang's roadblock at Elgin. Both said they were held at gunpoint, and their vehicles were searched. The gang took all of their guns and ammo from them. One of them had a few cases of hard liquor that was also taken. Each vehicle had to pay the 50-dollar fee to get out."

Kyle's phone rang. He spoke for a moment and then told the group, "Sgt. Burris will be landing in a few minutes. Eddy, get a 4-wheeler and meet them at our new air strip, then take them to a vacant trailer. I will meet you there."

Eddy jumped up and said, "Okay Dad, see you in a few minutes," and then left.

Kyle met Sgt. Burris and his pilot at the RVs. They shook hands, and Kyle said, "We are sure glad you came to help us. Put your stuff in the trailer and meet at the meeting hall. It's the building over there." Kyle pointed out the meeting hall. "Inside it is where the mission planning will be done. It also has a fulltime kitchen and restrooms."

"I told you we would come if needed. Eddy told us you have a bigger problem than you knew about yesterday."

"Yes sir, we do!" replied Kyle.

"Well, some better news from my end. I am allowed to involve Boise city SWAT. They have a converted armored truck from Wells Fargo. And we now have a second Bearcat, ready to roll if needed. So, it sounds like I should make a phone call and get both ISP teams and the Boise team to go on alert and standby."

"Yes, sir we will need them," said Kyle.

"I will get the two Bearcats and armored truck loaded up on low boys to trailer them to La Grande. They and the teams will be here within a 5-hour travel and prep time."

"Okay, see you in a few minutes at the meeting hall. We have a live drone, UAV video feed of Elgin on the big screen," said Kyle.

"Copy, we will see you there in about 15 minutes."

Back at the meeting hall, the guys now had assignments. A Ghost Team member with a Guard Sgt. would be watching the UAV feed at all times and taking notes in log books on anything important. Sgt. Burris and his pilot hung out near the big screen also taking notes and talking with Mac or Kyle. Lonnie was checking with Union County SO to get all of the known Snake Heads' personal information and arrest history. Jim and Tim were getting an inventory of all SWAT gear on hand and the lists of the deputies and Rapid Response Team gear. And then, would go through the list and get whatever may be needed. Rick with Eddy, Justin and Jimmy cleaned each Humvee and the V-150. They did maintenance checks on the vehicles and restocked them with the 3 B's (beans, bullets and bandages). Just a few MREs went into them, but lots of medical supplies and ammo for all guns. The Lt was calling or taking calls from the Governor, Major Westbrook, Sheriff McCabe or Sheriff Carlson all day.

Guard soldiers came into the meeting hall with cases of 5.56 ammo and boxes of empty thirty round magazines. Those folks not working on anything could be seen loading the ammo into the mags then stacking them into other boxes.

CHAPTER 30

In the early afternoon, the UAV went to a larger viewing circle checking homes and roads outside of the city. It had picked up three motorcycles approaching the city on Highway 204, the same roadway to and from the gang's ranch twenty miles away.

The roadblock of pickup trucks opened up and the three rode into the city. They rode over to the bar and parked out in front of it. From the drone image it was easy to read the top patch on the back of each one of the gang's jackets. The Sergeant at Arms came out of the bar and walked up to the President, Vice President and the regular patched (nonoffice holder) member of the Snake Heads gang.

Kyle said to the UAV Sgt., "Keep those three in the view. Let's see what they are up to."

On the ground, Ralph told the regular member who arrived with them, "Go get us each a cold beer and then find us. The beer had better be cold, understand?"

"Yes sir, Mr. President. I will be right back and the beer will be cold."

"Shaw, take us to the south roadblock and tell me what has been done," growled Ralph.

"Yes sir, Mr. President. I have got the buses in place like you wanted. The men have been outfitting the buses with armor plating. It should be finished by the end of the day. We found sheets of heavy steel that will end up covering the four large buses on the outside. After that, I will cut out the gun ports in the steel on each bus. We have water, rifles and ammo already inside each bus."

"Okay, that's a good start, Shaw. Conduct a drill so I can see how my men will respond to a vehicle coming to the roadblock."

"Yes, sir. Once we get over there, I will have the spotter sound the alarm."

At that moment, the gang member with the beer came running up to the group of three men. He stopped and held out three beers.

Ralph said, "Okay, they are cold, but you spilled some beer out of each bottle. Go back and bring us bottles of beer that hasn't had spilled out of bottle, you jackass!"

"Yes sir, sorry!" said the gang member before turning to run back toward the bar.

Ralph threw his bottle at the running member. It landed behind him, crashing and breaking on the road as the beer and glass splashed against his pant legs.

"Hold off on the test until I get my full… cold… beer. I hope that jackass gets it right this time, or we may be short a member! I aimed for the back of his head, lucky for him," said the very angry Ralph.

The V.P. said, "Mr. President, he is the best we have for working on the bikes. Perhaps another type of punishment would be better."

Shaw explained more of what was happening to their city as the member approached them again with beer. This time he had three unopened beers in a bucket on ice. He met the three and sat the bucket down. He picked up a beer, opened it and handed it to the president.

The President took a long drink, enough to empty half the bottle. He leaned back and let out a loud "Burrup" and wiped his mouth.

"Good, now the V.P. and Sgt. need their beer," said Ralph. Ralph pointed at the member and said, "Find us again with three more just like that, in ten minutes."

"Yes, sir Mr. President." And then the member ran back toward the bar.

"Okay Shaw, now do the test."

Shaw radioed the spotter, "Do the test drill."

The spotter was stationed atop the motel roof, so he could see the roadway beyond the buses. He raised a megaphone and turned on the siren. Twenty men came running from areas inside of the blocked off city. Eight went into each large bus and grabbed a rifle then took up shooting positions spaced throughout in open windows. Four others already armed with AR style rifles stood around the short bus. They were all in position in a couple of minutes.

"Very good, Sgt. Let's check out the other roadblock," said Ralph.

At the north Highway 82 roadblock, the results were about the same. That spotter was standing on the nearby gas station roof top. The men mostly came running from the bar to man the buses.

"Shaw, do those spotters have scoped hunting rifles up there so they can also be our snipers?"

"Yes sir, they're the best shots we have, both ex-army. They have bolt action 30-06 rifles each with a 3x9 power scope. They claim they can kill a man at 300 yards."

"Okay, at night split the guys up so some are awake, some asleep and some partying. Make sure they're not too damm drunk or smoke too much weed. They need to be able to shoot or fight at any time and to respond to their posts at the sound of that alarm. You got all of that!" Ralph again growled.

"Yes, sir. You can count on me to get things done around here and all done right," replied Shaw.

"Okay, one last thing, Sgt. Let the guys know I am working out a way to get each of them a night off from here to get drunk and stoned with one of our ladies at the farm. We need to get the defenses done first. I hope that will be in two or three days."

"Good news, I will tell them. Thank you, Mr. President," said Shaw.

"Okay, the V.P. and I are going to the bar to eat lunch."

Back at the ranch, everyone in the meeting hall stopped doing whatever they were doing to watch the big screen when Mac shouted for Kyle and Sgt. Burris to watch it. When Mac saw the Snake Head President, Vice President and Sergeant at Arms meet, he knew they needed to all watch whatever was about to take place in Elgin.

"Now, that was a learning experience," said Kyle. "I wish we could have heard what was being said on the ground."

"Yeah, but that would have just confirmed what we think happened," replied Mac.

"Guys, no sound was okay," said Sgt. Burris. "We now know where their lookouts are. That was a test, no doubt about it. They showed us what they plan to do when someone arrives at their roadblock. They plan on twenty armed guys in or around the buses at both Highway 82 roadblocks, and they are putting armor plating to stop bullets into their positions."

Kyle asked the Guard Sergeant who was in contact with the UAV operators.

"Could you get the UAV to zoom into the roof top sniper/lookout positions? We need to see what type of rifles they have. JJ, get up here and see what you think about taking them out."

"Hey, remember Kyle, I am a trained sniper. I have been looking at them already and searching out where any other likely sniper hides might be set up and where I will be to take them out," said JJ.

Another minute passed, and the UAV camera zoomed into the south sniper/lookout. It stayed on the location for a couple minutes then moved over to the north position.

JJ said, "Well, the close up is great. I like what I saw. Only one guy at each area with a blow horn, binoculars and a scoped hunting rifle. The last two items are completely useless at night. I already know that I can take them both out with the .50 caliber from a single firing position either north or west of the city, and I will do it in the day or night."

"Wow Kyle, she got you good," Mac said laughing.

"Hey, I was just testing her," Kyle said and looked around for support. "Anyone believe me?"

All shook their heads NO. Then everyone started laughing, including Kyle.

Mac asked the Guard Sergeant, "Could you have the UAV follow Ralph home? My guess is he will leave in an hour or two and head back to the farm. We need some intel on it for daytime and at nighttime. I am afraid we need to attack the farm and Elgin both."

Lonnie spoke up. "Mac, I was beginning to think the same thing. I have been keeping a head count on who's at Elgin. I believe there are about ten gang members still at the farm. About twelve known missing women from local police reports and four or more gang guys' wives might remain at the farm."

The Guard Sergeant asked, "Should we get another UAV up? One to stay on the city and the other on the farm?"

Mac replied, "Yes, let's do it. Best to have them both in the air until the mission is done. That might be a couple of days from now. Is that possible?"

"That's no problem, we have three UAVs. We stagger the takeoff times, that way the third UAV will cover each UAV when they need to land and refuel. If done right, we will have 24/7 coverage on both locations. But, we need another big screen in here," said the Guard Sergeant.

"I will go to the ranch house and get one of the Lt's," said Kyle. As he was walking out the door, He turned and said, "Be back in 30 minutes."

Throughout the next few hours the group noted every detail at both locations. Mainly at the city the gang was fixing up their defense, drinking beer and going through the homes and business buildings taking whatever they wanted. At the farm, they watched as some tended to their marijuana grows, and it appeared they had an active meth lab in the newer barns they built since Mac and Kyle's visit years ago. Women were being brought out under guard for walks or hanging laundry from one of two buildings that appeared to be like bunk houses. Ralph and his wife left the main house once to go into each outer building, likely doing inspections. By night fall, the group learned how many gangsters they would need to fight. All preplanning of the mission needs on manpower and equipment was done.

After dinner, Kyle said, "Let's make an overnight watch list. We need four people in here all night to watch the UAV feed at both locations. Let's do three hours per shift so we all get some needed sleep. How about we make the assault plans after breakfast?

As soon as the last plate of breakfast was cleared from the tables, The Lt got up and walked to the front and stood between the two-big screen TV's. "Folks listen up. A few of us have been working around the clock already to put this mission together. We will start the assault early AM. You each have information in front of you regarding your team assignments and duties. What you do not know is the Governor allowed the Guard to assist in a limited role. He is really pissed, mainly because of the gangs armored up roadblocks on the highway. He knows our bullets might not be up to the job of taking them out. The Guard has heavy weapons and they will be used. Remember, these are not normal times. We take out the leadership and anyone that is holding a gun. First, we breach the buses with force. If any of the members surrender, we will accept their surrender. That is from the Governor.

"Sgt. Burris is the South team leader. He will be leaving here soon to brief his teams. He will be bringing back 16 SWAT men from Idaho. Their back-up will be La Grande city police and Union County deputies, twenty total extra. Mac will be North team leader. All Ghost Team members are involved. Back-up will be troopers and Wallowa County deputies, fifteen total extra men. Major Westbrook will command all National Guard from the ranch meeting hall. Sgt. Best will be in the field. As of now, it is unknown how many soldiers will be in the field. I will be in command of all police teams and will also remain here. That's all I have. Rest and relax as much as possible. The North team leaves the ranch at midnight."

CHAPTER 31

At 1:00am at the SO, Mac conducted the briefing for the entire North team police members. "You guys each have a small packet of instructions showing each of your assignments plus maps of the farm and city. Please spend a few minutes reading through the whole packet. Closely read and reread your assignment duties and locations. I will start going over all of the details. Okay, before I start, any questions?" asked Mac.

No one raised a hand or said a word.

"Okay then, we will meet the Guard units on Highway 82 near the area where we go off-road to the farm. We will have Guard medics along with us and some soldiers to secure any prisoners. The medics will call in the Dust-Off choppers and set up landing zones if needed. Let's have the deputy who transports the sexual assault advocate to hang back with the medics. Likely, they will all be needed at the building where the kidnapped women are being held. We should assume the women will be highly traumatized and likely have physical injuries. The UAV image shows all lights are out at the farm, and no guards are posted just like last night. I will make the call on entering Elgin from Highway 82 or Highway 204 before we leave the farm."

Mac continued going over every detail of the mission with the whole group. After about twenty minutes, he was finished.

Mac told the group, "We pull out of here in ten minutes."

The north team convoy met up with the National Guard about ten miles from Elgin. All the vehicles parked along the roadway behind the Guard vehicles.

Kyle walked up to Eddy, Justin, and Jimmy and said, "Take this roll of duct tape and tape up every vehicle's taillights that is going to the farm. Make sure no light can be seen when the brakes are used. Check every vehicle and pull all dome light bulbs that come on when a door opens."

Mac walked over to Lonnie, Lenny and JJ and told them, "Good luck."

Lonnie replied, "The National Guard vehicles are moving. We better go, see you later."

Mac went back to the team vehicles headed to the farm. "Okay guys, no more vehicles light's on at all. They could be seen from the north lookout as we climb into the hills. We go in from here on with NVG only. We will travel on this gravel road for about five miles before we cut fences and then go cross county."

At 2:00am, Major Westbrook landed at the ranch with the two Dust-Off medevac helicopters. The chopper crews all went into the meeting hall to watch the big screens and the Major to manage the upcoming battle. The medevacs would be standing by at the ranch until needed or the battle was won.

"Major, before the bullets start flying this morning, I want to tell you about the Humvee windshield that had a bullet shot into it," said the Lt. He then told the whole story about when the Ghost Team met the three gang members with the two kidnapped women on Highway 82. He also included Kyle's history with Ralph.

"Thanks for the information. That makes sense why it needed to remain secret. God, I hope we get all of the women held at the farm out alive," said the Major.

The Guard north team parked about two miles away from the Elgin city limits. The Ghost Team members traveling with them also parked there.

Lenny and JJ geared up to leave on their hike. Lenny said, "Goodbye, big brother. I hope we see you in about six or eight hours."

Lonnie said, "See you later. JJ, you better take care of my brother." He then walked off with Sgt. Best and some soldiers to set up a firing and lookout position north of the north Highway 82 roadblock.

Lenny and JJ started their hike across country to the west side of Elgin. While using the drone earlier, JJ had found a house that would give them a perfect sniper hide. There she could take out both lookouts on the roof tops and Lenny the Highway 204 gangsters.

Mac's North team convoy had stopped at the point where a barbed wire fence ran next to the gravel road. A deputy from the last vehicle in line walked forward and cut the three barbed wire fence lines near a fence post. He then pulled the wires aside, and that gave them a ten-foot-wide opening so the vehicles could pass through. Once all the vehicles were inside, the convoy stopped for several minutes so that the same deputy could repair the fence before moving on. If the fence was not repaired, the rancher who owned that land could lose many head of cattle by morning.

As the group drove across fields through timber and on the land owner's dirt road, they passed many head of cattle, deer and some elk grazing. The animals only stopped eating for a few minutes to look up at the vehicles as they passed. The convoy finally came to the area to cut another fence and drove onto the gang farm property, still a mile from the farm house.

A short time later Mac parked the Humvee in a hidden gully away from the farm house. The other vehicles also parked in the gully. Mac circled up the team personnel, then said, "Only assault members go further from here. We don't have much time to be in our positions before 4:00am. Those staying here must be as quiet as possible, and do not turn on any lights. Listen for us to tell you when to drive to the house or outer buildings. The Guard diversion at Elgin starts at 4:30am. We should be engaged in a fire fight here shortly after that. Assault teams, let's head out." Mac, as always, led the way.

JJ and Lenny had made it into the city's western edge. In the near total darkness using their NVGs, they easily shifted around unseen by the two gang members standing at the Highway 204 roadblock. The two walked the last several blocks to the now vacant house that they would use as a sniper hide. JJ carried the massive .50 caliber rifle and Lenny an M-4 with a suppressor.

Lenny said, "We think the house is vacant, but let me clear both floors with the M-4 before you go in."

"Good idea, hurry up if you can!"

A few minutes later, they were setting up JJ's shooting position in the upper bedroom window facing east. JJ adjusted the bipod on her rifle. "This is perfect, I can get both roof snipers from right here. I'll have them ranged in a minute, then let's see about your position facing the 204 roadblock fools."

Upon checking the upper side bedroom window, they ranged the distance to the 204 roadblock. They found they were 200 yards away, with a clear shot to the "fools" standing guard there. Now, they just had to sit and wait for daylight and for the Goose teams to shoot the buses.

JJ radioed, "Long bow to command, #1 and #2 in position."

The Guard north team with Lonnie set up in a hidden location 700 yards from the armored bus roadblock. They were there to deploy a Goose team and observe the city. After that action, they would only engage any gang members that fled their way. The Goose teams had Carl Gustaf 84 mm anti-tank rifles nicknamed "The Goose." They too had to wait until daylight.

Lonnie radioed, "North Goose team in position." He then heard the reply from command and north assault team.

The south Guard Goose team had also set up well hidden, facing the armored-up school buses at the south roadblock. The Guard Sgt. there radioed, "South Goose team also in position."

Mac radioed, "North assault team copy, we're approaching the target."

The North assault team had silently and slowly approached the farm buildings. As they got close, Mac told the team, "Take up your assigned fighting positions."

"Jim and I will cover Mac and Rick as they set up that claymore mine in front of the gang's bunk house. The UAV guys said there are nine gangsters inside that place. That makes sense, since they left nine bikes lined up near the front door," said Kyle.

Mac and Rick went forward and placed the claymore mine 35 yards out in front of the gangsters' motorcycles. Rick placed some debris in front of the mine to hide it. As Mac unrolled the detonation wire, they found covered fighting positions away from any back blast of the mine at a place where they could still see the bunk house.

Kyle and Jim then went to the farm house. The motorcycles of the gang's President and Vice President were parked side by side alongside of the house. They found a downed log close to 100 yards away from the motorcycles and laid down next to each other behind it in sniper positions.

Jim said, "Well Kyle, soon Oregon will be rid of this gang forever."

"Yeah, they won't be victimizing anyone else. I owe Ralph, you only take out the VP."

"I figured. Man, I sure like this night scope on my 6.5. Can I keep it?" asked Jim.

"Only if you make a one shot, one kill," said Kyle.

"At this range, no problem. Remember, we wait til they get on the bikes," said Jim.

Mac radioed, "All North assault members, radio me your status."

Each member told him code-4, in position.

Mac radioed, "Command, north team in position."

Sgt. Burris radioed, "South assault team in staging position."

A short time later, Long Bow #3 and #4 had moved into sniper positions behind the Elgin motel and then informed command.

About a half hour later, Lt radioed, "All units, all units two minutes to diversion."

At 4:30am, two Guard APCs that had been hidden near Elgin were armed with 4.2-inch mortars in them. Instead of armed rounds, they fired night flares over the top of each roadblock on Highway 82. The flares popped open with a sound of a small caliber gun being fired and drifted down on parachutes. The whole area near the school buses was lit up like daylight.

Both roof top sniper/lookouts were likely sleeping because it took over a minute before each was sounding the alarm. Then, lights in the motel rooms started turning on. The gangsters started coming out into the street from the bar and motel. Some running, some walking, all in different stages of dress. Each going to their assigned roadblock school buses or over to the Highway 204 roadblock.

As the flares were nearly out, suddenly—*pop, pop*—two more flares were again lighting up the area. Shaw came out of the motel and yelled at the nearby south lookout. "What's going on!? Do you see anyone?"

The sniper/lookout on the roof yelled back, "I don't know, those are US Army flares fired from a 4.2- inch mortar. I cannot see anyone; the flares are blinding!"

"Keeping watching, I'm calling the boss!" yelled Shaw.

Shaw pushed speed dial #1 on his phone for the gang President, who was asleep at the farm house. After several minutes, Ralph finally answered.

Ralph yelled into the phone, "What's the reason you woke me up, you asshole!"

"Sir, we're under attack by the US Army!"

"WHAT! You're nuts! The Army is not allowed to attack citizens! What the hell is really happening?"

"Sir, we're getting flares shot over the city."

"Just flares? What about men? Do you see any vehicles or men approaching?" yelled Ralph.

"No sir, just flares. Hey wait a minute, they're going out now."

"Okay, the V.P. and I will be there soon. Phone me if you hear shots fired or see anyone approach."

"Okay sir, the men have deployed as they trained today. Everyone is in position."

Kyle and Jim looked through their NVGs and saw the upper level bedroom light turn on. A couple minutes after that, the main floor bedroom light came on.

Jim radioed, "Both targets in the house now awake."

A few minutes later, they saw the VP exit the back door of the house and walk with a flashlight to the bunkhouse where the gang members slept. Several more minutes passed, and the V.P. exited the bunkhouse to walk back into the main house. The lights remained on in the bunkhouse.

Kyle said, "Jim, I guess the diversion is working. I owe you for the suggestion, let's get into the rifle scopes."

"Copy."

About five minutes later, both the President and V.P. walked out the back door, both smoking cigarettes. They walked over to their motorcycles. Each one bent down, turned on the ignition and grabbed the handle bars before swinging their right legs over the seats. Before either had a chance to push the start button on the motorcycles, the V.P.'s body flew backward. That caught the attention of Ralph. He looked over at the V.P.'s body hitting the ground. Suddenly, Ralph felt terrible pain in his right foot as his right leg was jerked backward, causing him to fall off his motorcycle. Both Kyle and Jim had suppressed rifles, and no one had heard or seen the shots, including the targets.

Ralph looked down but could not see much in the darkness. He felt his right foot. He realized the front half of his boot and foot were missing. Blood was pouring out from the stump. While lying on the ground, he looked over at his Vice President. The V.P. looked like the back side of his head was missing. Ralph was now in a panic. He tried to stand up on his left foot and hop to the back door to safety. Suddenly, massive pain again. This time, in his left foot. He fell again, his mind telling him he had been shot in each foot. He can't think right and is still feeling drunk from the party earlier and getting dizzy from blood loss.

Kyle put down his R-25 and picked up his M-4. He clipped the sling onto his vest and ran toward Ralph.

Jim yelled out, "HEY, STOP!" to Kyle. Then radioed, "Both targets at house neutralized."

Kyle kept running without hesitation toward Ralph.

Jim put down his 6.5 rifle, grabbed his M-4, and then got up to run after Kyle. Jim knew this move was not right under any circumstances and very dangerous, but he had to follow his friend to cover him.

When Kyle got near Ralph, he stopped and drew his Glock, pointing it right at him.

Ralph, still laying on the ground, looked up. "Oh, it's you.... you asshole, you shot me. Get me to a doctor."

Kyle replied, "Not this time. No doctor is coming here, you asshole."

Ralph's face tightened up as his right hand lowered down to his belt, and he grabbed his handgun from its holster. He drew the gun out and started to point it toward Kyle.

Kyle pointed his Glock at Ralph's groin and fired a single shot.

Ralph screamed out in pain, dropped his gun and grabbed his groin.

Kyle said, "That's for the young girl you gang raped six years ago. This one is for trying to kill my family."

Kyle aimed the gun's night sights at Ralph's face and fired just as Jim arrived.

Jim was facing the house and yelled, "LOOK OUT!"

Kyle turned toward the house and saw a bright, blinding light and was knocked to the ground with massive pain in his chest. His head and neck were in real pain. He could not breathe very well; he was only able to get small amounts of air into his lungs. His chest muscles were not responding to his need to get air. His left hand was numb and felt useless. He remembered being in a bomb blast years ago. Maybe he was blown up again, but this time he hadn't heard an explosion. This time, it seemed he was in greater pain. He thought he might be slowly dying. Panic started to set in from the pain and lack of ability to take a full breath. He heard shell casings hitting the ground near him and the sound of a bolt on a suppressed M-4 opening and closing as the gun was being fired. At that point for Kyle, the world went black.

Jim shouted into the radio, "Kyle is down, he's been shot!"

Jim had aimed and shot the woman who had just shot Kyle. She was standing in the living room at the window. He then heard screaming inside the house and another woman appeared holding a shotgun. That woman started to aim the shotgun at Jim.

Jim fired his M-4 again, this time emptying the rest of the magazine into the second woman.

As Jim was putting a fresh magazine into his M-4, he heard the claymore go off with an ear deafening *BOOOOM*! Jim was close enough that he felt the pressure wave from the blast, and then the blowing dust covered him. He bent down and awaited any targets who may appear from around the house. In Jim's mind, it made no difference if Kyle was alive or dead. He was going to stand his ground and fight while kneeling over Kyle's body to cover his friend the best he could until all threats had been neutralized. He knew Kyle would have done the same for him.

Knowing that Kyle had been shot, Mac and Rick got up and ran to the bunk house right after Mac fired the claymore. They then shot anyone who was still moving.

Mac yelled into his radio, "Get the medics here NOW! OFFICER DOWN!"

Mac and Rick found a bloody mess of what used to be nine gang members who were struck with the high-speed small steel balls from the claymore. Hearing Kyle's shots from his Glock, the gang came running out of the bunkhouse door. Mac had counted until all nine gangsters were outside. He then hit the clacker that fired the claymore. The few who were still alive would soon bleed out, but Mac and Rick shot them anyway.

Mac radioed, "Main house assault team, form up at the rear door and clear the house. Gang bunkhouse team, move up and clear the bunkhouse. Then get to the kidnapped women's bunkhouse and free them."

Back at the ranch, all wives were watching the UAV video and listening to the radio traffic. They could see all Ghost Team members and the others on the ground at the farm. Upon hearing the radio call of a member being shot, Dust Off 723 pilots and crew got up and ran for the chopper that was parked not far away. It lifted off before even being told where to go. Claudia screamed out, "OH MY GOD!" and started crying.

The Lt waved Mary over to him. He told her, "Get Claudia outside and take the other wives. As soon as I know more, I will get someone to come out and talk to you. Make sure to tell her we do not know what his condition is at this time."

Mac and Rick had run over to Jim and found Kyle lying unmoving, face up on the ground. Mac yelled to Jim and Rick, "Provide me cover while I check on Kyle."

Mac got out a flashlight. He also passed the light over the other bodies lying nearby. The others were both clearly dead by gunshots to their heads. All three bodies were covered by dirt and dust from the claymore blast. He heard the convoy vehicles driving fast toward the house. Mac waved the flashlight toward them and radioed, "Get the medics over to the waving flashlight. All others, stage up and cover us in case of more gunfire."

The two medics got to Kyle, and after a moment told Mac he was unconscious. His left wrist could be broken, and he was shot in the center of his chest. One medic said, "His vitals are strange, but we normally deal with 20-year old's."

Kyle's brain was telling him he was floating away; he must be dying. Then, he was bouncing around, maybe on a stretcher, then he was laid on the ground. His head hurt really badly, and he could hear voices. He heard, "Wake up buddy, wake up. Damn you, Kyle. Wake up!"

Kyle realized he had a mask over his face. Oxygen was being forced into his lungs, and it felt good. He could breathe again. His mind was still fuzzy, but the fresh oxygen removed the panic he had moments before. He knew that one voice, who was it? He found the strength to open his eyes. He saw Rick standing over him repeating, "Wake up, wake up." Kyle heard another voice saying, "Dust Off is two minutes out." Kyle tried to move and realized he was strapped down. The straps were holding his legs, arms, chest and head.

Rick then said, "Buddy, don't try to talk, you need to keep that mask on your face. You were shot and may have broken or cracked ribs, you hit your head hard on the ground. Lucky, you were wearing a helmet. The ballistic vest panel stopped the bullet, it was a .44 magnum. Blink at me if you understand."

Kyle blinked his eyes open and closed as he heard a Blackhawk landing nearby.

"I got to go tell your sons you're awake," Rick told Kyle. "The battle here is over. See you later today, my friend."

Kyle was lifted again and his stretcher was pushed into the Blackhawk and laid on the floor. Moments later, he felt the chopper lift off. He was told they would be landing at the Enterprise hospital in less than ten minutes. The chopper medic injected him with something that was removing the massive pain felt throughout his body. He then relaxed and went to sleep.

Mac phoned the Lt and informed him about Kyle's condition. He also told the Lt, "All others here are code-4.

We have thirteen EKIA, of that number two were the President and V.P.s wives or girlfriends. We have rescued twelve women; the medics are still checking them out. They should be enroute to the Enterprise hospital soon. None of them have injuries beyond being beaten up and raped. Word is they got punched or slapped around a lot, mainly by Ralph. The entire farm is now secured."

"Copy, I will get Sheriff McCabe enroute to the hospital. He can interview the women and work on getting them back home," replied the Lt.

The Lt got up and rushed outside to where the wives where gathered around Claudia.

He told them everything he knew about Kyle. Then, he returned inside the meeting hall to continue monitoring the mission.

The Lt got on the radio and said, "Ghost Team member Kyle is conscious; his vest stopped a bullet. Unknown any further."

JJ and Lenny looked at each other and gave each other thumbs-up after hearing the Lt.

Mac circled everyone up for a quick pep talk. He told them Kyle's condition was really good considering being shot in the chest by a .44 magnum.

Jim told the group, "I really thought Kyle had missed with his first shot. But, he didn't. He shot Ralph's right foot, then his left foot. I would not believe it if I did not see it myself. Only Kyle could have done that. I knew he had a score to settle with Ralph. I don't blame him one bit for what he did. Ralph needed to feel pain and fear before he died."

"Okay, guys," Mac said, "You all did a great job here, but the next fight will be more dangerous. Get your heads clear, watch out for your buddy. We are going into Elgin through the Highway 204 to save time. JJ and Lenny will be able to provide better sniper cover for us than from going in on Highway 82. Recheck your gear, drink some water. We move out in about 20 minutes."

Mary told the wives, "Claudia and I are going to the hospital."

Mac's wife said, "I'm going, too."

The others gave Claudia a big hug; they were all crying.

Claudia said, "I need to get Dacoda and bring him with us. Kyle loves that dog, he's part of our family."

The three of them and the dog jumped into Kyle's F350 and took off for the hospital. Claudia sat in the backseat petting and hugging Dacoda. Through tears, she said, "Crap, three different times I had state troopers knocking on the front door at night, every time telling me Kyle had been injured and we needed to get to the hospital. Each time the trooper took off driving with siren and police lights on all the way to the hospital. I like the brotherhood that the state troopers have, but I was so scared riding to the hospital and not knowing what happened. The troopers do not talk much when driving code-3. I thought that would be all over with after Kyle retired."

Mary, while driving as fast as she could, said, "Our men are too damn old for this stuff. I can't sleep anymore worried about each one of the men. They are all family. Every day they put the uniforms on and go out the door, I'm scared until they get home."

Lonnie radioed command. "What does the UAV show the guys are doing at the buses?"

"Only half of them ever came out and took up fighting positions. My guess is the others are too stoned or too drunk to get up. Now only a couple remain at the buses. The others went to the bar or back inside the motel," replied the Lt.

In Elgin, Shaw was running up and down the halls of the motel making all the guys get up and come down to the lobby. After about ten minutes, they all showed up.

He told the guys, "We are being probed for an assault. You guys need to drink some coffee and take some meth. Wake the hell up! We need to be ready to fight whoever is doing this!"

After that, he then went to the bar to yell at the guys hanging out there. But, the biker gang men had been working hard the last few days and needed to get drunk and stoned. Few would even listen to Shaw at this hour.

A senior gang member in the motel lobby looked around and said, "Look guys, there are not enough cops around here to take us, and they can't get past the buses. We have the snipers on the roof with the siren to warn us if anyone tries to get inside our town. I'm going back to bed."

The others looked around and most of them then walked to their rooms and quickly fell back asleep.

Sgt. Best spoke to Lonnie about the flares. "We are coming up on thirty minutes since the last flares went out. Time to mess with the gangsters again. I will be having the APC crews fire some more flares off again." He then phoned the Major and told him.

The Lt radioed all units, "Two minutes to the next Elgin diversion," to warn the four snipers to turn off their

NVGs and turn their heads away so they are not blinded by the bright flares.

Pop, pop ... pop, pop, four new night flares were parachuted down onto the school buses.

The lookouts turned on the sirens, and the lights in the motel came back on again. Guys walked out of the bar and looked up at the flares. This time, no one ran. Instead, they walked to the buses. Only a few came out of the motel walking, not running, to the buses.

Shaw ran up to the south roadblock, and instead of twenty guys armed and in fighting positions, he found eight. Now, he was totally pissed off, thinking they might be attacked at any moment. Most of the guys were sleeping or passed out. Even the President and V.P. must have decided it was a fake attack and stayed at the farm because now his phone calls to the President were not even being answered.

After ten minutes with no attack, he decided the flares must be just a harassment. Shaw dismissed the guys and warned them not to go back to sleep. He again yelled at them, "You guys need to take a hit of meth and stay awake. The real attack will come at daylight. We need to be ready."

CHAPTER 32

Mac led the north assault convoy to a staging area several miles outside of Elgin. There they parked all blacked out and tried to relax. Each team member knew this might be a fight to the death for every gang member. They had to wait for daylight and then assault the city.

Major Westbrook turned to the Lt. "It's time to see if our diversions have been grinding them down. We will give them the flares for the third time in two minutes."

Lt radioed, "All units, all units, flares in two minutes."

It was going to be light soon; sunrise was about ten more minutes away. *Pop, pop,* flares over the school buses again. The lookouts sounded their sirens for the third time. The UAV video showed the gangs response was slower than before and with even less men moving into the buses.

Just as the flares were about to go out, Sgt. Burris said, "South assault team Bearcat #1 diversion moving to the target." The Bearcat pulled out onto the highway several miles from Elgin. The crew inside turned on the police lights and siren then headed for the south roadblock as fast as they could drive.

Hearing the police vehicle siren, Shaw called out to the lookout, "What can you see? Sounds like the attack is coming!"

"I see police lights on an armored vehicle driving this way. I can't tell what's behind it, if anything."

Shaw ran back past the motel toward the bar firing his AK rifle into the air and shouting, "WE'RE UNDER ATTACK. Get into the armored buses NOW! WE'RE UNDER ATTACK!"

His gun fire was getting most guys up and moving. The bar was cleared out, more came out of the motel, and guys ran to both roadblocks. A few tripped and fell due to being too stoned or too drunk, and the lack of sleep affected every one of them.

Shaw ran to the motel and went to the roof; he wanted to observe and direct the battle. He saw the Bearcat stop and its spotlights turned on. The lights were moving around pointing at the roadblock school buses.

Inside Bearcat #1 the radio operator said, "Bearcat #1 stopped 600 yards from roadblock, search lights now on."

Several gangsters inside the school buses started shooting their rifles at the vehicle. Shaw just watched. He could not decide what to do at the moment, so he let the guys fire at the vehicle, knowing it was out of range. Even if a bullet was to hit the Bearcat, the heavy armor would be enough to stop them. Shaw was glad, now, that at least all guys assigned to the buses were in their positions.

The Bearcat u-turned on the road and sped away.

All the gangsters raised their rifles, shouting and yelling. They ran out of the buses. They started jumping up and down still yelling and shouting, even giving each other high fives.

Shaw went down to the school buses and said to the guys, "We just won the first battle, we turned around their only armored vehicle. Those pigs are really stupid to think they can beat us. Let's wait and see if they try that again. Go back inside the buses and wait, we will be ready."

Now the sun was starting to show on a new day in Elgin. Major Westbrook told the Goose teams, "Fire in two minutes!"

The Lt repeats the warning over the radio to make sure everyone knows to expect to see and hear several massive explosions.

JJ set her stopwatch for 90 seconds then got into a shooting position. She switched off the giant gun's safety and prepared to take out the South lookout first. Through her scope she saw the lookout standing in the open. He was on the roof looking through binoculars toward the direction the Bearcat just went. Her stopwatch clicked at 90 seconds, and she squeezed the trigger on the .50 caliber rifle. That sent the 706-grain bullet into the lookout's chest and blew his body into several pieces. The top half landed on the street behind the school buses, but his legs and hips remained on the roof. She quickly pivoted the rifle to the north lookout who had just turned to look toward the sound of her shot.

He scanned the area with his binoculars and spotted an upper level open window in a house. He thought it might be 800 yards away from him, too far to get shot at. He could not see anyone in the room because the room was dark inside. He saw a bright light in the room, he thought it was a big fireball coming straight at him. Before his mind could hear the shot or even register that it was a gunshot, his life ended as he was struck by another 706-grain .50 caliber rifle bullet in the center of his chest.

Shaw looked around after hearing the first rifle shot. He heard the body of the lookout hit the ground near him.

He heard the 2nd shot and stood still looking around. Those were his last actions. Just seconds after JJs two shots, both Goose teams fired. The rounds hit the armored buses blowing them several feet into the air. Each shot caused a secondary bus gas tank explosion, and the fireball went over one hundred feet up into the air. Before anyone in the other nearby bus had a chance to escape, the Goose teams had reloaded and fired at the other armored bus in the line. The armored school buses were reduced to a mess of twisted, burning metal, each containing dead gangsters. Two Goose rounds fired at each Highway 82 roadblock was all that was needed. The rounds may have just killed half of the gang in just a couple of seconds.

Lenny had been watching the gangsters at the Highway 204 roadblock. Since the flares had been fired, they had increased the gang number there to a total of four.

The four heard the rifle fire and then the explosions. They turned and faced away from the highway. To their east was a fireball at the north roadblock. To their south/east was a fireball where the south roadblock had been just moments ago. Lenny aimed and fired at a single gangster standing behind the others. Because his M-4 was suppressed, they never heard the shot. The three others turned around after hearing their friend drop to the ground. One gangster quickly took off running toward the bar several blocks away.

Another gangster bent down to help the fallen friend up not understanding his gang brother had been shot dead. The last one raised up his rifle and pointed it around, searching for a shooter on the road beyond the roadblock. Lenny shot that one next. The gangster staggered back several steps and fell, landing hard on his back in the road.

The remaining gangster let go of his friend on the ground and stood up looking at his other gang brother lying on the ground. Lenny fired at him, but this time he missed. The gangster heard the bullet slap the ground near him and ricochet. He wasted no more time and ran away toward the bar. Lenny fired again and again and missed with each shot. It just made the lucky gangster run for his life faster as each bullet hit the road near him.

Lenny returned his scope to the two lying on the road next to their rifles. Lenny fired several more shots into each gangster just to be sure they were dead. He then shouted over to JJ, "I got two of four at the roadblock."

"Sounds like you and me need to spend some time at the range," was her reply as she kept her eye looking through the scope, her head on the stock and finger on the trigger, scanning for more targets near the motel.

Lenny said, "That sounds like fun."

Back at command the Lt was watching the UAV video. He radioed, "South team, there are about ten men still inside the motel and the couple in the house across the street. North team, you likely have the two couples in the upper level above the bar and the other two runners from the Highway 204 roadblock. Unknown how many were still in the bar, maybe five or so. Two more are in the gas station near the north roadblock. No one is moving at the buses."

"Bearcat #1 and #2 and armored truck moving to assault Elgin," said Sgt. Burris.

The Bearcats traveled fast toward the burning remains of the school buses with the Boise SWAT truck following behind them. As Bearcat #1 neared the city, they fired off smoke grenades into the street in front of the motel.

Equipped with angled blades on the front bumper similar to snowplows, they both pushed through the school bus debris and entered the city.

The remaining gang members in the motel had no leadership. Some were attempting to form a defense.

They still believed only one armored vehicle with the retired troopers was all they had to fight. No one in the motel could see anything but smoke. The four gangsters in the lobby heard multiple big diesel engines coming into the city. Two looked at each other and ran out through the lobby door and around the building to their parked motorcycles. Both were armed with AR-15s.

On the radio, all heard, “Long Bow #3 and #4 engaged, two EKIA behind motel.” Both used their suppressed, bolt action, scoped .308s and had one shot, one kill.

JJ and Lenny were still stationed in different windows. JJ said to Lenny, “Did you copy the other long bows?”

“Yeah, sounds like we might get runners. Can you see anything?”

“Just lots of smoke. They really have the street covered with the Bearcats’ smoke grenades.”

Bearcat #1 stopped near the motel lobby entrance. They fired off more smoke grenades across the street near the house that contained gangsters. Bearcat #2 had the gun turret with the 240B, and it stopped in the street to cover both Bearcat #1 and the Boise SWAT truck. The Boise SWAT truck drove slowly around Bearcat #2 and preceded to the house. Stopping just before the house, they radioed in position. “Bearcat #1 team unassing, moving to target.”

“Boise SWAT, unassed, moving to target,” was heard over the radio.

Both teams grouped up behind hand carried armor shields to assault their targets. That was the signal for north team to enter the city.

The V-150 hit the Highway 204 roadblock using the tractor blade. It easily pushed a pickup out of the way and entered the city with the Lt's Humvee and the gun Humvee behind it. The gun Humvee stopped just beyond that point and took up a fighting position.

The Bearcat #1 team moved to the motel lobby door. They looked like a modern Spartan warrior group dressed in black. Ducked down behind the shields, only the tops of their black helmets could be seen. The M-4 rifle barrels stuck out between the shields instead of Spartan warrior spears. In the lobby was one dumb gangster standing just inside the doors trying to see outside though the smoke, another behind an overturned table. Both had AR-15s aimed, ready to shoot.

As the ISP SWAT team came into view of the two gangsters, the two had no time to react. First, one M-4 opened up, firing, then another. The glass doors at the lobby entrance were destroyed by the SWAT team gunfire along with both gangsters in several seconds. The table ended up a poor choice for cover. That gangster had bullets and wood splinters blasted throughout his body. The team moved into the lobby, checking carefully for any further threats.

"Bearcat team #1, two EKIA motel lobby," was broadcasted through the radio.

Across the street, the Boise SWAT team had to use a police key, (hand held ram) to pound open the front door. While doing so, they heard shouting inside the house.

The team had just gotten inside the living room. Suddenly, a gangster jumped out of a side bedroom doorway facing the team. A woman followed, but she turned and ran to the rear door and outside. The man stood with a sawed-off pump shotgun leveled at the team and tried to shoot it as the woman exited the back door. The shotgun safety was still on. The guy fumbled the safety off and was shot by a burst of M-4 machine gunfire. As he fell dead, his finger tightened up on the trigger, and the shotgun fired one round. The pellets bounced off the floor and into the SWAT team. As the pellets hit the first shield, the officer was holding the shield above the floor, ready to step again. He was knocked backwards from the impact. The officer behind him caught him from falling.

He shouted, "I'M HIT! I was shot in my foot."

At that close range, the pellet had gone through his boot and deep into his foot. The team backed up and fired their rifles randomly throughout the room as cover and retreat fire.

From JJ's sniper position, she heard the shotgun blast and then saw the woman exit the back door of the house. The woman was holding a handgun and was wearing a Snake Head gang leather jacket. She stopped several steps from the door and raised the semi-auto handgun, aiming it with both hands as she turned looking for police to shoot.

JJ had the rifle scope centered on her.

She did not want to shoot, but it was clear this woman was not giving up and was ready to kill. JJ knew at this range there was no need to hold over for the bullet path. She also knew what needed to be done before another officer would have to face this woman. JJ squeezed the trigger; the woman's body was throw backward and into the air like she had been hit by a train. The massive shock of the big bullet dismembered the woman. Her body hit the outside wall of the house in pieces. Almost like a bug hitting the windshield of a car traveling on a highway.

Boise SWAT radioed, "OFFICER DOWN! Team retreating to vehicle. 1 EKIA, 1 female runner out through the back door."

JJ radioed, "Runner from Boise team EKIA."

At command, this time Dust Off 733 pilots and crew ran to their Blackhawk and awaited word to hear if they needed to fly to Elgin. The north team of Mac, Rick and two troopers had climbed out the back of the V-150 then formed a 360-degree circle at the same time JJ had taken her shot. Tim and Ike remained in the vehicle. Tim manned the 240B in the gun turret. Justin was in the vehicle driver's seat.

To their left, the Lt's Humvee stopped. Jim and three deputies grouped up.

The plan was for Mac's team to walk toward the bar on the right side of the road for the several blocks as Jim's team did the same on the other side of the street. The bar was located on the left side of this road. They did not carry shields due to the long walk to the bar.

As always, Mac led. They slowly walked toward the bar using the cover of parked vehicles and home walls as they traveled. Lenny was the over watch sniper covering them. Both teams had gotten one block when Mac stopped with a brick wall of a house beside him. He turned to look at the other team members across the road.

Automatic gun fire suddenly rained down on Mac's team from an upper window at the bar. Mac was knocked down and unconscious.

Lenny returned fire toward the bar, but it was too far for an accurate shot with his M-4. He just let loose with a whole thirty round magazine into the window area where he had seen the muzzle blast. Tim opened up with the 240B and fired off short bursts into the upper window area.

Rick shouted into his radio, “MAC’S DOWN! He’s been shot, he’s unconscious. Get the V-150 up here, NOW!” Rick and a Trooper dragged Mac away using his vest straps as the other trooper provided cover.

Dust Off 733 heard the radio traffic that Mac was shot and unconscious. They did not need to be told; they started the engines. A minute later, they lifted off and headed to Elgin.

Rick had Mac at the rear door of the V-150. The team lifted Mac into it and onto the stretcher. Mac was bleeding badly around his face, still unconscious. Rick told Justin, “Drive like hell through town past the South team. We need to get him to the medics outside the city with the other injured officer.”

While they drove, Rick was trying to assess Mac’s injury. He radioed command, “Mac was shot in the helmet, it may have been from ricochet off a brick wall. He has deep cuts on his face from the bullet or brick. He is still unconscious.”

Lt replied in a drawn-out voice, “Copy.” He turned to Major Westbrook. “Can you take over all command for a few minutes? I need to go outside.”

“Yes, of course. Anything else you need?”

“NO DAMMIT, my men are all getting shot up. I should have been there, not here. I’ll be back in a minute!”

The south team was very slowly clearing each room on the lower level of the motel.

So far, no one was found. They only heard sounds from above as the gangsters were running about in the upper level. The cover of smoke in the street was now clearing.

As the V-150 sped past the motel, JJ saw curtains move in several upper level windows. No one shot, so she held her fire.

Jim's team had stopped their assault. They stayed covering the street, but would not continue until different mission plans were made. Just them taking on the bar would end in a disaster.

The V-150 arrived at the aid station a couple minutes later. Several men ran over to the vehicle and helped unload Mac. An Army medic told Rick, "We got an ER doc and nurse from the La Grande Hospital right here. Mac will be in good hands in a minute." The doc got right to Mac. The shot Boise officer had his foot wrapped up and was talking while lying on a stretcher nearby. Dust Off landed a couple minutes later. They loaded the Boise officer on board on first.

The doc walked alongside Mac, followed by Rick, while Mac was carried to the chopper. He told Rick, "His helmet took a round for sure. Right now, I am not sure if any bullet fragments entered his head or not. The facial cuts are not as bad as they look. The face bleeds a lot more than other parts of the body. I cannot remove the helmet until in the ER. I gave him a drug to keep him knocked out. I am going with him. A hit like that can cause brain damage. We won't know anymore until at the hospital. The face wounds likely just need cleaned and stitched."

With that said, the Dust-Off Blackhawk took off and headed to the Enterprise hospital.

Rick phoned the Lt and told him everything the doc said about Mac and the Boise Officer. Rick then said, “I have an idea for a change of plans on the assault on the bar and the gas station.”

“Okay, as soon as you get the details worked out, call me.”

The Lt walked back into the command center meeting hall.

“Thanks for that break, Major. I am ready to get this assault done. The guys on the ground are making new plans.”

“Good, let the guys in the battle change plans as they see fit. That shows great leadership,” replied the Major.

“Thanks for your trust in me and my men.” The Lt then updated the Major about Mac’s known status.

CHAPTER 33

Rick talked to the Boise SWAT team about his new idea. They agreed it was good and they would do it. Rick then spoke with Sgt. Burris on the phone and he also agreed with Rick's plan. Finally, Rick discussed the new plan with the Lt, and he approved the changes for further assault on the biker gang.

The V-150 and Boise armored truck drove back through Elgin past the motel and to the Highway 204 roadblock area. Rick went over the change in plans with the other team members. JJ then went back to the same house and window where she would now be the over watch sniper for the south side of the bar with her .50 caliber rifle. Jim grabbed his .308 sniper rifle and went to a roof top three blocks north of the bar to cover the bar and the gas station area from that angle.

The V-150 traveled to a point near the bar and stopped in the middle of the street facing the turret gun at the upper level south side. The gun Humvee drove and parked facing the bar from the north side, training the turret gun on the lower level. The vehicles parked covering the bar from different angles. The Boise SWAT team drove their armored truck near the gas station and then stopped where they knew that two gangsters were still inside. That was several blocks away and out of sight from the bar.

Rick told the remaining guys, “We will wait until the Boise SWAT team is done at the gas station. They will then assist us when we assault the bar.”

When the south team had cleared all of the ground floor rooms of the motel, they had placed cameras at the foot of the stairs and in the lobby, then requested Bearcat #1 to back up to the lobby door. There, the team climbed in half exhausted from the work they had done on just one level. They pulled out and parked one block away, still in view of the motel front. Now they had to decide to send in the second team to clear the top floor with an unknown number of armed gangsters awaiting them or go to their plan “B.”

Long bow snipers #3 and #4 were still hidden behind the motel and had reported curtains opened and closed from different room windows. No one was seen with a gun and no one tried to escape. Sgt. Burris then conferred with the Lt on the phone about what he and Rick had thought up earlier.

The Boise SWAT team approached the gas station on foot. One member went around to the backside and hid. He got into a fighting position in case anyone fled through the rear door. The rest of the team moved up near the front door and placed a listening device onto the glass window. They then pulled back and listened for a few minutes to find out where the gangsters might be inside. Right away, they heard two men talking inside the lobby area of the gas station. The gangsters were talking about being afraid of getting shot. They did not know what was happening, but saw the smoke, heard gunfire and saw armored vehicles driving through the city. They decided to wait until dark and then sneak away. They want to give up the gang life and blend into the population of La Grande.

The Boise team leader said, "Let's form an arrest and cover team. We then use the PA in the vehicle to call them out, arrest them and take them to the prisoner transport soldiers. When done, we then assault the bar with the Ghost Team."

The Boise vehicle pulled up in front of the gas station and stopped. An officer's voice on the PA said, "You guys in the gas station, come out now, hands up or we will shoot you."

The front door opened, and two guys came out with their hands in the air. Both were shaking and one said, "Don't shoot, we don't have any guns. We left them in the building." They were quickly arrested and searched. Then the gas station was searched and cleared; no one else was in the building. The Boise SWAT team with the two prisoners were back at the Highway 204 roadblock area. The prisoners were quickly turned over to the prisoner transport soldiers and were later taken to the Union County jail.

A few minutes later the assault on the bar was on. This time Rick and Lenny with two troopers and three deputies approached on the sidewalk out of view of the bar. The Boise SWAT team approached the bar from the next street north. By using that route, Boise SWAT would approach the rear of the bar which had a service door facing that street. Once in well-hidden cover, Boise SWAT radioed, "In position."

Rick radioed to Tim, "Time to use the PA."

Tim said, "You in the bar, come out now. We have the building surrounded. Anyone coming out armed will be shot."

Ghost Team members in both vehicles reported seeing curtains moving in the upper and lower windows.

Tim used the PA again. "You in the bar can surrender, no need to die. If you choose to not surrender, you will die."

Glass was broken out of several upper level windows and lower windows; all gunfire was aimed at the armored vehicles. The Lt got on the radio and said, "Open fire with the 240Bs, fire a full ammo box. Long bursts throughout the whole damn building."

Both guns opened up, and Tim and Jimmy traversed the guns across the building. JJ fired her .50 caliber sniper rifle. She aimed and fired, moved the rifle a little and fired some more into the upper level. She then continued firing, now putting rounds into the lower level windows where some gunfire had come from.

Just moments after the vehicles started shooting into the bar, two women and a man ran out of the rear service door and into the street. All three were wearing black leather jackets with a patch across the top back area that read "Member" and another patch below that one read "Snake Heads." All three were armed with AR-15 type rifles.

The Boise SWAT team leader yelled, "STOP, stop NOW!" from cover. The three slowed and tried to find the officer that was shouting at them. The male gangster yelled, "Just shoot and keep running." He raised his rifle to shoot and was struck by multiple bullets before having a chance to fire. He dropped to the street dead.

Both women stopped in the street and aimed their rifles. They were pointing them around looking for the police but, could not see any.

Another officer shouted, “Put the guns down, NOW!”

Both women pointed their rifles toward the sound of the voice.

All Boise SWAT team members fired at the two women. No rounds missed their targets; the women were dead before they hit the ground. Even the rifles they had held were shot into pieces.

The two M-240Bs had finished firing an ammo can of 200 rounds each. They had to stop to reload and allow the guns to cool down.

Boise SWAT radioed, “Three EKIA, in street behind bar.”

The Lt radioed, “Everyone hold fire and stay in position. Any more gunfire from the building, they get another ammo can of 7.62. This is not a rescue mission. If anyone is still alive and bleeding, too damn bad. South assault team proceed with plan B.”

Plan B was to have no further officer assault on the motel. It was decided to be too dangerous. They would just make the gangsters come out shooting or surrender. Both Bearcats had tear gas and launchers. The big problem was the gas would likely cause a fire in the old motel building. La Grande Fire Department was called out and staged nearby, ready if needed.

Sgt. Burris using the PA in Bearcat #1 said, “Everyone in the motel come out now, this is your last chance.”

Upper level windows had glass broke out in several different rooms and gunfire was directed at Bearcat #1. Bearcat #2 had until that moment, remained hidden from the upper level windows. Sgt. Burris radioed Bearcat #2, "Move up and fire the M-240B at the rooms that we are taking gunfire from. We are shooting gas into the rooms now."

Bearcat #2 moved into position and came under the same rifle fire as the other Bearcat. Those inside the Bearcats could hear the bullets hitting and bouncing off the vehicles. The ISP SWAT trooper manning the machine gun then opened fire. He fired short bursts throughout the upper level.

In the rear of the motel, an upper level window had opened. A rope dropped out the window and soon a gangster with an AR-15 rifle slung across his back climbed out of the window. He lowered himself down the rope into the parking lot. At the ground the gangster grabbed his rifle and aimed it. He stood pivoting around the area while looking through the gun sights for any police to shoot.

The Long Bow snipers had remained hidden and unseen by the gangster. Long Bow #4 said to #3 "On three, two, one." Two rifle shots entered the gangster and ended his life. All heard on the radio, "Long Bow #4, one EKIA in parking lot."

Bearcat #1 by that time had fired gas into every upper level window. Suddenly, the cameras in the lobby showed two gangsters running down the stairs. They exited and ran around the building toward the parking lot, both coughing from the tear gas. Sgt. Burris radioed "Two enemy, both armed with long guns and handguns running to parking lot."

Seconds later on the radio came the report, "Long Bow #4, two more EKIA, parking lot."

More gunfire came down at the Bearcats from other windows. The machine gun in Bearcat #2 returned fire with large amounts of 7.62 ammo into the rooms. Smoke was now bellowing out of the first rooms that had been gassed. Clearly the rooms were now on fire. Sgt. Burris waited for several minutes to see if any more of the gangsters would shoot at them. At that point, half of the upper level was now on fire. Flames five feet and longer were seen in many windows and smoke was coming up through the roof. He then told the fire department to respond. Both Bearcats pulled back away from the burning building as the fire trucks arrived.

The teams inside the Bearcats got out and covered the firemen and trucks, scanning with M-4s pointed at the burning motel just in case anyone might still be alive and willing to shoot at them.

Rick radioed to Tim, "Fire at the front door until the doorway is opened." Tim fired the 240B until the front door was destroyed. All that remained was an open doorway. Rick had Tim crease fire. Lenny approached the doorway with a grenade ready as Rick covered him. Lenny tossed the grenade into the bar and jumped back to the outside wall for protection as the blast went off, shaking both of them. Everyone held their positions for several minutes until the dust and smoke settled down.

Rick radioed Tim again, "How about we send in Ike now and I will have two troopers cover you?"

"Have them meet us near the front door in a minute. We will move the V-150 over near you guys and I need to get boots on Ike's paws," replied Tim.

Tim and Ike led the others into the lower level, the actual bar. Tim kept Ike on a leash for the dog's safety. He had one hand holding his Glock, the other the dog leash. A tough way to shoot at a threat, but Tim trained this way for many years. The two troopers were aiming shotguns and scanning side to side as they walked behind the K9 team. Ike using his well-trained nose passed through the whole bar ten times faster than any human could search. The bar, restrooms and cooler were quickly cleared. No gang members were there, just a messy shot up bar. Never to serve another drink until a complete remodel if it was not torn down.

The troopers went up the stairs first. They cleared the area around the stairs, then the K9 team went up. Everywhere they looked was total destruction. All the officers could smell the blood still drifting in the air. The floor, ceiling and every wall had been shot up and were falling apart. In the first bedroom, Ike pulled Tim right over to a headless body. The floor was slippery with blood, and there was an M-16 lying nearby. Ike followed a blood trail, and he stopped at a bloody handgun on the floor. Ike then continued around the room and went behind the bed were another dead gangster was lying on his back that had been hit by three or more bullets.

They then went into the other bedroom with Ike in the lead. As they entered, they could see a body lying face down atop a bloody mattress that was on the floor. The wall behind the body also had blood stains on it. Tim told a trooper, "Go to the body on the mattress and roll it over and check for any sign of life." As they covered him, the trooper checked for breathing and pulse. He shook his head. There was a large pool of blood on the mattress from his chest area and a handgun nearby.

Tim said, "Look, this guy must have pulled the mattress off the bed and hid behind it as he sat against the wall. Bullets came through the wall behind him and through the mattress from the other direction. He never had a chance."

There was another body lying near the window. Blood had poured out of several large bullet wounds. Flesh and body parts were tossed about the room.

"Guys, let's get out of here. This level is so damn shot up, the roof may come down on us. We're done here. I think this old bar is a total loss," said Tim. As the team left the bar, Rick radioed, "Bar clear, four EKIA."

Down the street at the motel, the fire department spoke with Sgt. Burris. They decided to let the old building burn completely down and just standby to make sure the fire did not spread beyond the motel.

The Lt radioed, "All units, all units, enemy force neutralized. Take up assigned security positions. Union County SO enroute. They will then conduct the cleanup with their M.E. Because of the UAV seeing everything, we are sure there are no others hiding at this time."

Several hours later, the remaining Ghost Team members headed to the ranch. The teams from Idaho decided to spend the night at the ranch and debrief with the others in the morning.

CHAPTER 34

The next morning, the meeting hall was packed with all the police involved in the mission. The Guard soldiers and Ghost Team wives all enjoyed a big country breakfast. Most talked in small groups about the assaults. After they were finished with breakfast, they waited for the Lt.

The Lt came into the meeting hall and walked right up to the front and addressed the crowd. "First off, the information about our brothers at the hospital. Officer West, Boise SWAT. will be released today. After some rehab time, he is expected to have a full recovery."

Everyone shouted and clapped their hands.

"Mac is still in a medically induced coma. He may or may not have any brain damage. It is too early to tell. Neither the bullet nor any fragments penetrated his helmet. But, his head still took a hard hit. Doc said it was like someone hitting his helmet with a baseball bat. He has several facial wounds that have been stitched. We will not know much more until a day or two.

Kyle does not have any brain damage. He has a sprained wrist, 2 cracked ribs and a lot of bruising. The bullet sent his heart into flutter instead of normal beating. He nearly died. Without a ballistic vest on, the .44 round would have killed him. The doc said the oxygen helped get his heart beating right again. Without the medics giving him the oxygen and his quick delivery to the ER, he would have had full heart failure. Tests show his heart is working great now, but that could change for the worse. They want to keep him for a few more days. We owe a lot to the Dust-Off crews. Thank you, guys, for getting our men to the hospital."

Everyone stood and clapped.

"Now, about the mission. You guys saved twelve women from a living hell of further rape and likely death. The women told the Sheriff about three graves where other kidnapped women got buried after Ralph shot them. The SO found the three grave sites and even a few more. Two gangsters had surrendered and about 63 gangsters were killed, 5 were female members. The number is not positive because some bodies may still be found in the debris at the burned down motel. Also, the gangsters that died in the buses were only found in parts. They are counting feet to help find a correct number."

After a pause, he continued.

"Let's now debrief the assault with Rick, Sgt. Burris and Sgt. Best standing and telling us what worked and what needed to be improved. After they get done, anyone with a comment or question, I want to hear it. We have guests arriving here in about two hours who want to meet all of us."

The mission was gone over in detail almost minute by minute. Everyone had a chance to speak. Just like in the old days after a mission, the best way to get better was to hear of your mistakes and what worked and what failed. The Lt would later submit a mission report to the Sheriff, the Major and Governors of Oregon and Idaho.

Two hours later, Governor Madison was led into the meeting hall by Sgt. Anderson and followed by Sheriff McCabe. Both officers were wearing class A uniforms. Sheriff McCabe first stepped forward.

"Sheriff Carlson of Union County cannot attend today. He wanted me to express his deep thanks for ending the Snake Heads crime spree in La Grande. His office is still rejoining the kidnapped women with their families and destroying the meth labs at the farm. The M.E. is recovering the bodies from the graves and in the city. Sheriff Carlson signed a letter of thanks to each one of you and is sending the letters to your commanders." He then stepped back.

Governor Madison stepped forward.

"The Sheriff, Sgt. Anderson and I stopped at the hospital before coming here. What is it with you guys? Kyle was lying there in bed saying he is okay and wants to leave, but it was clear he was still in a lot of pain. He wanted to stand up to shake my hand. The nurse held him down and told me he refuses to take half of his pain meds. It is a good thing he has a tough old nurse. Claudia is at his side. She told me Kyle is just a bullet magnet. He has been shot too many times to die from a gunshot. The hospital let their dog Dacoda in the hospital room with them. The dog has made a lot of friends at the hospital."

He paused and looked around the room and into the eyes of every officer seated before him. "I asked Bill, I mean the Lt, has there ever been a SWAT assault that involved this amount of SWAT cops against that large number of armed bad guys. He told me no. Actually, he said hell no. It would never have been allowed to happen in the old days. Because such a mission would have been judged that what you guys had to do yesterday would be too dangerous. But, you guys did it anyway knowing full well of the danger. I am issuing medals of valor to each one of you. Because of the war, I only have letters to give you today. The medals have yet to be made.

"I cannot say enough about the action that you took and the courage you had to get the mission done. All of Oregon is grateful for your selfless action to rid Oregon of a large group of killers. I will now walk around to each of you to shake your hand and give you your letter. Everyone, please give the Old Men in Blue, the two Idaho SWAT teams, and yourselves a big round of applause. Thank you all, job well done."

After the applause ended, the Governor said. "As we all know, this war against the invaders and dealing with some really bad criminal groups is not over yet. I think the state may ask for your help again. As Governor, I hope you will answer that call."

ABOUT THE AUTHOR

Ken Moore has lived in Oregon his entire life. He has been happily married for the last 16 years to a loving wife. For recreation, he has visited many parts of the state, mountain climbing, hiking, backpacking, camping, boating, hunting big game and fishing. Ken also spent most of his teenage to senior years shooting rifles in various forms of rifle competition.

At home, he takes pride in being the maintenance guy by doing most carpenter, painting and plumbing jobs. For a relaxing evening, he enjoys reading real paperback books and E-books, usually with the family Labrador lying near his feet.

Ken chose law enforcement as his career and started police work in 1981 through the present day. He began as a Reserve Deputy Sheriff, later a Corrections Officer in a county jail. He was hired by the Oregon State Police in 1987, and in 2011 retired from that agency. During that time, Ken worked in the Patrol Division at the Portland office. He was also a department firearms instructor for revolvers, semi-auto handguns, shotguns and several different rifles. For five years he was assigned to the Portland Police Bureau in a plain clothes and undercover assignment working in a street crimes unit. During that time, he and others in that unit were awarded a unit commendation for "A substantial positive impact on the community" from the Mayor of Portland and Chief of Police.

He ended his career at OSP as a Senior Trooper assigned in the Fish and Wildlife Division in Portland patrolling in boats on the Willamette and Columbia rivers or patrolling in a 4x4 pickup in recreational areas outside of the metro area.

Being fully retired at age 53, Ken still felt he had many years left to earn a paycheck. So, before 2011 ended, he found a part-time police job working two days per week at a metro area city. He is still employed there. Ken is assigned to the traffic division and is happy to finally have a low-stress police job.

To contact the author: kmoorebooks@gmail.com.

Made in the USA
Columbia, SC
12 November 2021

48803970R00167